The Princess and I

As told by Megan

Written By: Rebekah M. Eddy

THE PRINCESS AND I

Published in the United States of America

ISBN: 978-1-365-73792-3

I would like to dedicate this book to everyone who picks it up and takes the time to read it. I hope it blesses you.

~Rebekah Eddy

Table of Contents:

1:
My New Job

I hadn't known peace like this for quite a while. The sky was blue and the grass tickled my arms and legs. I dreamily watched a bird swoop and dive through the trees. A happy sigh escaped my lips and I sat up, my hair cascading down into its original state of chaos. I felt as if nothing could go wrong, and wished the feeling never to go away.

From behind, a hand clamped over my mouth. The peace of the morning shattered, and I felt a chill of fear.

A merry laugh brought my senses back to me, and I wriggled from my brother's grasp, spinning around to confront him.

"Malcolm!" I scolded. "You ought to be ashamed of yourself; sneaking up on an innocent girl and almost scaring her out of her wits!"

My brother threw back his head with another laugh that bounced off the hills surrounding us. I sat with arms folded until he stopped and sank down next to me with a sigh of pleasure. "I did come out here for a reason, Meg. I found a job for you."

I let out an excited squeal, my temporary annoyance forgotten. "You did?"

Malcolm nodded. "Yes, come inside and I'll discuss it over our midday meal."

With an exclamation of horror, I clamped a hand on my forehead. "Our meal! Malcolm, I forgot to prepare our meal!"

My brother shook his head. "Oh, Meg! Whatever am I going to do with a sister who dreams as much as you do?"

I stood, dusting off the bits of grass and dirt that clung to my skirt. "Well," I said, "I might as well get started sooner rather than later!"

My brother grinned up at me, and stood up too. We walked to our small, but dearly loved cottage which sat nestled between the rolling hills of the countryside and a thick forest.

While I prepared our simple meal, my thoughts strayed to how my brother and I had ended up here: alone together in a cottage on the outskirts of a village surrounding the castle of our king.

So many things…I closed my eyes. So many things had happened to rip me from my carefree childhood, and thrust me into premature adulthood. I hadn't been the only one. The absence of our parents' wealth to cushion the simple lifestyle they preferred was far harder on Malcolm.

Suddenly, my brother became so much older. No longer was he my playmate, whose sole purpose was to entertain me; he was now a serious provider for us. Ever since that day our parents had died. So long ago it seemed, though but a few years.

Only a handful of times, during the last year or so, had I been able to see the playful part of his character shine through his heavy responsibilities. This morning had been one of those times, and I relished it now as I finished mixing the biscuit dough. Malcolm took an exceptionally long time with the animals, and came in just as I put the steaming biscuits onto the table. He removed his hat and jacket, pulling up a chair to sit in.

Glancing up at me with a smile, he licked his lips, the old twinkle of mischief appearing in his eyes. "You must have been really busy to prepare all this while I was gone."

I raised an eyebrow and sat in my chair opposite my brother's. "Perhaps," I retorted, "or perhaps you just took a long time with the animals to avoid having me put you to work in here!"

He rolled his eyes in a playful manner. "As if I would ever do that!"

"You would," I replied. My brother laughed. After a short prayer over our food, the meal began. There was a long silence, and I felt my curiosity come back. "Well? You said you found a job for me!"

Malcolm finished his mouthful of food. "Oh, yes…I did say that, didn't I?" There was another pause. I felt my impatience begin to rise, but controlled it as best as I could, realizing my brother was trying to excite me more by waiting before telling me the news.

At last, he finished another mouthful and spoke. "King Frederick and his daughter understand if you don't want to take it."

I jumped up from my seat in surprise, nearly upsetting all the food into my brother's lap. He steadied the table and I calmed myself and sat down before replying, "The king! His daughter! What do you mean?"

Malcolm grinned. "King Frederick's daughter, Christine, needs a lady-in-waiting. Her former one married and now has a family, so she can no longer care for both the princess and her newborn child. The king mentioned the problem to me this morning, and I suggested you. Are you willing?"

I sat a moment in shock. The king's daughter wanted me to be her lady-in-waiting? I was thrilled! "Of course, I'll take the job! It'll give me something to do other than cooking and cleaning."

My brother smiled. "I think you'll like the princess. She reminds me a little of you."

I smiled back at him. "I'm sure I'll like her."

"You don't mind coming with me tomorrow, do you? I thought that the sooner you could meet with her and get to know her, the sooner—"

I interrupted him. "Of course, I don't mind!" I felt anticipation bubbling up inside me. I would be going to the castle tomorrow! Malcolm went back to his eating, leaving me with much to occupy my mind. A ridiculous smile stayed on my face as the afternoon came and went.

Meanwhile, I kept busy with various household chores. Evening soon fell and I went to bed with a full mind. Malcolm snored softly in his bed on the other side of the room, but I lay awake, my eyes glued to the crack in the ceiling above my bed. I had so much to think about.

Tomorrow I would go with Malcolm to the castle. What would I wear? What should I say? What would I do? So many unanswered questions. My eyes started to feel heavier, and I yawned.

Our life had never been exciting...except when Father had his nobility thrust upon him for saving King Frederick's life in a storm.

Then they died. It was so unfair. Tears stung my eyes, even though they were closed in protest. My mother's long hair and dancing eyes—eyes that were the same color as mine—filled my vision, and I remembered what she always smelled like: lavender and the woods in which she so loved to walk. Father had claimed she would be the death of him, after being allowed to marry her because of his new title. But only in jest. Little did he realize how close he was to the truth.

My thoughts drifted to the man who had been both the solid foundation and the holding anchor in our family. Father was a strong, quiet man who mostly stayed at home with his nose in his books. Except when Mother managed to drag him off on a small adventure with her. His dark eyes that changed sometimes in the sunshine to lighter shades were always watching: sometimes with a faint smile of amusement, sometimes in deep thought, sometimes with stern reproof. I had only seen him angry once. He had caught Malcolm and I throwing rocks at an ugly cat that had been wandering through our farm. One look from him, his eyes snapping, and the quiet "cease" had instantaneously quelled both of us. We never picked on animals, well or sick, again after the talking to he gave us in his study.

Why did it seem like whenever I put my trust in people, God chose to take them from me? I sighed. At least Malcolm was still here. *Not that I would necessarily trust him with my life,* I admitted with a wry smile. My brother had enough on his shoulders as a part of King Frederick's Court without having to worry about being responsible for my every action. Not only had he gained our father's title after his death, but also knighthood for a brave deed done in battle. He held his place in King Frederick's Court and by King Frederick's side because of his extraordinary strategizing abilities. Often he had to be absent from our home all day, sometimes more than a day, when he had to be in conference with the king. I missed him, but had come to accept that we would lead different lives.

In a few months I would be turning eighteen… I sighed again. Why did everyone have to grow up? Malcolm would be turning twenty-three just two months after my own birthday. I smiled sleepily. Perhaps Malcolm would marry soon and I would gain a new sister and maybe even become an aunt, if the Lord so allowed. My last thoughts before I fell asleep were muddled, and soon all memories were lost for a while: I was asleep at last.

2:
The Princess

Blinking, I awoke to my brother throwing open the wooden shutters that had effectively kept rain, snow, and all other varieties of weather out for years. The bright morning sunshine streamed into our home, and I let out an involuntary groan, throwing an arm over my eyes in a mute appeal to this disturbance of my rest.

After a few moments of silence, I lifted my arm, reluctant to face my brother. Malcolm was looking at me with the grin I knew so well. "Rise and shine, Meg, you have to come with me this morning, so there will be no sleeping in today!"

I rubbed my eyes and yawned. Malcolm disappeared outside to milk the cow, and I took advantage of his absence, dressing in privacy.

Recalling that I was to visit not only a princess, but also a king, I dressed into a more elegant, although still simple, gown. I smoothed the folds of the dress and fixed my hair in a practical bun that would keep my somewhat wild hair in place for my first day as the princess's lady-in-waiting. I gave myself a satisfied nod in the mirror standing beside the wash basin. I looked respectable and sensible. Just as a lady-in-waiting should. With one more excited smile at my reflection, I put on an apron and made our breakfast.

A few minutes passed and I worked quietly, humming a few bars of a favorite folk song, *Greensleeves*. My brother came in with a bucket of milk. I carefully strained it, and we sat down to eat.

Malcolm glanced over my outfit approvingly. "That's the dress I bought from the peddler, William Price, last year," he said, smiling. "It becomes you well."

I blushed, remembering the delightful surprise I had enjoyed when my brother had gifted the gown to me for my sixteenth birthday. "Thank you. I keep forgetting what his name is. Does he still peddle in this village?"

My brother shook his head. "No, he became an excellent swordsman, and now gives lessons to nobles of the king's court."

I gasped. "A peddler?"

Malcolm nodded. "One would not think that a peddler could teach swordsmanship skills to nobles, and yet I am being taught by William, and can attest to the fact that he is truly a great swordsman. I don't think there is one in the kingdom who could best him with their blade."

I smiled. "You take lessons in swordsmanship?"

My brother laughed. "Of course I do! How else would I know all I do about wielding a sword?"

A teasing light appeared in my eyes. "I just assumed you were a born swordsman, just as you were a born strategist. I've only seen you practice outside amongst our chickens, so how should I know you were being taught actual lessons?"

"You might have drawn a logical conclusion from my steady improvement each week," Malcolm answered with a raise of his eyebrows.

"Perhaps," I said, a sudden idea coming to me. "You don't suppose I could learn, do you?"

Malcolm looked doubtful. "I'm not sure…you're a lady."

I shrugged. "A lady should be able to protect herself." My eyes twinkled. "There's not always a handsome knight in shining armor to be had when I'm alone here at the cottage so often."

My brother smiled at my jest. "True, and I'm sorry that I cannot be here with you as often as I should like." A slight frown creased his forehead. "I did make you a bow, and arrows with which to shoot. You are very skilled with them, why would you desire to also learn swordsmanship?"

"Well, a bow only works for long-distances, Malcolm. What if an enemy was to come close? There are such things as surprise attacks. Then how would I protect myself if no one were near? If I knew how to fight well with a sword, imagine the surprise it would give them! An enemy would not suspect a woman to have a sword, let alone know how to use it. I would feel much safer."

I felt slightly ashamed of myself for begging to learn in such a fashion, but I *did* wish to learn how to use a sword. I watched my brother practice upon occasion, my eyes wide as he swung the gleaming weapon around with so little effort, the blade flashing in the sun. I am a hopeless romantic at heart and I confess to idolizing my older brother. After seeing him with his sword, I had set my heart on learning how to use the sword just like Malcolm.

My brother rubbed his chin as he did when thoughtful. "Very well, Meg, I'll see about having you take lessons."

I smiled, grateful to him for letting me, and perhaps with a small feeling of triumph. "I really do think it will come in handy someday."

We went back to our breakfast, finishing it in silence. I cleaned up while my brother saddled our horses. My horse was all black except for a single white stocking on his left hind-leg. His name was Duke, and we often went on long walks together through the woods and fields, a passion I inherited from my mother. My brother's horse was a handsome bay, with a blaze. His name was Prince.

After the horses were saddled, we mounted them and rode toward the castle, which sat high above the village and was surrounded by rolling hills and beautiful valleys.

As we rode closer, my mouth dropped open at the size of our king's home. No matter how many times I was taken to visit the king throughout my life, the awe never faded when I looked at the castle's majesty.

Multiple towers raised their mighty heads into the sky, and intimidating walls connected each pair. I could barely make out the heads of passing soldiers as they marched their rounds on the top. I felt my neck snap a little as I gazed upwards in astonishment, and quickly jerked my attention forwards again. I snuck a look at my brother, and found him watching my reaction to the castle in silent laughter. My cheeks burned, and I ducked my head in embarrassment.

The guards let us in after an exchange of greeting with my brother whom they knew well. We left our horses in the care of one of the stable boys, and walked through the fortress' gate.
The castle was far more magnificent on the inside than it was on the outside. Stubbornly, I kept myself from looking around me in astonishment, though I wanted to, and it was difficult to keep myself from gasping out exclamations of delight. We walked through huge hallways lined with tapestries illustrating gory battle scenes, or portraits of kings and queens in past generations.

One in particular caught my eye as we passed it: a painting on stone of King Frederick's wife who no longer lived. Her face held both grace and beauty as she smiled down upon me as if blessing me on my way past. With a sting of sorrow, I realized that the queen reminded me of my mother. All too soon my brother took me beyond it, but the face would remain etched in my memory forever.

Malcolm didn't seem impressed at all and kept walking with confidence down the hall as if he belonged there. I followed him through hallways and up staircases. The castle was alive with people, rushing to and from unknown jobs and appointments. Servants, nobles, and ladies swept by without

18

giving me a second glance. Another guard let us in, and Malcolm continued toward the throne while I hung back, standing behind my brother's sturdy figure.

King Frederick greeted my brother with a warm handshake and smile. Malcolm turned to me, and I took the cue, stepping out from behind him and introducing myself.

"I'm Megan, Your Majesty; Malcolm told me that your daughter, Princess Christine, needed a lady-in-waiting."

King Frederick smiled warmly at me, melting my shyness. "Yes, she is in need of a new lady-in-waiting to replace Sophia. I'll summon her now, and then you can be free to get right to work." The king whispered something to a nearby guard, and the guard responded by exiting the room.

My brother and the king walked over to the throne together, leaving me standing uncertainly. To my surprise, the king didn't sit on his throne though, instead taking one of four seats around a table to the right of the throne. My brother took another and motioned for me to take a third.

They were both soon lost in a political discussion, which went over my head, so I was able to observe my surroundings undisturbed.

If only Father could see me now, I thought. *Here I am in a castle, not ten feet from the king, in order to become a lady-in-waiting for Princess Christine herself!* I tried in vain to understand what on earth my brother and the king were talking about. Their voices were lowered, and I felt guilty of eavesdropping despite having been invited to sit next to them. After catching a few words like "the Duke", "Princess Christine", and "tribute", I gave up trying to hear what was said and returned to looking around me.

A detailed tapestry of Christ on the cross adorned the stone wall above the doorway, and my unblinking gaze watched the long-suffering face of my Savior until tears came to my eyes. My thoughts turned heavenwards even as I beheld His suffering. *Why did my parents have to die? Why did that fever that killed so many people come to that village just when they happened to be visiting my grandparents? Couldn't You have waited until they had left?* Ashamed, I let out a quiet sigh and closed my eyes, turning away from the king and my brother so they wouldn't see the turmoil in my face.

I know You're in control...You always have been. But I still don't understand Your timing sometimes. I wrestled with my emotions, pushing them down and back into a safely locked part of my heart. I could be strong. I had to be. With determination, I turned to face the door and kept my mind free of such sad thoughts until the princess arrived. Perhaps this job with the princess would help me forget the pain I still felt from losing my parents.

In a few moments, the guard reappeared. A beautiful young woman followed him. She looked about my age, and every inch a princess. For this, without a doubt, *was* Princess Christine. She advanced toward the throne gracefully, and I suddenly felt plain in comparison to the rich beauty of the king's daughter. She had long black hair that fell in waves over her shoulders. Her gown was long and full, and around her neck were sparkling jewels. However, after I finished surveying her gown and jewelry, I caught a look at her face. An impish smile arrested my attention, and I caught a twinkle of fun in her eyes.

Malcolm and the king stood ceremoniously when she entered, as did I. The princess walked up to the table and greeted her father with a kiss on his cheek.

"You wanted me, Father?" she asked with a sweet voice.
The king nodded. "Your new lady-in-waiting came this morning with Malcolm."

My brother turned on his charming smile he always had ready for use and nodded, introducing me to the princess as if I were also the daughter of a king. Christine glided over to me with a warm smile, much like her father's. Her eyes continued to twinkle, and I found myself beginning to like her.

"So you're Malcolm's sister. I've heard a lot about you from your brother."

I raised my eyebrows with a suspicious glance towards my brother, who managed to look like a perfect angel of innocence while avoiding eye contact. "You have, Milady? I see…"

The king looked from me to his daughter and back again. "My dear, perhaps you should have this first day with your new lady-in-waiting be a day to get to know one another, and begin work tomorrow."

The princess clapped her hands together, her eyes sparkling. "That's a wonderful idea, Father!"

I followed the princess from the room, and walked to her quarters. The princess chattered on as we went, but I do not think she really expected any reply, so I just nodded every once in a while and smiled upon occasion.

We arrived at her rooms, and the doors opened to reveal a room far more magnificent than even the throne room. The stone walls were almost completely covered with beautifully woven tapestries, but these mostly pictured blooming roses and intricate designs from some faraway land. I was a little glad there wouldn't be soldiers with missing limbs or weapons sticking out of them decorating the room where I would be spending the majority of my time.

A fireplace crackled in the center of one of the walls, and a large bed took up a great deal of space in the middle. Four wooden chairs cushioned with soft furs of an unknown animal were arranged around the fireplace, and a table with a few more chairs sat in another of the corners. To complete the luxurious quarters, a washbasin and pitcher sat atop a dresser on one side of the bed and a closed wardrobe stood against the wall on the other. A window, currently open, let in the early midday sunshine and the tempting smells of a garden in bloom. I was going to have to get used to being amazed if I was to survive working in a castle.

The princess led me over to one of the chairs situated in front of the fireplace and gestured for me to sit down and make myself comfortable. She sat in another facing me, and smiled in excitement.

"Today I am free to treat you as guest, but I hope that I shall always be able to treat you as a friend and advisor."

I returned her smile, knowing I was going to enjoy my new job. "You can treat me as a friend at all times, and I shall enjoy it!"

The princess looked at me in thoughtful silence. "I am a princess..." she began after a moment. I glanced at her as she continued, "But please treat me as you would treat any of your village friends. I may be royalty, but I hate to be looked up to." I laughed, but she gave me such a look of reproach that I stopped. "No, it's true! I don't like to be treated differently. Your brother was the first person other than Father and Mother who treated me as an equal." The princess gazed into the fire. "I enjoyed it. I never felt as if he would flatter me into a wrong decision or ask me for something. I want you to do the same. Pretend I am not a princess at all."

I shrugged. "Very well. It will be easier for me, I think, to treat you as an equal. I was worried you would make me bow to you or something."

The princess's merry laugh pealed across her quarters. "I would not make you bow to me," she said, and then looked over at me again. "May I call you Meg?" I nodded. She smiled. "Call me Christine. I can't stand it when people call me 'Your Highness' or 'Milady.' I just know they're trying to get me to do something, and it bothers me every time."

There was a short silence, but my curiosity showed itself at last.

"What exactly *did* Malcolm tell you about me?" I asked.

Christine smiled, dimples appearing in her cheeks. "He did mention that you were a dreamer and sometimes forgot to cook his meals."

My mouth dropped open. "He didn't!"

Christine nodded and continued. "But he also mentioned you were an excellent archer and that you were very pretty like your mother." She paused, regarding me with a thoughtful expression. "I can see that you're pretty, but how can you shoot one of those heavy longbows?"

I smiled. "I don't. My brother made me my own special bow. It's designed to be lighter than a regular longbow, but it shoots just as far, and is as powerful and accurate."

Christine looked genuinely interested. "Could you teach me how to shoot with your bow?"

I nodded. "Of course I can! I'll bring it tomorrow when I begin my work."

"That's splendid!" Christine replied. "Do you practice any other weaponry?"

"Well, not exactly," I said with a laugh. "However, Malcolm promised to let me take lessons from a professional swordsman soon."

Christine smiled. "Will he allow you to take lessons from William Price? Father told me he was a very good teacher." I nodded. "Well, you may be able to meet him. Father invited him to the feast tonight."

I raised my eyebrows in surprise. "There is to be a feast tonight?"

Christine nodded. "I thought Malcolm told you!" I shook my head, so she continued, "Father decided to put on a feast in honor of my eighteenth birthday. You and your brother were both invited. I'm surprised he hasn't told you yet. Will you be able to come?"

I smiled. "I've never been to a royal feast before. I'd love to come."

Christine clapped her hands. "Wonderful! I shall let Father know. He likes to keep track of who we have at any given feast." Silence fell again. Christine looked into the crackling fire, her face flushed from the heat, and her head resting in her cupped hands. A smile played about the corners of her mouth. She glanced up at me. "Your brother must like giving nicknames."

I gave her a puzzled look. "Why say that?"

Christine laughed. "He gave you a nickname: Meg. And he also gave me a nickname."

"What's your nickname?"

Christine groaned. "He started calling me Chris the first day we met."

I laughed. "Chris? Did you tell him that was a boy's name?"

"I tried to, but he just laughed and said he didn't care. When I told him that *I* cared, he promised to only use it in private, never in public."

I grinned. "Well that was nice of him, I must say!" Christine returned my grin. I continued, changing the subject, "When is the feast beginning tonight?"

"It will probably begin about an hour before the usual suppertime, for Father usually has several nobles give speeches, and we all know how long that can take!" Christine replied. "He asked your brother to make a speech, and he said he would."

My eyebrows rose again in surprise. "Malcolm?" I asked. "He doesn't like to be the center of attention. I'm surprised he would want to give a speech."

Just then, we were interrupted by a knock on Christine's door. I got up and opened it to find my brother standing in front of me.

"I was told to come down here and see if you both were all right," he said. I bade him enter and he walked in, a lopsided grin on his face. I sat him down on a chair.

"We haven't been kidnapped yet, if that's what Father wanted to know," Christine said, her impish grin returning.

Malcolm chuckled. "I'm sure he'll be glad to hear that. He puts great store behind you, Chris."

Christine's eyes met mine, and she sighed. "If I've told you once, I've told you a hundred times... stop calling me that! It's very unladylike."

Malcolm laughed. "When were you ever ladylike, Chris?"

24

She smiled, a twinkle of mischief appearing in her eyes. "I was ladylike when you acted like a gentleman," she replied tartly. My brother gave me an I-told-you-she-was-like-you look.

Suddenly, my brother slapped his forehead with a gasp. "I forgot to tell you, Meg, we're both invited—"

I finished for him, "—to the feast?"

He nodded, glancing at Christine. "She told you already then?" I nodded. He gave a sigh of relief.

"Good!" he said, standing up. I took the hint, standing as well. Malcolm gave me a grin. "Come, Meg, we must leave early today or the king will put us to work on his feast preparations!" He turned to Christine. "Besides, Chris must make her own elaborate preparations, and so we mustn't intervene with that!"

I cleared my throat and turned to Christine, suddenly remembering that I had other duties, not just being her companion. "Do you need my help Prin…Christine?"

The princess waved away my offer. "Not today. Sophia wanted to help me one last time before retiring," she answered with a smile. "I could hardly refuse her. Besides," the princess shook a finger at me, "you were to be treated as a guest today. I forbid any work whatsoever until tomorrow."

The twinkle in her eyes was contagious. I returned the smile. "Well, then, I suppose we ought to take our leave. I'm excited to attend my very first royal feast this evening."

"I'm excited too," the princess said. "For though I have been to many feasts because I'm a princess, I've never had a feast for me! It's going to be wonderful!" She came over to me and gave me a hug. "I believe we are going to be the best of friends," she whispered.

I smiled. "Aren't we already?"

She squeezed my hand. "Of course we are!" Malcolm broke our goodbye with a polite cough, and we took our leave.

3:
The Feast

The ride home was quiet, and my brother's previous cheerfulness sank into a serious silence. I looked at him out of the corner of my eye, frowning. He was worried about something... if only there was some way I could help.

With a sigh, I steered my horse around a fallen tree, and tried to enjoy the gentle rocking of his walk. I ran my hand through Duke's thick, black mane and breathed in the fresh country air as we rode out of the village surrounding the castle.

My brother woke from his deep thinking to comment briefly on the day. "Excellent weather, eh?"

It was obvious that my brother hadn't put much thought into *that* sentence. "Yes," I answered before lapsing into silence again. I didn't annoy him with useless comments. There was a mutual understanding between us as for when to speak and when to keep silent.

My thoughts returned to the feast, and I pondered what preparations I would make. This kept me occupied until we arrived at our cottage. I unsaddled Duke and led him to our barn.

Filling his manger with hay, and a bucket with some water, I rubbed him down before going back to the house and beginning my preparations for our dinner.

Once we finished eating, Malcolm disappeared outside. It was what usually happened when something was on his mind; for some reason he could think better while caring for our animals (which always needed care in some way or another). Upon occasion, I wouldn't see him again until the next day. With the feast tonight that wouldn't happen.

The afternoon went pleasantly enough, although Malcolm wasn't there. I spent my time quietly mending the endless pile of my brother's shirts and jerkins that needed a tear sewn shut or a hole patched.

Time passed, and a few hours slipped by before I heard the familiar sound of Malcolm stomping the dirt from his boots outside our door.

I rose from my chair and put away the mended clothing. A splash of water told me my brother was washing up just outside our door where we kept an extra wash basin for just such occasions. I took his que and smoothed my gown, fixed my hair, and washed my own face. My hand went to my special box, filled with my few valuables, many of them given to me by my mother before her death. I took from it my mother's locket and golden ring that opened up a river of memories, which washed over me, leaving me with a lump in my throat and tears in my eyes. Putting them on, I admired myself in the mirror.

"They look nice with the dress."

I spun around, but smiled when I noticed my brother, leaning against the wall with his arms folded. "They do add more elegance to it," I agreed. Malcolm nodded. I spun around in a circle, watching the dress twirl.

My brother grinned at my antics. "Make sure you're ready in an hour," he said.

I looked at him, still in his grimy farm clothes. "You had better make sure *you're* ready in an hour."

He laughed. "Very true! Your wish is my command. I shall go get ready now, my fair lady!" With a sweeping bow he left, and I finished my preparations in peace.

An hour later, after one last smoothing of my dress, and one last touch to my bun, I was ready. A call from my brother outside caught my attention, so I quickly threw my cloak over my shoulders and walked outside.

Malcolm was standing with the horses already saddled. I looked him over with admiration. He was wearing a black doublet over his chain mail, and decorating that was our country's silver coat of arms, a rearing unicorn with mane and tail billowing in an imaginary wind. A dark green cloak thrown over his shoulders and held at his throat by a silver clasp completed his outfit. Even his hair, usually in a semi state of chaos, looked neat and tidy for once. He swung up onto his horse, grinning down at me.

I smiled. "You look nice."

My brother laughed. "Of course I do! Don't I always?"

I raised an eyebrow in mock disdain. "You vain thing!"

He tilted his head with his eyes still twinkling. "You look nice too."

"Thank you," I answered. "Now will you please help me up onto Duke?"

"Of course."

After tucking me and my dress carefully onto the back of my horse, we rode to the castle.

Upon arriving, our horses were again taken by a stable boy as had happened this morning. We walked into the castle, being escorted by a guard to the banquet hall.

Huge chandeliers hung from the arched ceiling with lit candles adorning them like the jewels which sparkled at every woman's throat who occupied the same room. I counted at least seven long tables covered in a wide variety of food-many of which I had never seen before. With wide eyes I caught a glimpse of exotic birds, stuffed in all their glory, and an entire roasted pig with an apple in its mouth. Even the servants, who milled about refilling silver and burnished brass goblets, were well-dressed. Each lady's gown seemed finer than the last. In vain I hoped they wouldn't notice my own scuffed shoes and simple dress. My mother's necklace, which had seemed to very fine to me at home, paled in comparison to the other jewels.

My brother saved me from embarrassing myself yet again as he led me to the high table. "Your Majesty," he murmured, placing a fist over his heart and bowing to the waist. I followed his example and curtsied.

King Frederick welcomed us with gracious majesty before motioning for my brother to sit on his left side.

Christine, positioned at the king's right side, beckoned me to sit with her on the benches that stretched out along the length of each table. Welcoming me with a warm smile, she said, "Oh, Meg, you look beautiful this evening."

I ducked my head, suddenly shy as I sat in front of all those people. Inwardly, I thanked my mother for making me learn all the manners a lady ought to have.

"As do you, Christine," I said with sincerity.

Christine was breathtaking in her gown of dark purple. Golden highlights in the dress brought out the rich beauty in her dark hair, and her eyes sparkled with new brilliance in contrast.

"I wouldn't be surprised if you were to find a suitor tonight," she continued as if determined to make me blush. If that was her wish, she was accomplishing it easily.

"I hope not," I said with firm conviction. "I have no intention of marriage anytime soon. Malcolm still needs me." I glanced over at my brother and noticed his eyes were finding their way toward us far oftener than anywhere else. "No, my brother would need to find himself a bride before I can consider marrying myself," I concluded.

To my relief, the princess let it go at that and began pointing out a few important nobles and their wives to me by name. I recognized a few as old friends of my father and mother, and told myself to remember to greet them before we left.

The first speeches were made before the meal began. Malcolm was asked to stand for his speech, and I leaned forward eagerly in my chair to catch all his words.

"My fellow subjects," he began, "I was honored to be asked by our dear King Frederick to give a speech to you all. However, I know that I am terribly hungry, as are you all, I am sure, so I promise to keep it short." There was scattered laughter, and I smiled.

My brother continued, "I hope that you all will enjoy the food and entertainment provided by our generous king. I would like to say that it has been a great honor, and a great joy to have known the king personally for three years now, and his daughter, Christine, for whom this feast is for, as well. I wish to congratulate Christine on reaching her eighteenth birthday and King Frederick on having put up with her for that long!"

Again, there was laughter, and even Christine and King Frederick had a difficult time keeping a straight face.

Malcolm grinned. "As promised, I shall keep this speech short by stopping here, after a toast to the princess!" All rose from their seats and my brother held his glass in the air. "A toast to Princess Christine: May she live happily for many, many more years!"

He sat down amidst applause, and the meal began. I was in the middle of eating a leg of what looked and tasted like chicken, but was probably some exotic bird, when I felt a prickly feeling on the back of my neck: someone was looking at me. I frowned, putting my knife on my platter before scanning the room.

Our eyes met across several tables, and I saw at a glance that the someone was a young noble. I looked away quickly, a blush beginning to spread over my face.

The onions and venison on my plate suddenly demanded my attention. I let a few minutes pass before I risked another glance only to find that he was still looking at me! He caught my eyes and smiled. Determined to not show anything other than civility at his boldness, I gave him a stiff nod and turned away towards the princess. I hoped that he would translate my body language and stare no longer when he realized I disliked it. Returning to my meal, I tried to ignore the feeling that I was being stared at.

The feast ended at last, but I never had a chance to ask Christine who the young-noble-who-stared-at-me was because she stayed busy in conversation with my brother until we left. Our horses had been saddled already, so we merely swung onto our horses and rode off into the night.

I arrived home exhausted, but I continued to think about the mysterious young-noble-who-stared-at-me. Even when I was in my warm bed and drifting off to sleep, I asked myself questions about him. Who was he? Had he known my parents? Did I only imagine he was staring at me? What if he had really been looking at the princess? After all, I knew Christine's beauty far exceeded my own. Would I ever see him again? Even as the last question passed through my mind, it faded into oblivious dreams.

4:
Archery & Swordsmanship

The next morning came quickly, and I crawled out of bed still exhausted from the previous night. Malcolm looked just as tired as I was, and while I fixed our breakfast, he cared for our animals, bringing in milk from our cow as usual.

The seriousness that had overcome him yesterday seemed to have disappeared completely, and his cheerful smile was sent my way more times than I could count this morning, which was odd even for Malcolm. I was glad that he wasn't worried anymore, but I wondered what on earth could have him in such good spirits. It wasn't until after our meal that I found out the answer.

"Meg," he said, breaking the stillness of our meal.

I looked up at him across the table.

"I have something for you."

My curiosity was piqued. "Oh?"

I watched with undivided attention as he walked over to the chest where he kept his most prized possessions and pulled a beautiful sword. I dropped my fork in surprise.

Malcolm smiled. "It's for you. I spoke to William yesterday and he agreed to teach you. In fact, since I'm already paying well for my lessons, thanks to the King's generosity, he said he would teach you without pay."

I looked at the sword, noting it wasn't Malcolm's. "But, this sword..." I began.

Malcolm nodded, agreeing with my unspoken thought. "No, it's not mine. This sword belonged to Father. He gave it to me, but I already had one. I've kept it these years because it was his, but for no other reason. Now, if you are to learn swordsmanship, you shall need it, and the sword will be useful at last."

My brother handed it to me as he spoke. Gently, almost afraid to touch it, I took it from him, and I felt a thrill go through me as my hand clasped the silver handle. Slowly I drew the sword from its sheath, watching, as inch after inch of shining metal caught the sun and threw light across the house. Malcolm watched me with a small smile of satisfaction. I returned the sword to its sheath and glanced over at him with dancing eyes.

"Oh, Malcolm!" I breathed.

He chuckled. "It was worthwhile, giving the sword to you."

I smiled dreamily. "It's perfect for me."

"I thought you might say that. It is a beautiful sword. Because of the metal used, it's not as heavy as mine, so it'll be easier for you to use."

"I'll have to think of a name for it."

Malcolm snorted. "Meg, you don't name *swords*."

I looked over at him. "*I* do."

Malcolm shook his head helplessly. "Girls will be girls," he muttered. I threw him another look and began cleaning up after our breakfast, my eyes often returning to the sword.

It wasn't until we were already well on our way to the castle that I thought of a name. I smiled, looking down at the sword hanging by my side. The name was perfect. Wait until Malcolm heard it; then he would want to name his own sword too. Duke's easy gait almost rocked me to sleep, but I kept myself from the foggy drowsiness by thinking; I was finally on my way to learning the art of swordsmanship!

We arrived at the castle right on time, and the same guard let us in. As had happened the previous day, the princess brought me to her chambers, and we left the king and my brother in discussion over the kingdom's politics.

Christine dragged me outside immediately, eager for her first lesson in archery. I smothered a smile and allowed her to take me out where her father's targets were set up. Once there, I took my bow from my shoulder and slipped an arrow into place. Motioning for the princess to watch me, I drew back the string, holding tightly to the shaft. I closed one eye, focusing on the bulls-eye with the other. I took a deep breath, and then let it out slowly. I let loose my arrow, and a solid *thunk* told me I had hit my target.

Christine squealed, as if forgetting that she was an eighteen-year-old princess. "Oh, Meg! You got it right in the middle! It's a perfect bulls-eye!" she said.

I smiled, lowering my bow. "I've had lots of practice," I admitted. "Once you've learned and practiced with a bow, you'll be able to hit bulls-eyes more and miss less."

Walking over to where she had been waiting, I showed her how to hold my bow, how to notch the arrow properly, and how to hold the arrow in place. Christine was a fast learner and soon felt she was ready to try to shoot my bow. I gave it to her, and stepped back, out of firing range. Christine brought the bow up to her shoulder after notching an arrow carefully. As I had taught her, she steadied her aim by taking a deep breath and letting it out slowly. She suddenly let go of the arrow and it flew towards the target. My eyes followed it, and with another *thunk*, the arrow landed in the target.

I clapped. "Well done! You got the arrow in the target!"

Christine frowned at the target and pursed her lips.

"What's wrong?"

She sighed. "I didn't get a bulls-eye."

35

I smiled. "No, but you hit the target on your first try." I suddenly chuckled, remembering my first shot with my new bow. "You did much better than I did."

Christine perked up. "Oh?" she asked, with ill-concealed interest.

I laughed. "On my first try the arrow didn't even get as far as the target; I accidentally shot it right into the ground in front of me!"

Christine forgot her disappointment, and insisted I show her again how to do it properly. I took my bow back and slipped another arrow into place. A slight breeze warned me to shoot with care. I held the arrow back a moment, aiming towards the tree slightly south of the target, canceling the effect of the wind. I let out a deep breath and loosed the arrow. Another squeal from Christine told me I had again gotten a bulls-eye.

She came over to me with her eyes shining. "Your brother was right! You are an excellent archer. Better than some of my Father's best!"

I blushed at her compliment, though I knew from experience that she was exaggerating. Glancing back at the castle, not far behind us, I noticed the figure of a man standing just above us. His arms folded; his hair blowing in the wind. I looked quickly away, but as our lesson continued, I wondered, who was he? Moreover, why was he watching us?

Christine shot a few more arrows, as did I, and soon Malcolm arrived. Our lesson ended for the day, but I promised to bring my bow again the next day to continue our progress. The man I had noticed was now gone, and I felt secretly glad, for I had never enjoyed being watched without knowing why I was under such scrutiny. It made one feel jumpy.

Malcolm brought me to the courtyard. "William said he enjoyed teaching swordsmanship more if he could do it in the southern courtyard where the sun shines longer into the evening. You don't mind, do you?" Malcolm asked, leading me over to a bench.

I shook my head; nothing would please me better than a lesson in sword fighting out in the sunshine and fresh air.

My brother smiled. "I thought you might not, so I already told him to meet us here. I'm afraid I won't be able to stay long; King Frederick needs my help in his council chamber. I know William well, though, and I'll be leaving you in good hands. Perhaps the best hands in all the land besides mine and the king's!"

I nodded, a small thrill of excitement running up my spine. I was at last going to learn how to swordfight! There was a short silence, but it was soon broken by footsteps clattering down the stairs that led from the top of the wall to the end of the courtyard. I vaguely wondered what William Price was doing on the wall when he arrived, breathless in front of my brother, clasping Malcolm's arm in the traditional greeting of friends.

His hair fell wildly about his head from the running he had been doing, and he looked to be no older than my brother was. During his peddling days, Malcolm was the one who usually conducted business with him, and only caught a glimpse of his comings and goings. Now, years after his peddling was over, he looked younger than I remembered.

My brother was busy explaining that he was not able to stay for his whole lesson, and William assured him that it was all right. He planned on letting me have a longer lesson this once, giving me the extra time that my brother wasn't able to have. They seemed to have forgotten me temporarily. I stood, my arms folded, waiting for my brother to realize that he was forgetting something.

At last, he realized he hadn't introduced me properly yet and turned back to William Price. "William, this is my sister Megan. She is to be your student."

William turned to me, and for the first time I got a good look at his face. We both recognized each other at the same instant. William was the young noble whom I had caught looking at me, and he was the man that watched me give archery lessons. I felt my face growing red, and I hastily put out a hand in greeting. He bent over and gently kissed it. I took this moment to scrutinize him further without embarrassing myself unnecessarily.

The sword master was of medium height with light hair and...blue eyes. Or perhaps gray? I would find out later. He was standing up now and I halted my surveyance for the moment.

"How do you do?" I asked civilly. The hearty disapproval of his staring at me the night before and during the archery lesson leaked icicles into my polite question.

William ignored whatever coldness was in my tone and grinned. "Fine, thank you. And how are you?"

"Well enough, I suppose," I said.

My brother glanced from William to me and back again, but offered no comment.

"I suppose you brought your own sword?" William asked after the short, awkward silence.

"Of course," I said.

"Then we shall begin. Come over here." He motioned me over to a certain spot on the ground and I stood. He went to stand about two yards away from me. "Now, unsheathe your sword," he commanded. I slid the sword from its sheath.

William seemed almost as impressed as I had been upon first seeing my father's sword and slid his sword back into its sheath before walking over to me.

"May I see that?" he asked. I looked over at where my brother had been, searching for some sort of wordless permission from him, but Malcolm had already gone back into the castle. I nodded, handing it to him. William took the sword in his hands, feeling the weight of it as he swung it through the air. He let out a low whistle of admiration before handing it back. "That's a beautiful sword. Is it yours? Or are you borrowing your brother's?"

I smiled. "This sword belonged to my Father."

"It's an amazing weapon," he repeated. There was a pause, and suddenly William broke it. "I'm sorry for staring at you last night. I was wondering who you were. I usually know

38

who's who at castle feasts, but I couldn't place you. I didn't find out until later that you were Malcolm's sister, and my new pupil."

I raised an eyebrow. The excuse was good enough…still, I wondered. "What is your excuse for watching me teach archery this morning?"

William laughed. "Excuse? Well, I always walk along the wall at that time. I saw you and the princess shooting, and out of curiosity I stopped to watch. I won't if you don't want me to."

"Well…" I replied slowly. "I suppose you can watch, but I always like to know why someone is watching me, otherwise it makes me nervous."

He laughed again. "Very well. Now you know: I shall be watching you. So when a prickle goes down your spine, you can rest easy knowing it's only me watching."

I smiled and raised my eyebrows, teasing him in a way I usually reserved for my brother only. "Are we going to stand here talking, or are you going to give me the promised lesson?" I surprised myself with how easy it was to treat my new teacher as a friend.

William's mouth twitched and he drew his sword again. "Begin by doing exactly what I do," he said, circling slowly.

I copied his every move, step after step, feint after feint, and thrust after thrust. Once an hour had passed, we were both ready for a rest. I sat, panting, on the bench, my arms screaming protests.

He grinned down on me. "You've done well," he said, offering me a drink from his water skin.

I returned his grin after a long sip of the refreshing well water. "Thank you, I've enjoyed learning."

"You're a quick learner, like your brother. He almost knows as much as I do about swordsmanship. I'm surprised he asked me to teach you when he could have done just as well by teaching you himself." William ran a hand through his sweat-darkened hair, pushing the sticky strands off his damp forehead and retying the loose ends with a strip of leather he pulled from his belt.

I shrugged. "He is busy most of the time, talking with the king about the kingdom's affairs. I think he likes it though...it gives him a chance to use his gift for military strategy."

William sat down on the bench too, and leaned his head back against the wall. "Your brother is a good friend of mine, ever since he bought that dress for you from me."

"Why did you stop your job as a peddler to become a swordsman?" I asked. "Besides the obvious reason of better pay and a higher standing in King Frederick's Court," I added quickly.

William smiled. "It was far too dangerous to be on the road all the time with robbers and bandits practically behind every tree and stone."

I gave him a look of disbelief. "Surely that can't be your only reason. It's not as if swordsmanship isn't dangerous. You can't make me believe that."

"That's not what I meant." William laughed. "Of course, swordsmanship is dangerous, but as a swordsman, I have a chance to protect myself against any enemy. As a peddler, all I had was a dagger and my cooking pan as weapons. Though I could throw the dagger with decent accuracy, having a sword would protect me much better." My new teacher chuckled suddenly, his face lighting up for a moment.

I turned to him. "What's so amusing?" I asked, not bothering to hide my curiosity.

"I was remembering something that happened to me as a peddler once."

I settled into my seat, giving him my whole attention. "Tell me," I pleaded. I had a weakness for good stories, especially ones as entertaining as this one appeared to be.

"Well, I had just finished selling most of my wares in a village's marketplace one day," he began, folding his arms and closing his eyes as if picturing the event in his mind. "Darkness was just beginning to fall, but like the headstrong young man I used to be..."

Here I turned a disbelieving snort that he wasn't *still* headstrong into a polite cough. Unfortunately, the polite cough got stuck halfway up my throat and a rather strangled sound came out instead, which bore an odd resemblance to a dying chicken. William regarded me in concern for a moment until I caught my breath and urged him to continue.

"I thought I could most certainly make it to the next village before stopping for the night. However, night fell a great deal faster than I thought it would and I found myself alone in the middle of a wood. Darkness hid most of the things around me from my view, and I was barely able to see the path in front of me." My teacher paused and lowered his voice, his gaze flitting furtively around the sunlit courtyard that seemed to have darkened a few degrees throughout his tale.

"That," he whispered, "was when I felt a boney hand clamp onto my shoulder."

Taken in by the story, I sucked air into my lungs and my eyes widened. "What did you do?" I asked.

William seemed immensely pleased at the effect his tale had on me. "I took the nearest weapon, which happened to be a large pan I used for my own cooking, and swung it at my enemy."

I could almost hear the hollow *tang* the cooking pot surely made when it connected with the body of William's enemy. "Did you kill him?"

William's laugh rang out at this question. "No," he answered gleefully, "the pan's handle came off from the impact and I turned around to see the hand I felt was merely a branch of a sapling tree which, to my knowledge, still holds a scar in its bark from my faithful cooking pan." He looked over at me with a smile. "Even though that particular pan is no longer useable due to the dent in its side and its lack of a handle, I still have it as a reminder to never push my luck." He turned serious for a moment. "I thank God that my foolishness didn't end up getting

41

me killed that night. I believe He put that tree there to teach me a lesson I shall never forget."

He sighed. "I didn't want that situation to happen to me ever again. So I began learning how to protect myself better with a sword I managed to buy with what little extra money I earned as a peddler. However, there are other benefits to teaching others in the art of swordsmanship," he added, a twinkle appearing in his eyes again. "Not only is it so much more fun than peddling things about the countryside, but I get to meet important people, I'm invited to feasts in the palace, and, obviously, I earn far more money teaching others than I ever did peddling."

William turned to me again. "Why do *you* want to learn swordsmanship?" he asked. "It's not a common thing for a lady."

"Well," I said, "I decided to learn for the same reason as you did. I wanted to protect myself."

"But you know how to shoot a bow accurately," William said. "Why do you need to learn swordsmanship as well?"

"Because if an enemy comes too close, then I'd still be able to fight it off, and I'd have the advantage of surprise. They wouldn't expect me to have a sword, let alone know how to use it, just like you wouldn't."

William smiled. "It makes perfect sense when you put it like that."

We both jumped when the sound of footsteps came to our ears. Then we looked at each other and laughed.

"It's probably Malcolm," I said.

"Time for his lesson already?" William asked no one in particular. "Time has flown!"

Malcolm arrived and walked up to us. "I have to have a very quick lesson, William. There's important business to discuss with the king."

William nodded. "We'll start right away then." He turned to me. "Farewell until next time, Lady Megan."

"Farewell," I answered. "And please, just call me Meg like everyone else does," I added.

"Certainly, if you wish it," my teacher answered with a respectful bow.

"The princess said she had no further use for you today, and that you could go home whenever your lesson was over," Malcolm said. "I have to stay until supper. Do you mind riding back home alone?"

I shook my head. "No. Duke is fast, and I have a sword," I answered with a confident smile.

"Godspeed," Malcolm and William both said together as I walked from the courtyard.

A stable boy brought Duke to me at the front gate of the palace already saddled. I didn't forget to thank him before mounting up and riding back through the village to our home.

5:
I Learn More

Malcolm came home just as I had finished putting supper on the table. Now would be the perfect time to tell him what I had decided to name my sword. As he walked in, I looked up at him with a welcoming smile.

However, he seemed oblivious to it and merely murmured, "Is supper ready, Meg?"

I would have none of this moping about anymore. It was getting on my nerves. I knew he was hiding something from me, and I intended to find out what it was. I wanted to fix it. I wanted to make him happy and carefree again. Planting my fists in my sides, I faced him. "Malcolm," I said, "something is wrong. Tell me what it is."

Malcolm avoided eye contact. "Nothing's wrong, Meg," he answered.

"Furthermore," I continued, "it is wrong to lie to your sister. Now, tell me what's wrong."

My brother gave in with a sigh. He sat down in his usual chair and ran a hand through his already untidy hair. "The king has heard some disturbing news, and it has me worried as well."

I sat down, confident that my brother would tell me all. "Go on," I encouraged. "What news?"

"Meg," Malcolm replied patiently. "I can't tell you that. It's confidential."

I frowned. "Surely our king knows that I would do nothing to betray him!"

"I know, but these are dangerous times. Our kingdom may be forced to wage war, and the very walls have ears to bring news to our enemies. Peace and serenity have come to an end for now, and it's time we faced that fact."

I saw that argument would never change his mind, so I switched tactics. "How can I help?"

My brother smiled wanly. "Keep Christine safe," he answered simply. "The king knows that if and when there is a war, he will have to go and lead his army. However, the enemy might take advantage of his absence and find a way to capture his daughter, thereby forcing him into giving up his kingdom because of his love for her. These are only possibilities, and slight ones at that, but it worries the king nonetheless."

My brother paused, and I watched concern for the princess come into his own eyes. "I might as well be completely honest with you, Meg," he continued with a sigh of resignation. "I'm worried about the princess too."

Suddenly I understood, and wondered how I could not have noticed it before. "You love Princess Christine, don't you?" I asked, though it was more like stating the obvious.

For the first time in his life that I can remember, Malcolm blushed. First, his ears grew darker and darker, and soon his whole face was as red as the cherries growing in our orchard. He nodded, but I had already gotten an answer from his reaction to my blunt question. My brother looked so much like a boy I saw once that was caught stealing apples in our marketplace that my sense of humor got the best of me and I burst out laughing.

Malcolm recovered himself, and looked slightly injured at my laughter. "Why is that so amusing to you?" he asked indignantly.

"Your face," I gasped out between outbursts of mirth.

My brother's face twitched, his mouth curled into a smile, than a wide grin. He must have realized what a spectacle he had made of himself for he was soon laughing along with me.

We recovered ourselves and with one last grin at each other, we began our meal in silence. I remembered that I was going to tell Malcolm the name of my sword, but as I opened my mouth, Malcolm began speaking.

"I'm sorry I didn't tell you right away that I loved Christine," he apologized, turning red again.

My mouth twitched, but I restrained myself. "That's perfectly fine, Malcolm," I assured him. "I understand, really." Even though I didn't understand, and to be completely honest, didn't *want* to understand.

"I didn't know myself until about two days ago," Malcolm continued. "Of course, I knew that I enjoyed her company and liked her as a friend, but when the king laid out his worries about her if there was a war, I suddenly realized how much I needed her companionship. I knew that without her my life would seem incomplete."

I tried very hard not to be wounded by these words. Hadn't his life with me been happy? Hadn't we always been the best of friends? Why would he prefer Christine to me? Bitter, jealous thoughts against the princess began piling up in the back of my mind. Quickly, I kicked them out, mentally of course, and smiled sweetly at my brother.

"I would love to have her as a sister," I said, leaving out the 'in-law' that I felt tempted to tag on to the familiar term. "She and I are already good friends. Where will you live?"

Malcolm smiled. "We'll live in the castle at first...just so the king can have his family around him in his old age. Once he has left his earthly castle for a far better one in heaven, we will move into a smaller, cozier home. Castles aren't the best place for raising children."

I hated how selfish the next question sounded, but I really did need to know... "Where will I live, Malcolm?"

My brother look surprised. "With us of course! We'll keep our home for a place to move into after the king has died and build larger rooms as needed." He laid a hand on my shoulder. "I hope you know that we would never dream of not having you around. Besides," he added, "Christine will need lots of help raising our twenty children."

Had I not caught the twinkle in his eyes, I would have gasped at his outlandish expectations, but having seen it, I merely shook my head in a helpless fashion and smiled again. "I don't believe Christine knows what she's going to get herself into if she promises to be your wife. However, I am very happy for both of you, and if you need it, you have my blessing to continue getting to know her better."

Malcolm gave me a look full of gratitude. "I knew you would support me in this," he said, squeezing my hand.

There was a pause. Finally, I would be able to tell him the name of my sword. "Malcolm?" I asked.

He looked up. "Yes?"

"I named my sword."

He showed interest. "Really? What did you call it?"

"His name is Safeguard."

My brother nodded as if he understood the perfection of the name, but I felt he was not giving me his full attention. "It's perfect."

I gave up. He was in love. There's no way he was paying attention to small things like what his sister named her sword. I sighed inwardly, knowing that from now on, nothing was going to be the same as it had been.

* * † * *

"Good shot!" I applauded. Christine and I were practicing her archery out at her father's target and she had just finished a set of arrows. Several of them were extremely close to the center; only one completely off the target.

48

Christine gave me a doubtful look. "I didn't hit a bulls-eye," she said woefully.

"That will come in time," I reminded. "I've spent hours and hours practicing over the years to finally get to this point."

"The point where you hardly ever miss," Christine finished wistfully.

I felt the hair on my neck tingle and smiled. Pausing our practice for a moment, I turned and waved at William's silhouette. He returned my wave and continued on his walk along the wall.

Christine frowned in puzzlement. "Who is that?" she asked.

"Sir William Price," I answered. "He's taken an interest in your archery."

"Or perhaps yours," the princess retorted.

I shook my head and stole a mischievous look at the princess out of the corner of my eye. "He wouldn't want to watch my archery. It's not nearly as exciting as yours."

Christine's impishness rose to the surface immediately. "That's true," she agreed. "My archery is far more mysterious. You never know where my arrow will hit, whereas with your archery, you just hit bulls-eye after bulls-eye. Quite boring, really."

We laughed. I could never be mad at Christine for long, even though I did feel as though she was stealing my brother from me.

"All the same," the princess continued, "I don't suppose you think that William prefers your company over anyone else's?"

I felt my face grow hot with embarrassment and hurriedly changed the subject back to archery.

* * † * *

Weeks stretched into months as I got used to working alongside the princess. My job was easy, really. All that was required of me was to be a companion and assistant for Princess Christine: to help her choose outfits, and to accompany on her rides or walks in the forest around the castle. I learned to copy the graceful way she carried herself, as well as the gentle way she treated the multitude of servants.

I watched as my brother formally courted her, and was often the chosen chaperone when they decided to walk in the gardens or ride their horses across the countryside. The king was obviously delighted that his daughter accepted the advances of my brother, and whispered rumors of their inevitable betrothal began circulating the castle and surrounding villages.

While my brother grew his relationship with Christine, I grew in my knowledge of swordsmanship. My lessons with William came and went with rigid regularity. One evening, William boasted of my fledgling abilities to Malcolm, and, in turn, my brother asked to see a sample of what I had accomplished. With his head in the clouds so often as a man in love, I wasn't surprised that he hadn't noticed any improvement in my skills. Reluctantly, I agreed to have a mock duel with my teacher the next morning. However, when the hour came for us to fight, I already doubted myself again, but I was determined not to show the inward struggles to my teacher and brother.

"Are you ready?" William asked, slicing the air with his sword as he bowed. "Or are you going to be too nervous to fight me with your brother watching?"

"Of course I'm ready!" I exclaimed hotly before noticing the teasing twinkle in his eyes. "And having my brother here only makes my swordsmanship improve," I added after seeing it. "His presence always makes my courage soar to mountainous heights."

"We shall see," my teacher said, but smiled at my words.

We began our duel. I forgot the fact that my brother was watching. I forgot where I was and how much time went by. My thoughts were instead centered on William's quick thrusts, and the speed of my own counter moves. Our blades both flashed in the sunlight, and I dodged and stepped forward too many times to count. Finally, the bell was rung by Malcolm and I stopped, panting for breath.

Our fight was over. At least for now.

Malcolm came up to us both with a wide grin. "That was simply marvelous to watch!" he exclaimed. "You are both magnificent with your swords."

I bowed to my brother in mock formality. "That is true praise coming from you, my brother."

Malcolm threw back his head with a laugh that bounced off the stone walls surrounding us. After a moment, he turned to William. "I do believe that she is better than I!" he said, still chuckling.

I gave both my teacher and brother a look of disbelief. "I don't think I could possibly be..." I trailed off when I saw the looks on their faces. "You mean that you really think that I...! No, I couldn't!"

William was looking at me as if a sudden idea had dawned on him. "I think you might be able to, Meg. You've got skill enough, I suppose."

"When shall she duel me?" my brother asked, clearly enjoying my discomfiture.

"In a fortnight?" William asked me.

"Oh, that seems so very far away," I replied, my voice filled with sarcasm. "Why not have it tomorrow?"

"If you wish it," Malcolm answered with easy grace.

I was in for it now. "Tomorrow then," I said.

6:
The Duel

Why, oh why do I get myself into these terrible situations? I asked myself for the umpteenth time on the way home from my swordsmanship lesson. I had been chiding myself about it ever since I agreed to the duel the next day. My brother was even now sitting astride his horse with a smug look on his face, knowing he would obtain victory already. *I* was certain he only wanted to have the duel with me because Christine was sure to come, and he knew it would be an easy win.

"Show off," I muttered.

My brother turned to me with a quizzical look on his face. "What did you say?"

I shrugged. "Oh, nothing."

He let it go, much to my relief. The remainder of the ride home was silent.

Once home, I began supper preparations, determined to not show how nervous I really was about the fight tomorrow. It was a difficult thing to do, and I had to check my desire to run outside and scream in an effort to relax my nerves.

Malcolm spent less time with the animals than usual and I put him to work setting our table. He did this cheerfully and whistled a catchy tune while doing so. I began humming the harmony to it almost automatically. My mother had sung that song to me whenever she put me to bed so I was very familiar with it.

Greensleeves is my delight
Greensleeves is all my joy
Greensleeves, my heart of gold
And who but my lady Greensleeves?

I have been ready at your hand
To grant whatever you would crave
I have both wagered life and land
Your love and good will for to have

Well, I will pray to God on high
That thou my constant sea may see
And that yet once before I die
Thou will doth say to love me

He caught my eye and winked. I smiled, forgetting my troubles for the moment in the joy of having him there; a treat I knew now that I would not have forever.

Supper was laid on the table and we sat down to eat after a prayer. Once my brother had finished his plate, he folded his arms, leaned back in his chair and studied me. I finished my own meal before he spoke.

"Meg, you don't have to do the duel," he said. "William would understand."

I raised an eyebrow. "Do you think I would back out now? After all the work I've put into practicing?"

Malcolm's face clouded for a moment. "Meg, I'm worried what might happen. I don't want to injure you."

"Well then, I guess you'll have to let me win!" I grinned.

54

"Please, Meg," my brother pleaded, "I'm serious."

I sobered. "I am too, Malcolm. If I don't fight the duel with you, William will find someone else that won't bother about being careful. Having a duel with you is really the safest way for me to get better."

He sighed and pushed his chair back from the table. Lowering his voice suddenly he whispered, "Meg, the Duke of Devonshire has just declared that he will no longer give King Frederick the tribute that he has in the past. This means war. Our king will be summoning troops in the next few months to march on the Duke's castle before winter comes. He wants you to stay in the castle with Christine while we are away. Are you willing?"

Slowly my mind wrapped around the information. "Of course I'll stay with the princess. Does he really believe that she might be in danger?"

Malcolm shrugged. "A king can never be too careful. It will ease his mind to know that she is not alone."

"Much help I'll be if the castle is stormed," I answered ruefully. "How will I help keep her safe?"

My brother grinned. "Let's just say that there was another reason I let you learn the art of swordsmanship."

"How long is the king planning on fighting this Duke?" I asked.

"Until he gives up and gives the king a formal agreement that he will continue paying his tribute. We may come back for short periods of time, but the king knows his men will do a better job fighting if he's right there, fighting alongside them."

A worried frown creased my forehead and I began twirling my hair in an absent-minded fashion, a habit I had been striving to break. "When does the king leave?" I asked, jerking my hand away with an inward rebuke to myself.

"Within the month." Malcolm ran a hand through his hair and stood up. "I thought I would warn you."

"My thanks," I said drily. *Within the month? Within the month!*

Malcolm grinned suddenly, the worry melting from his face. "We'd better get some sleep tonight so we can duel our best tomorrow."

I groaned. "I don't know how I get myself into these predicaments! Why do I even open my mouth?"

He laughed. "Just go to bed and try to get some sleep. I'll check on the animals one more time before also going to bed." He winked at me again as he shut the door. "Good night!"

I sighed, cleaned up after our supper, and went to bed as he had ordered me. Laying on my back, the soft mattress and scented pillow beneath me, I suddenly realized just how tired I was. Only a few minutes passed before I shut my heavy eyelids and drifted off to sleep.

* * † * *

"Ready?" Malcolm asked me, his eyes twinkling, and a grin spread across his face like the butter I had spread on my biscuit that morning.

I sighed. "Let's just get this over with."

"William, you'll act as judge?" My brother turned to my teacher with a quizzical expression.

"I will," he answered, "but I have one question for you both. I know this isn't going to be a fight to the death—"

"Most definitely *not*," I said.

William grinned. "—so how will I know when the fight is over?"

My brother rubbed his chin while eyeing me. "I don't want to have it be whoever inflicts the first wound wins either though..." he said.

"No," I said with conviction. "No wounds."

"Is there such a thing as a fight to the point of losing?" Malcolm asked William.

My teacher frowned. "You mean a fight where whoever knows he is losing will call an end to the fight?"

56

"Not exactly. I was more thinking that we could make two lines in the dirt of this courtyard on opposite ends and have each opponent start on one of them. Then they would come to the middle and begin the duel. Whichever duelist manages to get their opponent over the opposite line wins. Can you understand that?"

William worked out what my brother was saying for a minute before nodding his head. "I understand. What about you, Meg?"

I shrugged. "I understand as well. To win I will have to force Malcolm over his starting line. It's simple enough."

"When you put it like that!" my teacher agreed with a laugh.

Quickly, William took a handy stick and drew the suggested lines on opposite sides of the court.

"Ladies first," my brother offered gallantly, giving me the choice of which line I wanted to start on.

The whole courtyard was shaded, currently, so that made the choice relatively easy. I knew I didn't want the sun in my eyes if I was fighting, and direct sunlight on one's back was also extremely uncomfortable since it would make one's hands sweaty and unable to wield a sword as well as one might in the best circumstances.

I chose one and Malcolm took the other. Both of us looked at William. He dropped a piece of cloth that had been dyed red for similar duels and my brother and I stepped to the center of the courtyard to begin our duel.

I had come knowing that my brother was good, and as the duel began, I could see that I had been right. I was immediately backed towards my line for at least ten feet before I was able to gain back some of the ground I had lost. Our blades both flashed so fast I could hardly watch my own, let alone where Malcolm's was going next as I tried vainly to be ready to counter his moves with my own. It was almost a miracle that I was able to back him towards his line at all.

Why did I ever listen to Malcolm and William when they said I had a chance at being better than they are? I thought to myself as I grimly tried at least to keep Malcolm from pushing me back to my line. *Well, they were wrong. I cannot hold a candle to Malcolm's swordsmanship. I can at least have the satisfaction to say "I told you so" after my brother beats me.*

Suddenly, things got easier. Malcolm's blade stopped flashing as quickly, and his eyes were not watching my sword...they were focused on something behind me. I didn't bother glancing away from him though. I took advantage of his temporary distraction and pushed him farther and farther away from my line. His eyes suddenly snapped back to the fight and widen in slight panic. He had realized that the fight was in my favor now and he jumped back in desperately trying to turn the fight back.

Hope had come to me though, and I was unwilling to let go of it now. Malcolm's own line was only twenty feet away now. Mine, though I could not know for sure, was at least thirty feet behind me. I was not going to give up now. I had a fighting chance at last.

If possible, my sword's blade flashed faster and my eyes darted back and forth in effort to keep up with it. My attack methods became almost reflexes as I advanced another yard or so closer to Malcolm's line.

He pushed me back two strides.

I gained another four.

He pushed me back again, this time at least three strides.

I gained seven strides.

His line was so close, and yet I knew this would be the hardest stretch.

I pushed him back again for a gain of five strides.

By now, we were both exhausted and I silently wished that our lines had been drawn closer together. *Although,* I thought, *if they had been closer, I probably would have lost by now.*

With less than ten feet left to go, my brother fought almost wildly. I was surprised how well we had both managed to keep from hurting one another. Our swords had been so fast during the entire fight, and our fighting so frantic most of the time that it I was surprised that neither of us earned so much as a scratch.

Finally, with a breathed prayer for strength, I gave one last effort. Forcing my exhausted muscles to swing my sword one last time, I pushed Malcolm over his line.

We stopped immediately, panting for breath. My arms felt like clay and I barely had the strength to sheath my sword and sink to the ground.

William came over to congratulate me as did my brother, but my face was buried in the soft ground and I merely groaned and waved them away. "Give me some time," I ordered into the sweet-smelling grass.

After a few minutes of rest, I sat up and smoothed my hair, redoing the bun that had fallen out during the course of the fight.

Presentable at last, I stood up, still slightly weak-kneed and shaky. I shook William and Malcolm's hands meekly, but shook my head at their compliments and praise.

"I didn't deserve to win," I said. "Malcolm is still better than me."

"Then how did you win?" William demanded.

"I don't know," I answered. "About half way through the fight Malcolm got distracted and I didn't so I was able to take advantage of him. That is how I won. I wouldn't have had a chance other than that distraction."

Malcolm grinned sheepishly. "She's right about the distraction. Princess Christine came out of her room onto her awning to watch us for a moment. The movement and color of her dress against the grey stone did take my focus away from the fight."

William smiled. "Well in that case, shall we have another fight some other time when the princess isn't around?"

I shuddered. "No thank you. I want to stop while I'm ahead." I gave my brother a teasing smile. "Not everyone can say that they've beaten Malcolm in a sword duel. Besides," I added mournfully, "the way my arms feel, I doubt if I'll ever be able to lift a sword again, not to mention actually be able to fight with one."

Just then one of the king's many knights came out onto the courtyard, interrupting our laughter. "King Frederick wishes to see you in his apartments, Sir Malcolm," he said stiffly.

"Tell him I shall come immediately, Sir Alfred," my brother answered.

"I will do so with all speed," the knight replied. "I have a message for your sister as well: Princess Christine wants to congratulate her on winning the duel."

I blushed. "It wasn't really a—"

"My sister thanks Her Royal Highness for the congratulations," my brother said.

The guard, Alfred, left us and Malcolm followed soon after.

"Be sure to go to the princess and stay with her until I come to go home with you," Malcolm ordered. "If she offers you dinner, accept. This business with the king might take a while."

I nodded. *I hope nothing has gone wrong yet,* I thought to myself. "I'll be ready," I promised. *Ready for trouble,* I added mentally, seeing the worried look in his eyes.

As I had suspected, though hoped against, trouble was coming...and it was coming sooner than any of us had expected.

7:

Worries & Plans

"Oh, Meg, you were wonderful!" the princess gushed as soon as I stepped into her quarters. "I didn't think it was possible for anyone to beat Malcolm in swordsmanship, but you did it! His own sister!"

I sat on the chair she offered me and shook my head at her praise. "But I didn't, Christine," I answered, knowing it was useless to tell her there were several men in the castle I could name who were better than my brother, including my teacher William.

The princess gave me a confused look. "I saw you do it though," she said.

"Well, yes," I replied, "but only because he got distracted. He was winning."

"Distracted? How was he distracted? He fought you almost furiously!"

I smiled. "That was after he regained his focus. When you came out to watch, the bright color of your dress against the gray stone balcony threw him off."

Princess Christine frowned. "I am so very sorry. I knew I shouldn't have come out to watch unannounced..." she trailed off. "I thought that I would be less of a distraction by slipping out to watch than by announcing my presence at the beginning. I thought it might make you or Malcolm nervous to have me watching." She sighed. "I didn't think that the color of my dress would distract poor Malcolm and make him lose!"

With a shrug, I waved away her apology. "It's alright. I don't think Malcolm minds very much."

Suddenly, the princess let out a giggle. "How his pride must have suffered. To be beaten by his own sister!"

I grinned. "I think he knows that he would have beaten me had the distraction never occurred. That thought will keep his pride from being flattened too much."

"Would he have?"

"Oh yes. He was well on his way to winning when he lost his focus for a few seconds."

"And that's all it took for you to turn the fight in your favor?" The princess shook her head in amazement. "I wish I were that good with the sword."

Sparing me from further embarrassment, a knock sounded on our door. Princess Christine opened it to find Malcolm standing outside. She started to apologize for distracting him, but he held up a hand to stop her.

"I have no time for a friendly chat today, Chris. Your father wishes both you and my sister to come with me to his council chamber."

A line formed between the princess's eyebrows. "What's wrong?" she asked worriedly, forgetting to remind Malcolm not to call her by the boyish nickname.

"I think he wants to tell you."

"So be it. I shall come right away."

Together we walked behind Malcolm to the king's counseling chamber, which was located behind a large door just down the hall from Christine's chambers.

The king looked up as we entered and waved us in. "Christine, Lady Megan…I need to talk to both of you." He turned to Malcolm first. "Close the door please."

My brother did so, and the princess and I walked closer to the king and sat down in front of him on the bench to which he motioned.

A worried look had settled into the princess's eyes, and she leaned forward to take her father's hands in her own. Their eyes met.

"Father, what's wrong?" she asked. "I know something is wrong. Please don't keep me in suspense any longer!"

King Frederick gently stroked his daughter's hands and glanced in my direction. "Malcolm told me that you know what I need you to do," he said.

I shot a bewildered look towards my brother and answered, "I'm not sure I know what *exactly* you expect me to do, Your Majesty."

The king turned back to the princess. "The Duke of Devonshire finally stopped paying his tribute."

Christine's frown deepened. "That scoundrel," she hissed vehemently. Then suddenly, her eyes widened. "But, Father, he knows your armies are greater than his! That Duke is a bad man, but not a fool…why would he stop paying tribute if he knew you could come and force him to pay it again on penalty of death?"

"Because he might have help," my brother answered on the king's behalf.

Princess Christine turned to him. "You think he has allies who would fight with him against Father?"

Malcolm nodded. "Yes," he answered. "Your father, though he is a good man, one of the best in my opinion, does have enemies; enough enemies to build a dangerous army."

The princess turned back to her father. "And you think the same as Malcolm on this matter?"

King Frederick nodded. "I do."

Sudden understanding came to the princess and she gasped. "That means you'll be going to war with him!"

The king nodded. "I had hoped to spare him, but the Duke of Devonshire has called this on himself. If I try to make peace quietly, other parts of my kingdom will also try to pull away. This is the only way I can keep my kingdom from falling to pieces around me."

Tears sprang into the princess's eyes. "Oh, Father!" she moaned.

"Your Majesty?" I asked tentatively.

The king turned to me. "Speak, Lady Megan."

"When will this war be? How long are you planning to be away from this castle? What will happen to the kingdom if you never return? How can I be the most help to you? What—"

King Frederick held up his hand to stop my questions that would have continued to flow from my mouth as I tried to sort out what was happening around me.

"Lady Megan," he said, "let me answer these questions one at a time." A glimmer of a smile came to his face and he continued, "Now, please repeat the first one."

I took a deep breath. "When will this inevitable war be?"

"Soon. I cannot wait much longer. My armies should be marching within the month."

"And you'll be with them?"

"They need me," the king answered simply.

Princess Christine gasped. "You-you're leaving the castle, Father?" she cried.

"I have to, Christine; the men need me beside them. I'm their leader, and I can't lead them properly while still in the castle."

"But if you're gone, and Malcolm with you, I'll be here—" her breath caught for a moment before she finished whispering, "—alone."

The king smiled at me while patting his daughter's shaking shoulders. "You won't be here alone," he promised.

"Th-the servants d-don't c-count!" Princess Christine sobbed out from behind her hands.

"I wasn't speaking of the servants," he answered calmly.

The princess lifted a tear-stained, confused face from her hands. "Who are you speaking of then?" she asked.

"Lady Megan has agreed to stay with you in the castle while I am away," the king said. "Since I was worried about you being all alone in the castle while I was away, I came up with this plan. A plan that will keep you and Megan both safer while we are away fighting."

Future sobs died away before escaping the princess's lips. "Meg is going to stay with me?" she asked in wonder. "She's going to stay with me while you're gone?"

"Yes," the king replied.

"Oh!" The princess was astonished...so astonished that she could find no better word than "oh" to say. I was impressed.

Malcolm spoke again. "Then you're willing to have her with you?"

Christine found her tongue at last. "Oh, yes! I would love to have her stay!"

My brother let out a sigh of relief. "Thank you! I was worried about Megan being by herself in our cottage while I was away...this takes quite a load from my mind."

The king chuckled. "Well then, that's settled. Lady Megan, you had another question?"

I nodded. "How long are you going to be away from the castle?"

He sighed. "I can't be sure. Especially since this Duke seems to have allies. This war could drag on for quite a while. If all goes well and we have an easy victory, we will be back within a couple months. Otherwise, it may stretch into a year."

"So long..." Princess Christine moaned. "What will happen to us...to me...to the kingdom if you die?" Another sob tore from her throat as she clung to her father's arm. "I can't be there to make sure you're safe! I won't lose you like I lost my mother!"

I felt tears sting my own eyes. Watching Princess Christine and her father interact was reminding me painfully of what I had lost when my parents died. I no longer had a father to worry about. I hadn't even been able to say goodbye to them before they died. Malcolm and I had come too late, him from his training as a soldier and me from visiting a cousin in another part of the country. The hole in my heart that they had filled, the hole that had been stitched shut so carefully, was torn and beginning to leak again.

He placed a hand around her shoulder and drew her into an embrace. "We have to prepare for the worst while hoping, and praying, for the best," he said solemnly. "If the worst does happen, you will become the queen and rule in my place."

"I don't want to rule, Father!" the princess protested. "Surely someone else could instead!"

"We will all hope that things don't come to that, but if they do, you need to prepare yourself to rule." The king placed his hands on her shoulders and looked into her eyes. "I think, should the need so soon arise, that you will do a very good job. Even so, while I am away with my army, you will have to be in charge temporarily. There will be people who need to be judged, and persons who will need advice."

The princess looked frightened. "I don't think I can do it, Father!"

"I think you can."

I waited for a moment while the princess processed this before adding, "I'll be here to help you whenever you need it as well, Christine. You won't be alone."

She smiled at me. "Thank you. That means a great deal to me."

The king let out a deep breath and smiled, though his smile was touched with sadness. "Lady Megan, you will want to bring the things you think you might need to the castle within a week so you can be ready to move into the chamber we will prepare for you."

I nodded. "I'll be ready, Your Majesty."

"Now that that's settled," Malcolm said, "Meg and I really should be getting home. I will be back here early tomorrow morning to discuss more of the strategy details and planning."

I stood up, as did the king and the princess. "I look forward to seeing you both tomorrow then," King Frederick said.

"As do I," the princess added wiping away her drying tears. "You are both such good friends. I don't know what I would have done without you!"

"Know that we'll stand by you no matter what," I assured her with a tight hug. "Don't you forget that. Ever."

8:
A New Friend

A crash in the small hours of the morning startled me awake. I bolted from my warm covers in alarm only to see my brother standing sheepishly in the doorway, his foot poised in the air above a now-empty pail of milk and a boot in his hand.

"What happened?" I inquired moments later while mopping up the mess from our floor.

"I set down the pail of milk for a moment so I could take off my boots, but then knocked it over because my boot gave me some trouble." He sighed and regarded the guilty boot with a frown. "It's always been hard to pull off, but I think it's been getting worse this past month."

"I think my pies are making you fat," I said impishly, then quickly ducked away before my brother could revenge himself.

"Your pies are good, but I don't think they're to blame," Malcolm answered. He rubbed his stomach thoughtfully, then shook his head. "It's not fat, it's muscle."

I laughed and rolled my eyes in obvious disbelief. "Of course."

Malcolm came over while I made our milk-less breakfast and gave me a pinch on my cheek and a brotherly hug. "I'm sorry to have awakened you. I was going to go to the castle by myself this morning so that you could get the few extra hours of beauty sleep before following me with your belongings you think you might need during your stay with Chris."

I smiled. "Thankfully, I'm not in need of beauty sleep. However, I may need some extra time to get the things I'll need packed. I wasn't able to do that yesterday."

"You won't mind traveling to the castle alone?"

"I don't mind. I enjoy rides on Duke in the quiet of the early morning. Let Christine know that I may be a little late."

Malcolm nodded as he finished his meal. "She'll understand." He swallowed his last bite and stood, belting on his sword and pinning his cloak to his shoulder. "I spoke with Mr. Weaver, our neighbor, last evening, and he said he wouldn't mind caring for our animals during our absence."

I nodded at the sense of this. "We will pay him?"

"Of course. He refused a large payment, in remembrance of a kind deed our father did years ago, but I am sure I'll get him the money somehow." My brother winked at me, and with one last hug, he left me standing alone at the doorway of our cottage.

"I only hope we will be here to thank him for his kindness," I whispered. I watched him until he disappeared, then walked back into our home with a sigh. I had packing to do.

* * † * *

Packing was quite the task. I had to divide the items I knew I couldn't live without and the ones which would stay safe here in the cottage. Then, of course, there was the unpacking and repacking of bags that I felt hadn't been packed properly the first time. The hours slipped by until finally, it was completed.

I looked over my work with a satisfied smile. Duke stood patient and still with all my bags of girlish necessities piled on his back. There was barely room for me to sit, but I was loath to leave anything behind...not that I had much to begin with. After all, I didn't ever make it a habit to collect things and hoard them

70

over time. Most of my worldly goods were packed into the three bags that adorned my noble steed. Just before mounting Duke, I strapped on my beloved sword, Safeguard, and threw my cloak over my shoulders. Now I was ready to face this day.

The ride to the castle was beautiful. It was light out now, unlike when I had first been rudely awakened, but dew still sparkled in the early sunlight. I munched on my own breakfast, trusting Duke to follow the worn path to the castle's gates, and threw some of the crumbs to the birds which followed me in that hope.

I was greeted at the castle doors by a new stable boy. He looked vaguely familiar, as if I had met him before. To satisfy my curiosity, I asked his name.

"I'm Steven," the dark-haired boy replied with a shy smile. "I just got hired to work as a stable boy." Noticing my hesitation, he added more eagerly, "Don't be concerned about your horse, I take good care of animals…horses in particular. Gerhard, he was the old stable boy, but he's too old now and so I have taken his place."

"How old do you have to be before you're 'too old' to be a stable boy?" I asked next.

"Well, when you're old enough to become a squire, many boys prefer that to being a mere stable boy. But not me. I was offered the position as a squire a couple months ago, but turned it down for now. I prefer being with horses personally."

I raised an eyebrow. "You prefer horses to fighting? That's certainly a rare thing in boys. May I ask why?"

The stable boy shrugged. "I like animals." He paused before adding, "Naturally I like fighting too, but my mother prefers to keep me at home to work on our farm, so it doesn't really matter which I like better."

The logic in his statement made too much sense for me to bother inquiring further. But I had to ask one last question to satisfy my curiosity. "Would you become a squire if your mother allowed it?"

"Perhaps," the boy said after a moment of thought, "but I don't need to make that decision yet." He smiled up at me. "Is the interrogation over now? Do I qualify as good enough to look after your horse for you?"

I couldn't help but return the hauntingly familiar smile. "Yes, you're quite qualified. I need to take these bags into the castle, but once that's done you're welcome to take him off my hands."

Steven gently rubbed Duke's muzzle. "He's a handsome boy all right. What's his name?"

"Duke," I answered. "Not my choice—my brother named both our horses—but I think the name fits him."

"I think so too. Shall I find someone to help you with your bags?"

I shook my head. "Thank you, but no. I'm sure I'll be able to carry them myself, I would hate to bother anybody."

The stable boy gave the three overstuffed bags and then me a doubtful look, but shrugged to himself as if dismissing the thought before leading Duke to the castle stables. This left me and my belongings standing just outside the castle doors. I took a deep breath, hefted two of the bags over my shoulders and one beneath an arm. This accomplished, I staggered past the amused guards.

Just inside, I felt someone lift the bags from my shoulders with a disapproving sound. "You should have asked for help."

"I was doing just fine," I said rubbing my sore shoulder, more irritated at myself and the realization that I really should have taken the stable boy's advice than my good-natured teacher. I swallowed my pride, something I knew I would need to do more often. "Thank you for your help, William," I finished.

"What were you talking to my brother about?" my teacher asked while walking down the long hall to where he knew the princess would be waiting.

"Your brother? I didn't talk to a brother of yours!" I instinctively glanced backwards.

William smiled. "Yes, you did. The stable boy."

I stopped in astonishment for a moment. Replaying the conversation with the new stable boy in my mind, I finally realized what I should have known all along. "That would explain why he looked somewhat familiar."

"I thought you already knew he was my brother," William added. "You seemed comfortable talking with him."

I shrugged. "He was easy to talk to. Besides, he shares something in common with me."

"Which is…?"

"We both love horses," I finished.

"He certainly does," William agreed. "Horses…or rather, all animals, but horses in particular have been his passion since he was four years old."

"How old is he now?"

"Fourteen." William stopped in front of the princess's chambers and placed my bags carefully on the stone floors. He looked hardly winded at all from carrying the bags I knew were terribly heavy.

I fingered my shoulders again, realizing that the muscles I used for sword fighting and the muscles used for carrying heavy bags were in very different places. Silently, I thanked God for putting a brother and a friend in my life who would save me from making myself more of an embarrassment than I already had.

When my teacher turned to walk back through the hall, I asked him a question that had come to me suddenly. "William, have you other family? I mean, other than Steven?"

"I have no other siblings, if that's what you're asking," William answered.

"But what about parents?" I persisted.

"Oh," William said, an unreadable mask coming over his face. "I do have a mother, but my father died a few years ago. It was a riding accident." The short, clipped sentences stung like a slap across my cheek. This was an entirely new side of William, one I hadn't seen in all my weeks of training under him.

For a moment I was speechless. "I'm so sorry. I shouldn't have asked."

My teacher shrugged and the emotionless mask relaxed. Not by much, but by enough that I could see William's old self again...just under the surface. "Our time of grieving has passed. Of course I'll always miss Father, but he's home, truly home, now. I wouldn't have him come back to experience the pain of death again if you were to offer me the entire kingdom. Are you planning on having your lesson today at the usual time?"

I chose to ignore the abrupt change of subject, recognizing a sensitive topic when I saw one. "I wouldn't want to miss it," I said.

"I'll be seeing you soon then." William walked swiftly away without another word.

I turned back to the door and knocked on it gently, still mulling over what William had said. Princess Christine ushered me in with a smile and helped me carry my bags over to the next chamber where she had arranged for me to stay when the men leave.

"There." The princess looked around her with an air of satisfaction. "Make yourself at home...at least, as much at home as you can be somewhere that's not actually your home."

I glanced over at her with a smile. "Thank you. I really do appreciate your kindness in letting me stay here while Malcolm was gone. I was worried to be in our cottage by myself."

Princess Christine waved away my thanks. "Oh hush! I'm the one who should be thanking you! After all, I don't think I could have survived being here in the castle alone."

"Thank you all the same," I repeated.

"Do you need my help putting your things away?"

I looked around and shook my head. "I think I can manage. Thank you for your offer."

"You're welcome of course. Let me leave you to your unpacking in peace."

The door separating our rooms was shut and I was left to my own devices. I stared at the closed door for a moment, then shook my head and began the long unpacking process.

I was going to be living in the castle, next to a princess, and at the king's request. It would take some getting used to.

9:

<u>And so it Begins...</u>

Once I finished the unpacking, I gave the princess another archery lesson. Afterwards we ate together in her room.

"How are you enjoying being a lady-in-waiting?" Christine asked after I told her I had settled myself in the adjoining chamber.

I smiled. "Very much indeed," I said. "The feast was absolutely wonderful, and being able to spend so much time with you is more fun than I ever imagined such a job could be."

"What's your favorite part?"

"Doing your hair," I answered promptly.

A puzzled frown appeared between the princess's eyebrows. "My hair? Why, may I ask?"

"Your hair is a great deal easier to work with than mine is," I answered ruefully, tugging at the shorter hairs that had already found their way out of the orderly bun I had put them in that morning. "It does exactly what it's supposed to do. I can do so many more things to yours than I can do to my own. I feel like a little girl again, doing the hair of a doll."

Christine's laugh was a pleasure to listen to. Her eyes almost disappeared as they narrowed into blue slits of color. How I loved making her laugh. No wonder Malcolm was so obviously smitten by her. I waited for her giggles to die away into an amused smile. I wished hard for the moment to last forever.

But, alas, my wish was not to be granted. Malcolm knocked quietly on the partially open door, coming in at the princess's invitation. His somber face stole the sparkle from Christine's eyes. The moment died a quiet, but significant death, foretelling that future moments like it would be few and far between.

Somehow, even before my brother could say it aloud, I realized that the war had begun. Nothing could ever be the same again.

"It's happened, hasn't it?" Christine's quiet voice sounded louder in the silence around us. From outside the window, I heard a bird sing out its song with a cheerfulness that seemed to mock us.

Malcolm nodded. "The Duke of Devonshire has just declared war on the King. We'll be marching out to fight him within the week."

We. Malcolm had said *we.* My brother would be leaving. I had been expecting war ever since the conversation the other day. But so soon? Worried thoughts began tumbling through my mind as I processed this news. I forced them away and focused on what I knew would be needed of me at the moment.

The princess made a choked sound and fled from her room toward the counseling chamber where we knew she would find her father. My brother made a move to stop her, but I grabbed his arm and shook my head, somehow understanding that Christine would want some time alone with her father.

"I'm ready to move into the castle at any time." I read the question in Malcolm's eyes and answered it before he had the chance to ask. "Everything I might need at any point during your absence is in the chamber adjoining the princess's apartments."

My brother smiled, but his smile was touched with worry. He turned to me, laid his hands on my shoulders, and studied me. "Are you going to be all right?"

The question took me by surprise. "Of course!" I exclaimed, pasting on what I hoped was a believably cheerful smile.

He looked skeptical. "You looked worried." He forced me to look him in the eye. "You still do...despite the smile."

"I'll be fine," I promised.

"I'll write you, whenever I get the chance, while I'm away," my brother continued. "That way you'll know what's going on. I expect you to do the same," he ordered with a grin. "I'll be counting on all your news to keep me cheerful."

I groaned. "I'm terrible at writing anything interesting."

My brother laughed. "I know, but Chris will help you with that. She's pretty good at writing interesting letters."

I raised an eyebrow. "And just how would you know that?" I queried, just for his reaction.

I wasn't to be disappointed. Malcolm blushed as if on cue. "Oh, she's written me before...a few times. But just from a friend to a friend, you know."

"Of course," I answered, stifling a snicker.

"I'm planning on asking Chris to marry me tonight," he whispered confidentially. "Her father just gave me permission."

My eyes widened. "That's...wonderful," I said, surprised by the suddenness. How long had Malcolm been courting Christine? I shrugged, my mind too busy with the matters at hand to bother counting months. No one cared much about the proper amount of courtship during times of war. Too much was at stake. Many men would be rushing to marry sweethearts before leaving for war. Many of those same girls would likely be left young widows by the time it was over. I shut that thought from my mind. Christine would not, *could* not, be one of those young women.

"Do you think she'll say yes?" my brother asked, breaking into my thoughts.

I raised an eyebrow before smiling. "I don't think you need to worry about that," I said.

"Do you suppose Chris will—" Here my brother broke off when he heard footfalls and the swish of dress material over the stone floor in the hall outside the door.

"Did he just call me Chris again?" the princess asked, coming from the hall and closing the door behind her. I noticed traces of tears on her cheeks, but she smiled past them in a valiant effort to remain herself.

I nodded in answer to her question and she shot an accusing look at Malcolm. "If I've told you once, I've told you a thousand times..." she began.

Malcolm's good-natured laugh drowned out the rest of her protest. "It won't work, Chris, I've made it a habit now."

The princess groaned. "I suppose I'll have to put up with it then," she said.

I smiled, leaving the two of them alone. It was time for my lesson in swordsmanship.

The following days went by in a blur, despite the slight pause in order for the king to host a small feast in honor of his daughter's engagement. As I, along with half the kingdom, had suspected, Christine was just as in love with my brother as he was with her.

Malcolm and I had few times together. He was busy talking with the king or helping with the preparations for the war; I was busy closing down our cottage and helping the princess remember everything the king was telling her to do during his absence.

The day arrived that signaled the beginning of all our men going to war. Well, not *all* the men. Some had been ordered to stay behind and guard those at home. Selfishly, I wished that my brother had been chosen as one of *those* men...but the king needed his strategic genius beside him during the battle. I knew only too well my brother's abilities; I had fallen victim to his gift of strategy during countless chess games in our childhood. Every single one of them I had lost. The memories brought a temporary smile to my face, which was soon touched with sadness. I was watching him leave...perhaps never to see him again.

"I'm going to miss him so much." A voice jerked me from the past and I realized that the princess had joined me beside the window in my temporary residence that overlooked the men who were lining up and marching from the village. The king rode to and fro between the lines of soldiers, giving words of cheer and courage. My brother rode close behind him.

I nodded wordlessly. Looking out at the other women saying goodbye, I was struck by how selfish I was acting. While it was only right to feel grief when seeing a loved one leave, it dawned on me that I was being blind to everyone else's. My eyes filled with tears as I watched the men being called from their homes, some of them even younger than my brother...a few not much older than myself. Mothers, sisters, and sweethearts were giving their men what could be the final goodbye. Many of these men would never return.

"You're not the only one," I said suddenly, half to myself, half to the princess beside me. "Look." I gestured towards the weeping wives and daughters.

A tear trickled down Christine's cheek. "Why?" she whispered. "Why does there have to be war? Why do people have to be so stubborn? Why do people like the Duke have to disobey those they should obey?"

I didn't know how to answer this onslaught of questions...questions that I myself was wondering. I sighed, wishing I could say something cheerful, but finding no appropriate words to speak.

"If God cared about us as much as He says He does, why does He allow war?" the princess demanded, more tears dripping down her cheek and off the end of her quivering chin. "Why can't the human race live in peace with one another? Isn't that what God wants? Peace?"

I sighed wearily and leaned against the window. "Yes, God wants us to be at peace with one another. But we ruined our chances of living in a perfect world when we sinned in the Garden of Eden. Now we have to live through the consequences of that sin. War is a choice. Men don't have to fight...but because we live in a fallen world, often they choose to declare war between one another and lives are lost because of their rash decision." I felt as if I was repeating myself, as well as filling the empty air with senseless words, so I stopped talking and watched the recruiting of men in silence.

The princess also was silent, and for a moment I could hear the faint shouts of the higher officers getting their men into their places for the march out of the village.

"Thank you," Christine said quietly. "I needed to hear that."

I looked over to her in surprise. "Why do you say that?"

"I've been struggling these past few days with those questions. My faith has been weak. Your answers have built it up again." The princess smiled through her tears. "I think you being here is going to help me have enough courage to last while Father is gone."

I returned her smile. "I'll be as much help as I can."

We both turned back to the window. Enough had been said. Right now both of us wanted to be silent.

Our men were now lined up, and with King Frederick in the lead they marched out of the village, leaving everyone with a feeling of loss. Who knew when we would see them again, if ever? We could only wait, while praying and hoping, for their survival during the ensuing battles.

10:
The Reluctant Ruler

During the next few days, while the princess began to learn how to become the ruler her father's kingdom needed while he was gone, I did my best to help her with her burden.

I stopped my lessons with William, even though he hadn't been taken with the other men. This was mostly so I could be closer to Christine in case she needed me, but partially because it made me miss my brother more when I was near William. He reminded me so much of Malcolm that it pained me to watch him safe and sound in the castle while my brother was in constant danger.

I hated myself for it, but I felt angry with William for being chosen as one of the men to remain behind. It wasn't even his fault. The king wanted him around to help protect the castle because his reputation with the guards as a sword master had earned him their respect. Though a leader without a title, he still was the best choice when it came to choosing someone to stay behind and keep the king's daughter safe while he was away. Most of the soldiers were his friends, and all of them would do anything to have a chance to fight by his side.

Not only was he influential, but he knew the people of the kingdom from his wanderings around it in previous years as a peddler. This made him an essential part in any of the court hearings. However, I blamed him for obeying the order to stay. I tried my best to avoid him as much as possible, foolishly thinking that it would help. Of course, it didn't, but I made myself believe that it would all the same.

One afternoon, about three weeks after the men had left, I found the princess sitting alone out on her balcony. The wind was playing with a few strands of hair, which had somehow escaped her bun despite my best efforts at keeping her looking regal, at least on the outside. Tears had made small rivers down the side of her face, and she looked miserable.

I came up behind her, my dress swishing against the stone floors, and she turned when she heard me approaching. "What's wrong?" I asked softly.

"Me," she answered bitterly. "I'm wrong."

The answer took me by surprise. "Why do you say that?"

A sob tore from the princess's throat, and fresh tears began flowing down her cheeks. "I'm a horrible ruler!" she wept. "I simply can't do it anymore. I need someone else to take over. I'm spent. Father didn't know what he was asking me to do. He should have found someone else who could shoulder the responsibility better. Someone who could always know how to deal with all the people properly…someone who is a great deal wiser than me."

I waited until Christine had finished. Obviously, she needed someone to release her emotions on, and frankly, I didn't mind bearing the brunt of it. Part of me could understand—even feel to some extent—what she was going through.

During the pause she took to take a breath I said, "I don't see why you think you're such a horrible ruler. You've been doing a fine job in my opinion."

Christine searched my face. "You really think that?"

I nodded confidently. "Most definitely!"

"But this morning, when I tried my hand at settling a dispute, William Price came up to me afterward and told me that I hadn't made the right decision! He tried to explain, but it all went over my head. Then," the princess's breath caught, and a few more tears made their way onto her folded hands, "he gave me such a scolding…I'm not likely to forget it in a long time."

Christine looked up at me with pain-filled eyes. "I felt so humiliated, Meg. As he spoke to me, I almost wished the ground would open up and swallow me."

As I heard her story, I felt my insides boiling in anger at William's act. How dare he be so presumptuous towards the princess? How dare he make her feel so ashamed of herself? The princess felt unworthy enough already without his added insults to her ruling abilities. If only the king were here, or Malcolm. They could talk some sense into him. Only they weren't. A fact I grieved almost every waking moment. Much as I disliked it, I knew I would have to take care of it. Christine was too softhearted to voice her protests to William herself.

When Christine finished her woebegone tale, I spoke. "Christine, I shall go talk to William and tell him *exactly* what I think of his actions. Don't let them worry you again. I doubt that they will be repeated after I'm through."

The princess gave me such a look of gratefulness; I felt repaid right there for the trouble William was sure to give me later. "I can't thank you enough, Meg!" she said with a smile. "But please, don't be too hard on him...I don't think he realized that he would hurt my feelings as deeply as he did."

I grunted my doubts, and stood to go right then, but the princess detained me a little longer. "I wish my father had put you on the throne instead of me," she began wistfully. "You seem so good at telling people what to do."

There was a moment of silence. I wasn't sure whether the princess had meant that last remark as a compliment or as a subtle hint that I was being too rash in my decision to chastise William. I tried to come up with something vague as my answer, but nothing came.

With a startled look, Christine seemed to realize how that statement must have come across. "I-I'm so sorry!" she gasped. "I didn't mean to—that came out wrong. I'm so sorry. I *meant* that you would make a much better ruler than me. Ordering people around comes so much more naturally to you—" She covered her face with her hands. "I'm only making it worse, aren't I?"

I chuckled. "Never mind. I know what you're trying to say, and that's what really matters."

The tension melted and I left the princess in a much better mood than when I found her. I, however, was glowering darkly by the time the door to her chambers shut behind me. William was going to get an earful...if only I knew where to find him.

After a great deal of wandering around the castle and its surrounding courtyard and walls, and asking people if they had seen him go by, I found William practicing his sword with someone I didn't recognize. I waited until the other person left before approaching him.

"Lady Megan?" he asked in puzzled concern as I came closer. "Are you alright?"

My glower would have deepened if that was even possible. "I'm fine," I answered flatly. "It's the princess I came to talk to you about."

Worry sprang into his eyes. "Is she sick? Does she need a doctor? Should I ride to the king?"

I shook my head. "Nothing like that. I want to talk to you about your conversation with her this morning."

Relief that nothing was wrong flooded across William's face, and he broke into his smile that reminded me so painfully of my brother. I was annoyed to find my anger cooling...even disappearing slowly.

Before I lost it altogether, I demanded, "Well? Have you anything to say in your defense against her accusation?"

The puzzled look came back again. "Her accusation?"

"I was told that you not only pretended to be a better ruler than her, but also humiliated her and wounded her feelings. Is that true?"

"I did give her my opinion this morning after the Devin versus Filer trial was brought before her. And I do vaguely recall giving her advice lest the same thing ever happened again." An annoyed edge appeared in William's voice, and his face lost its smile. "Was I wrong in that?"

I braced myself. "You were certainly wrong in humiliating her," I replied.

"I most certainly did *not* humiliate her," William answered hotly, showing me that he *did* have a temper, a fact I had doubted before.

"Now you're calling the princess a liar!" I declared just as angrily.

William's eyes narrowed and he gave me as stern a look as someone easygoing could manage before steering me away from where we were currently attracting attention. "Let me set *my* side of the story before you...then you might not judge my advice to the princess as light as you do now."

He sat me down on a nearby bench and began: "Before King Frederick left, he asked me a favor...to give his daughter advice on how to take care of court matters whenever I could, knowing that wasn't one of your duties.

"The last few months I have spent a great deal of time near Malcolm and taught swordsmanship to several of his chief advisors, so he knew how well I understood the court and its systems. I began attending court a few weeks before he was to leave so I would understand it even more. Since then, I have been keeping an eye on the princess and her dealings in the court.

"This morning, a case came before her that was two men fighting over the boundary of their lands. One accused the other of intentionally letting his flocks graze on his fields that his own sheep desperately needed. The other man claimed that he had fallen asleep while watching his flocks, and that they had wandered off while..."

Here William waved a hand in front of my eyes and jerked my attention away from the squirrel I had been watching run back and forth between two trees. When I looked over at him again, I saw a flash of irritation pass through his otherwise placid face. "Pay attention to me, Megan, I'm trying to explain why I was giving advice to the princess!"

"I was," I said stubbornly.

William's good humor, ever near the surface, appeared, and he chuckled. "It *looked* like you were watching that squirrel."

I wanted to smile, but for some strange reason was also loathe to find my temper again after losing it. "I can listen while watching something else, you know," I said instead, my arms folded defensively.

"Very well," William answered, his smile fading again, "let me continue: The other man claimed that after he had fallen asleep, the sheep had wandered off into the other man's land. After hearing each of their stories, the princess decided that the first man, Devin was his last name, was being greedy with his land, and should therefore share with the other man, whose last name was Filer."

Here William's voice became softer, less like stating the facts of a trial and more like he knew these men and wanted to help them. "What the princess didn't know, and it was here where she erred, was that Devin is a poor farmer with half the amount of land and sheep that his neighbor Filer has. Filer, though also moderately poor, was considerably better off than Devin and therefore should have been the one to apologize and pay for any damage his sheep did to Devin's fields.

"I tried to explain this to the princess, but she didn't seem to be taking me seriously so I began telling her the seriousness of her position and how great a ruler's responsibility is." William sighed and ran a hand through his hair. "I wasn't trying to humiliate her," he finished. "Or hurt her feelings. I was only trying to help."

I succeeded in finding my temper, and my anger died away quickly afterwards. This left me with a humiliating sense of regret over my ridiculous actions. I rose shamefacedly and offered my hand to William before apologizing like the lady I was trying so hard to become. "I understand now," I said. "Please forgive my abominable behavior. I will tell the princess that you meant no harm."

William smiled before ducking down to kiss the back of my hand, a strange act I was getting used to now that I had been in the castle and around nobility long enough. "I forgive you wholeheartedly. I understand what you must have felt. Never mind about telling the princess, I'll come with you and apologize to her," he answered. "I truly didn't mean to offend."

"She'll appreciate it," I replied, knowing I would, had I been in her position.

And so our friendship was patched. For the first time in three weeks, I slept all night...and my deep sleep was scattered with beautiful dreams of days before war.

11:
News from Afar

Every day I looked for the promised letter from Malcolm eagerly. Over four months had passed since they had marched off into the distance, and my worry for his safety grew as the weeks went by. Before falling asleep, and even in my dreams, I would invent all sorts of horrible circumstances that I imagined must have kept him from writing me.

Even the passing and celebration of my eighteenth birthday did little to cheer me up. The princess told me I reminded her of a mother hen, and William declared that he had never seen anyone worry so much in his life. I ate little and haunted the castle gate in order to pounce on the first knight the king sent as a messenger to us.

But, as it turned out, my worries were without cause, for I finally received a letter in Malcolm's handwriting. It came from a soldier who was promptly whisked off by the princess to hear all about the progress of the battle and how her father was doing.

I shut myself in my chamber, settled down next to the window so I could read by the dying sunshine, and opened the precious note.

Dearest Meg,

I hope this letter finds you and Chris both happy and well. I long to hear all the news you have of dealings in the castle and all the trouble you have managed to get into while we responsible ones are away.

I smiled and treasured each word he wrote...I could almost hear his voice in my head as I read his loving, teasing sentences. My eyes dimmed with unshed tears. Oh, how I missed him! More than he could ever realize. *We are well,* I thought to myself in sorrow, *but hardly happy without you.* I continued to read:

Let Chris know that her father is doing very well. He contracted a slight fever after having to stay out in a bad rainstorm while we were marching, but he seems to have recovered quickly, and is now back to his normal, busy self. However, it took us a few weeks waiting for the men who had fallen ill to regain their strength before marching on. We have a few days left before reaching where we believe our enemies lie in wait, but God has blessed us with fine weather and even better company.

Prince lost a shoe about a week into our march, so now he goes barefoot. I think he likes it, but I am worried that his hooves might be quite worse for wear when we return. He would not let me get near enough to see, so I hope you will give me some advice as to how to manage him. You always were better at taking care of him than me.

Oh Meg, I cannot tell you how much I miss you and your funny outlook on life. Every day when I wake up I think about you and how much I wish you were here with me. This morning we were awakened by the most beautiful sunrise. It was your favorite colors, Meg, and I wish I could somehow capture its beauty in words, but words fail me. I pray for you and Chris as well as all the people at home every day. May He bless you with the best that life can offer.

Tell Chris that I send my love. I wrote as soon as time allowed. Chris will be getting her own letter soon after this one I hope. Alfred is coming after Flannigan with her letter. I do not have time

92

before Flannigan leaves to write another letter; this one I will only be able to get to him barely. His baby is being born soon, so the king gave him temporary leave to go back for a few days and then return with Alfred.

This march has taken its toll on all of us. We are tired and worn, but God continues to give us strength to face each new, exhausting day. Somehow, we all keep a stiff upper lip and courageously keep going, but already we have fought a few battles with some scouts and left dead men behind us, both ours and the enemies. It pains me to speak of the hardships of war, but you have to know that not all is sunrises and buttercups along our march.

Please send a reply back to us with Alfred and Flannigan whenever you get this letter. I long to hear about everything. If you cannot think of anything to say, at least send your love in the letter I know Chris will send.

I hear Flannigan mounting up, so I will end this letter now, with promises of another one soon.

I love you Meg, and I cannot wait until I hear from you and Chris.

Your loving brother,

Malcolm

I finished his letter with a sigh, and smiled. The door to my chamber was opened softly and Christine poked her head in.

"Meg?" she said.

I motioned her to come over to me. "Malcolm says he sent a letter to you, but that it will arrive later. He sends his love in this one."

Christine's eyes were suspiciously damp. "Did he? Oh, how I miss him. I hope they return soon."

I stood and hugged the princess. "I do too," I whispered, tears threatening to spill from my own eyes. I stepped back and handed her my precious letter. "Here, you can read this. It won't be as good as reading your own, but it'll suffice until yours arrives."

A sparkle appeared in the princess's eyes that had long been hidden and she hugged the letter to her heart. "I can't thank you enough Meg, this means more than words can tell."

"I'll want it back," I added teasingly as she walked away. "Be careful with it."

Christine looked back at me before going into her chamber. "I will treat it like gold," she promised.

* * † * *

Dear Malcolm,
I miss you. And I hope you return home safely very soon.
Much love,
Megan

I stared at the paper in disgust. This was going just as badly as I thought it would. My reply sounded short, dry, and extremely boring. Rubbing my forehead, I tried hard to think what I would want my letter to sound like. I wanted it to sound like what I wished I could say out loud to him right now. I threw the fifth letter under the desk and began yet again.

My dearest brother,

I can't begin to describe how happy I was to receive your letter. Christine and I have been longing to hear from you ever since we saw you disappear from our sight. The princess has yet to get your letter, but she now looks forward with great anticipation to Alfred's arrival.

We have been doing fairly well, all things considered. The princess did get a little humiliated after a scolding from William the other day, but after hearing his side of the story, it really was her fault. She's fine now though, and we haven't had any other wrinkles in our life. And no, we haven't got into any trouble. Not yet at any rate.

I will keep you and the other soldiers in our prayers for safety. Oh, I wish I could put how much I miss you into this letter, but Malcolm, you know only too well how bad I am at getting what I feel into words on a page.

Tell the king that Christine wishes for him by her side every day, and that she is doing a fine job running the kingdom while he is away, for even though she thinks she is doing a horrid job, she is really quite good at it. William tries his best to help, but with most of her father's advisors gone at war, it's been a bit tricky to say the least. I think we'll manage though.

I look forward to your next letter. I think they'll be the only things to keep me from worrying my life away while stuck here at the castle. You know I hate being cooped up without anything worthwhile to do with my time except helping the princess. And she does such a good job by herself, I hardly feel needed.

Well, I hope this letter cheers you, even though I'm not half as good at filling you in on news as Christine probably is. I hope it finds you as well as your letter found us. I won't bother sending Christine's love, since I'm sure she wishes to send you her love herself in her own letter.

I miss you, and I hope to see you back home and safe very, very soon.

Much love,

Megan

P. S. About Prince's hooves, just give him some sugar and soft words and he shouldn't give you any more trouble. I'll be prepared for the worst when you return.

I sat back and stretched my arms, suddenly tired. My hands, wrists, and arms were shouting their complaints up to my brain, but I ignored them and carefully sealed my reply before setting it upright on my desk.

Sir Alfred, one of the king's many knights, was expected tomorrow, and I looked forward to the news he would bring of our loved ones. I could hear Christine's soft snores through the open door between our chambers, and I smiled.

Blowing out the candle I had been writing by, I felt my way to bed in the darkness and undressed as quickly as possible in the sudden chill. I slipped into my nightgown and under the warm covers.

Within moments I drifted off to sleep, welcoming the escape from reality and pang of loneliness.

12:
More News

Sir Alfred didn't arrive until after our supper was finished. He swept off his horse, bowed stiffly, and presented Christine her letter from Malcolm with a thin smile.

"I hope Your Highness is doing well?" he asked.

Christine returned his smile and took the letter. "Yes, thank you." She paused for a moment before continuing, "My father...is he still doing well?"

For a brief moment, so slight that I fancied it was my imagination, a shadow of a smile passed over the soldier's grave face. "Your Highness," he started slowly, "I dislike being a bearer of bad news...but your father is not doing very well. He caught a bad fever a few weeks ago, and we thought he made a turn for the better up until just after Flannigan left. That very night the fever returned and has been gradually getting worse."

A small moan escaped the princess's pale lips and she covered her mouth with a trembling hand. "Oh no...no, no, no."

The knight placed a hand on her shoulder and sighed. "I'm sorry I had to be the one to tell you this, but we don't have much hope for him."

Christine let out a choked cry and fled to her room. Sir Alfred made a move as if he would follow her, but I stood between him and the fleeing girl in the effort to stop him.

"Sir, you must understand that she needs some time to take in this news, not to mention the time she'll need to read my brother's letter in peace."

Sir Alfred nodded. "I wish there was something I could do to help."

I smiled, any trace of suspicion gone when I saw his concern. "I'm afraid only time alone will help her right now. I'll check on her in a little while. She may want more details from you after the first shock is over."

"I'll be here to give it," Alfred answered. "If she needs me, I'll be in Tumbler's Tavern and Inn."

"Thank you again, sir, the princess will appreciate it."

The knight took his leave, and I began to walk to my chambers in order to await the princess's inevitable request for my presence. William slid from the shadows to join me with a thoughtful frown knitted across his brow.

"I don't trust him," he said.

His words drew a sharp glance from me, since I hadn't seen him listening to the messenger's conversation, but then a warm feeling of security washed over me. I knew if the knight ended up being an enemy of some sort, which I doubted he really was, then William would make sure the Princess and I were kept safe at all costs. After all, this was why the King had left him behind.

I waited for more but when he only returned my silence with silence, I asked, "Why do you say that? He seemed truly concerned about the king's ill health, and sorry that he had to be the bearer of bad news. It was good of him to tell the princess the truth about her father, even if it wasn't what she wanted to hear."

"Malcolm said that the king was doing much better in his letter," William said out loud, as if speaking his thoughts, "Why would Malcolm lie to his own sister...or the princess for that matter?"

"How do you know what my letter from Malcolm said?" I demanded.

"I asked the princess about it since I knew you probably wouldn't tell me," William answered matter-of-factly. "You and the princess aren't the only ones hungry for news."

"Well, anyways, Alfred didn't lie," I continued, determined not to let him win, and feeling a bit peeved by the fact that he assumed I wouldn't tell him news from my brother. "Malcolm's letter came with Flannigan, and he said the king got worse *after* Flannigan left. And Malcolm himself mentioned that the king had gotten a fever, but thought he was on the mend, which matches Alfred's story."

William's face stayed in a frown as we kept walking towards where I knew the princess would be, and he sighed heavily. "I don't know exactly why I'm so suspicious of him. He just seems, oh, I don't know…false somehow. Call it a fancy if you like, but there's something about him…" he trailed off into silence as we neared the princess's chambers.

"I think you're worrying too much over absolutely nothing," I answered. "You've had a lot of stress recently, perhaps you need a rest. Surely someone can replace you as the princess's court advisor."

William shook his head. "I don't think so, though I appreciate your concerns for my health." He gave me a cocky grin.

I felt my face heating into a blush, which only made things worse, so I turned to the door quickly. "Just stop all the useless worrying, nothing is going to happen."

Just before closing the door, I heard William whisper a reply more to himself than to me: "I hope not."

* * † * *

I found Christine lying on her bed, staring at its canopy with a blank look on her face. I saw traces of tears on her cheeks, but they were nearly gone. The forgotten letter from Malcolm lay on a chair, but she was obviously not in the mood to scan its contents.

"Christine?" I whispered, tiptoeing closer until her blank eyes met mine. "Do you need anything?"

"No." The word seemed as dry and empty as the cupboards of the poorest families in her kingdom.

I sat on the bed, which creaked under my weight, but the princess turned her face away from me. "Christine," I said again patiently, "you know you can talk to me freely."

The drawbridge dropped across the vast moat that had been between us because of her grief from having her father dying somewhere she couldn't be. She crawled over to me, the tears once again streaming down her face. "I don't want Father to die!" she sobbed. "I can't stand the thought that I may have to rule this kingdom by myself. I'd rather *die*," she added, placing a hand over her heart in a dramatic fashion. "To be completely honest, I'm terrified of having to rule a kingdom. *Terrified*," she repeated in distress. "And if Father was to die…" her head sank onto my shoulder. "I can't lose him like I lost Mother."

If I had been anywhere else, in any other situation, it would have been humorous how frantic the princess was not to rule…but as it was, I hugged Christine without a word. For a few moments, we simply sat there on her luxurious bed. Christine wept out her store of tears, and I received them, my dress soaking them up until I was as wet as if I had been out riding Duke in a rainstorm. The sobs died away gradually into hiccups, and I looked out the window only to shock myself at how late it was. I stood up and moved away from the bed, throwing more logs into her fireplace and hoping that the glowing embers were still hot enough to catch the new wood on fire.

The princess came and joined me next to the warmth, hugging herself. I fought back the sudden shivers that wracked my body, and gave her a tight-lipped smile that I hoped was convincingly warm in the firelight. "Hungry?" I questioned.

Christine nodded. "Yes, thank you."

"I'll get you some food," I said, turning to go.

The princess detained me with a hand on my shoulder. "Meg," she said softly. I met her gaze. "I-well, thank you for

102

being here with me. I was acting childish I know. Your presence was such a comfort. Your shoulder to cry on meant more to me than a hundred words." After a moment of silence, she continued, "Meg, I haven't told anyone…not even Malcolm, how my mother died."

A small frown settled between my eyebrows. "Nor do you need to. Not if you don't want to," I added. "I understand, really, I do."

Christine shook her head. "No, no…I want to tell you. Because you will understand. It's part of why I act the way I do." Her eyes met mine across the circle of firelight and I noticed tears gathering in them again. "I know how people talk about me. How I balk away from positions of leadership. A lot of people think I'm a coward. No," she held up a hand at my protests, "it's true. I've heard it with my own ears."

Tears had begun falling again, and she took my hands in hers. "Meg, I don't want you to believe the rumors."

"I never would," I assured her from the bottom of my heart.

She smiled at me. "Thank you for that…but I want to tell you."

"If it will make you feel better."

The princess's eyes closed and a cloud passed over her fire-lit features. I could almost watch the memories pass through her mind.

After a heavy sigh, she began, "My mother was a wonderful woman. She had that queenly air about her that made everyone respect her, listen to her, and obey her every command. Yet she was a gentle and loving wife and mother at the same time. I grew up wishing with every breath that I could grow up to be like her.

"Not long after my seventh birthday, my mother became ill. The healers tried everything, *everything,* to help her. Nothing worked. She began to waste away. Every time I visited her, she was more thin and more weak than the time before." The princess took a deep, shuddering breath.

"During what turned out to be my last visit, my mother took my hands in hers and looked at me with the same bright, intelligent eyes that no sickness could ever dim. I'll never forget what she told me for as long as I live. She said 'my sweet, precious Christine…take care of your father for me. Leading a kingdom isn't ever an easy job. Responsibility can never be taken lightly, and is not a job for weaklings.'

"Here she sighed and gripped my hands harder. 'Kingdoms rise, and kingdoms fall, but the best rulers are the ones who follow our God and use His wisdom to lead. No one should ever have to lead alone. When someone tries to rule by themselves, they will fall, and their fall will be great. Make sure your father never has to rule by himself. Make sure he always has someone to help, otherwise the power will turn them to tyrants.

'Christine, if I die before speaking with you again, please remember these things of all I just told you: being royalty is not merely an honor, but a heavy responsibility. Ruling a kingdom is a task that should never fall on a single pair of shoulders, because if it does, their human nature will take over and they will become monsters.

'Oh, my precious daughter, take care of your father. I love you.'" Christine's face was full of pain when her eyes finally opened.

There was a long silence. Then she turned to me. "And that, Meg, is why I'm terrified of leading our kingdom. I'm afraid of what I might become."

I wrapped the princess in a hug, my own eyes stinging with unshed tears. "No," I whispered. "You will never become a monster, or a tyrant, or anything else terrible."

"How can I be sure?" she said.

"Because you will never be alone," I answered with a smile. "That's why I'm here. It's what all your friends are for." I headed towards the door again, but she stopped me.

"Meg?"

"Yes?"

"Send that messenger…what's-his-name." She frowned in concentration, trying to remember the knight's name.

"Sir Alfred," I offered.

Her brow cleared. "Yes, Sir Alfred. Send Sir Alfred up here, please, along with my dinner. I'd like to talk to him for a moment. Alone."

It was my turn to frown. William's words echoed in my mind. "Are you sure that is wise?" I asked aloud.

Christine nodded. "Sir Alfred must be a trusted knight of my father's to be allowed to bring letters from Malcolm back to the castle; he wouldn't harm me for the world. But if it makes you feel any better, you can have a few of my men guard outside the door." She gave me a hopeful look. "I just want to find out how my father is doing…how he is *really* doing, and I forgot to ask about how the rest of the army is coping with Father sick. And I want to know how Malcolm is doing," she admitted.

"I'll find him," I promised. I handed her the still unopened letter. "You can read this while you're awaiting Sir Alfred."

She took the letter from my hand and I walked down to the kitchen to retrieve her some food. I saw William talking with the cook, and waved to him with a smile. He returned the gesture and came over to where I stood.

"How is the princess?" he asked.

I sighed. "Well enough, considering she practically got told that her father is dying," I answered.

He motioned to the damp spot on the shoulder of my gown. "You should change out of those and into something dry and warm."

"They'll dry. I'm here to get her food; she hasn't had dinner."

"Neither have you, I'll wager. Sit down; Samuel can bring Princess Christine her meal."

I sank into the offered chair with a grateful sigh. Almost immediately, my stomach growled loudly, much to my embarrassment and William's silent amusement. The cook's assistant, Samuel, came over at William's beckon and looked at him respectfully with his hands folded in front of him.

"Sir?" he asked like the polished servant he was.

"Princess Christine would like dinner served in her room tonight," William said. I was impressed by his ability to make an order sound so nice. "I was hoping you could bring it to her?" It wasn't really a question, but Samuel nodded.

"To be sure, I'd be honored, sir."

"Thank you."

I caught the man's sleeve as he turned to obey William's orders. "Oh, and Samuel?"

"Yes, Milady?"

"She wishes to have a talk with Sir Alfred, the soldier and messenger from our king. If you wouldn't mind fetching him as well?"

A shadow stole over William's face and a frown darkened his brow. "Are you sure she should do that? Why does she want to meet with *him?*"

"She wants more details on how the army is doing and her father's condition. But, have no fear, I'm having two of her guards watch outside her door while they're in conference."

That seemed to lessen his worries some, but not much. He dismissed Samuel with a nod of his head and his frown faded and mixed with the shadows on his face.

Samuel filled a tray with food and started on his way to executing his orders. William gave me a tray and then proceeded to watch me eat it, much to my chagrin. Finally, after choking down a few mouthfuls, I looked up at the half-smile tucked around my teacher's face and decided I had had enough.

"Could you please go somewhere else while I'm eating?" I asked.

"Am I making you nervous?" he asked as if he rather fancied the idea. A twinkle appeared in his eyes and he grinned. "Sorry." He didn't fool me in the slightest. The man wasn't sorry at all.

"I just don't like people watching me eat," I mumbled. The truth was he *did* make me nervous, and I was furious at my nerves for betraying me so. Inwardly, I rolled my eyes. *Next thing I'll be blushing,* I thought with a grimace and took another bite to cover my mistake. Too late. He had noticed.

"Are you unwell?" William was all chivalry the next moment. How a man could change that quickly baffled me. "I warned you about those wet clothes of yours."

"I'm fine," I began quickly trying to think up an excuse. "I only—"

Suddenly, Steven, William's brother, burst into the kitchen along with the distinct smell of manure. His face was red from exertion and his eyes were wild. Frantically, he searched the faces of everyone in the kitchen before noticing me and William over by the table. Relief mixed with the panic and he ran towards me, upsetting several dishes and people in the process.

"Milady!" he said in a hoarse whisper once he dropped breathless at my feet. He gulped air into his lungs before gasping out, "Milady, Sir Alfred is planning on kidnapping the princess!"

13:
A Traitor in Our Midst

I felt the blood drain from my face. Instinctively I glanced up at William, who looked exactly how I felt at the moment. He was an unnatural shade of gray.

William and I rushed away from our forgotten supper with Steven close behind. My teacher led the way down the torch-lit hallways, past the startled Samuel, who almost dropped the tray of food he had in his hands, and to the princess's quarters where the two guards I had told to stand watch gawked at us in startled confusion.

William reached the closed door first. It was locked, but that didn't stop him. He heaved himself against the door until it crashed apart under his terrific onslaught. Thankfully, the two open-mouthed guards and Samuel had enough sense about them to stay out of his way.

Once the door gave in, he burst into the room with me only a few feet behind him. When I arrived, he was standing stalk still with his sword drawn in the middle of the princess's private chambers. The fire was still blazing from the same log I had put in it less than an hour ago, but the window was open, and a slight evening breeze chilled my still damp gown. Steven was

109

right behind me, and the three of us stood in the deafening stillness that shrouded the room like a cloud.

"No," I said softly. Disbelief and horror finally made it past the numbing shock. "No, no, *no!* There has to be some mistake! Sir Alfred is one of the king's soldiers! He's a knight! He's supposed to have undying loyalty to his sovereign!" I began pacing around the room, trying to work out in my mind the confusing turn of events.

William sheathed his sword and a dangerous look came into his eyes. "He may have had undying loyalty to his sovereign, but I doubt his sovereign was King Frederick."

"No," Steven agreed, coming up to me. "He's one of Duke of Devonshire's men."

I turned to the boy and sat him down. "Tell me all you heard," I said.

Steven sent a questioning look up to his brother, and William replied with a curt nod. The younger boy had sudden fire leap into his eyes and he began speaking in a hushed whisper.

"I was bedding down a few of the horses in the stable tonight, and one of the mares was near giving birth so I was planning on staying the night in her stall just in case...but I must have dropped off to sleep, because the next thing I knew, two men were talking in the stall next to mine.

"I remembered that the horse in there belonged to Sir Alfred, the knight who had just arrived, and I was about ready to get up and ask if I could do anything to help them when Sir Alfred mentioned the princess's name."

A cold feeling settled into the pit of my stomach when I heard this. After all, I had spoken in Sir Alfred's defense when William mentioned his distrust...and I was repaid with *this?*

Steven continued, "He mentioned that the whole story about the king being sick was just a ruse to give him a chance to get the princess alone and that he had some sedative seeds from some healer somewhere in case the first plan of tricking her into coming with him to the king's camp didn't work."

Why had I left the Princess's side? Why had I trusted Sir Alfred? Why hadn't the guards done something? Why? Why? Why? I blamed myself for this. It was *my* fault the Princess was kidnapped.

"When the other man asked when he was planning on doing the kidnapping, he said, 'Kidnapping is an ugly word, and I prefer the term "borrowing for political reasons" myself.' The other man shrugged this reproof off and mentioned he didn't think there was a difference.

Sickening. I shook my head in disbelief. How could I have been so blind? William must think me such a fool.

"That's when Sir Alfred said the princess had asked for him to meet with her and talk to him about the king's condition among other things. At that time he was planning on taking her to the Duke."

I was angry now. Angry at myself as well as the Duke and the traitor, Sir Alfred.

"At this point I had heard enough," Steven said. "I thought I would come to you before Sir Alfred and the other man had time to carry out his plan. Unfortunately," the boy sighed in deep disappointment, "Alfred and his friend heard me leaving and the last thing I remember after trying to outrun them is sparks flying in my eyes and everything going black.

"As soon as I regained consciousness, I came to you as fast as I could, hoping desperately that I wasn't too late...but I was." The boy looked downhearted, and I gave him a smile.

"You did your best," I said in hopes of cheering him up. "Better than I might have done in your place." I couldn't even keep the Princess safe when she was inside her own room.

"They must not have hit you very hard," William put in. "We didn't miss the abduction by much."

"Is there a chance we can catch them before they reach the Duke's castle?" I asked, summoning a spark of hope in my desperate soul.

"A small one." William became business at once. "Steven, saddle my horse, I'm going after Christine."

111

"And mine," I added as Steven left the room.

William looked at me in surprise and with a small amount of displeasure. "I don't think you should..." he began.

My eyes pleaded with him silently. "I need to see that she's not hurt," I said. "Let me come. Please." How could I face Malcolm or the King after failing my duties as her protector?

A resigned expression came over William's face. "Very well, saddle Lady Megan's horse as well."

Steven gave us both a quick nod and bolted towards the stable. William followed him and told me to get ready; we would be leaving as quickly as possible.

I didn't need much, simply changed into a riding dress and slipped Safeguard onto my belt. I looked longingly at my bow and arrows, but realized they would only encumber my riding, so left them behind. Who knew what circumstances we would face in rescuing the princess...? I would hate to take chances with her life in danger.

I met William and Steven in the stable and was surprised to find not two, but three horses ready and saddled. My face must have registered the confusion I was feeling because a determined light sparked in Steven's eyes.

"I'm not being left here," he stated in a firm tone.

I glanced at William, who shrugged and grinned. "I doubt Steven will slow us down, he's a better horseman than I am!"

"I don't doubt his abilities," I returned with a weak smile. "If you're willing to have him along, I would feel safer with both of you."

With that we rode from the castle with the wind in our face and night falling about us. Clouds hid the moon's faint light and darkness fell like a cloak to veil the deeds done by the night creatures which now made their noises around us. Our horses fled through the forest as if chased by a thousand mad dogs.

William had not lied about his younger brother's horsemanship. Steven rode in the front and it seemed as if he knew by instinct whenever a tree, rock, stump or any other manner of roadblock came across our path. He warned us of each in low tones, leading his own horse skillfully around them and slowing his frantic pace only twice when crossing bodies of rushing waters that I could hear more than see.

I rode in the middle, thanking God for giving me a father and brother who had been willing to take the time to teach me the fine art of horsemanship. This and prayers for our safety soon became as regular as breathing while we journeyed through the dark trees.

In the back, I heard William offering up his own prayers for our safety, and more than once he asked me if I was all right when we stopped our horses for a brief rest before traveling onward towards the territory of the Duke of Devonshire.

Twice, we stopped long enough to eat some food, which William had somehow remembered to pack despite the circumstances.

"Are you all right?" William asked for at least the tenth time that day and the night before.

"I am as fine as I can be with the princess in danger," I answered, the same as I had the previous times.

William's eyes were filled with concern. "Tell us if this pace is too fast," he said. "We'll slow down if it is too much for you to take."

"You're a wonderful brother," Steven noted sarcastically from where he sat building a fire. "I'm just fine. Thank you for asking."

A grin popped out from where it had been hidden, and William's eyes lit up. "Just build the fire," he said. "I would ask about you if I was worried, but I'm not."

"Thanks?" Steven looked up from his handiwork after one last puff of air from his mouth. The fire's growing flame caught onto the bigger sticks and he stopped just long enough to feed it some larger wood to work with. He leaned back on his feet as he crouched there and squinted up at us where we were sitting on a fallen log.

"You're welcome," William answered. "Yes, it was meant as a compliment." He leaned over to ruffle up his brother's hair, but Steven successfully dodged away.

"I'm a little old for that, don't you think?" Steven joked. "How would you like it if I did it to you?"

William held up his hands in surrender. "Very well, you made your case. I'll stop."

The fire's comforting heat was making me sleepy. I pinched my arm in the effort to keep awake, and when that effect faded and my eyes drooped again, I shook my head violently to clear it of all fog.

My teacher noticed my exhaustion and ordered a few hours' sleep for all three of us, him and Steven taking turns at the watch. Anything further he said was lost to me, for the minute he said I could sleep, I did.

14:
The Journey Continues

I awoke to Steven shaking my shoulder when the gray beginnings of dawn touched the edges of the horizon. William was saddling the horses and I sat up, realizing that sometime during my sleep someone had laid a blanket over me where I slept over by the log. I pulled it around my shoulders. The chill of the fog that had enveloped the forest, during the hours we slept, seeped through my dress and made me shiver.

"Come, we must go," Steven urged. "The princess is only getting further away. It's light now, so we should be able to make better time."

I nodded, rising to my feet, still stiff from sleeping on the ground. My hands were almost too cold to hold the reins, but after I breathed on them for a few minutes, the feeling returned, and with it the sharp pain of reality.

Steven led us through the swirling mists, finding a path only God knows how. I followed his lead with confidence, trusting him and God to leading us safely out of the forest. The prayers, which had stopped only during my sleep, now continued as I dedicated almost every thought to pleading with the Almighty for our safety and the safety of Princess Christine.

More prayers were added as I thought of my brother, and for the king as he led our men in battle with someone who held his daughter as prisoner.

Only God could help us all out of the mess we were in.

After four hours of weaving our way through the forest, which kept us captive, Steven pulled his exhausted horse to a stop. Lather coated its sides, which were heaving with every breath the beast struggled to take. The boy jumped from his horse and took off the saddle and blanket and began walking his beast around in circles to cool it down.

I followed his example, but slid from Duke's saddle instead of jumping. It was a good thing I did, for my legs felt like jelly, and I would have crumpled into a heap on the ground if William had not caught my arm and steadied me.

"Are you all right?" he asked again.

I simply nodded.

"We can slow down if we need to," he said.

I shook my head. "No, the princess's life is in danger right now. I'll manage."

"Brave girl," I heard him mutter to himself as he led his unsaddled horse over to where Steven's was tied. I had to smile to myself. William didn't give compliments to just anybody.

I unsaddled Duke, speaking to my horse in soft tones and rubbing his muzzle affectionately. With his things off, I led him to the tree the other horses were tied to and added his reins to the knot.

William came over to me and handed me some bread. "I'm afraid that's all we have for now," he apologized. "Steven and I can't risk hunting right now and possibly alert those who hold the princess captive. I've rationed it out to last us until we reach the mountains. Hunting will be easier in the foothills."

I nodded, taking the bread with a grateful smile. "That's fine. I understand." I whispered a prayer over the sparse meal and ate it, realizing I was famished. Fresh meat would have been wonderful, but I was ready for anything to fill my demanding stomach. It's amazing how hunger can bring out the grateful side of people.

A light rain began to fall and William sent the sky a worried look. We saddled our horses and began the next leg of our journey that would take us through a mountain pass. Steven again took the front and made his way up the path that was beginning to grow more and more rocky and steep. I took my place in the middle and tried to focus on finding safe ground for Duke to climb on and help him not trip on the loose rocks that Steven's horse occasionally sent down our way.

The wind had been steadily getting stronger, and the rain began falling harder. I blinked the water from my eyes and pushed my wet hair back from my face. Patting Duke's broad shoulder, I encouraged him to keep up his spirit. We would get through this together. Lightening flashed somewhere nearby and thunder ricocheted off the mountainsides. Even Duke, who usually wouldn't startle at anything, was shocked at the sudden noise and shied sideways with a toss of his head, nearly pulling the reins from my hands.

I felt raw skin open and begin bleeding. Wincing, I kept my hold on Duke's reins and whispered to him. "Hush big boy, you're all right, noise never hurt anyone. It's only thunder. No need to worry, Steven and William know what they're doing. We're all going to be all right."

The rain and wind seemed to work together against us in order to stop our efforts to rescue Princess Christine. Lightening lit up the darkening skies around us, some of the bolts landing too close for comfort. Thunder bellowed angrily at us as we hunched over our horses in order to be closer to the ground. It was no good. I knew we would have to stop before long.

From the back, as if he had read my thoughts, William hollered towards his younger brother that he would need to find shelter, that we wouldn't be able to keep going in this storm. Steven hollered something back, but the wind tore the words from his mouth. A moment later he disappeared from our sight, the rain effectively hiding his figure from my water-filled eyes.

"What did he say?" William yelled at me.

I shook my head. "I don't know. I think he must have found somewhere for us to wait out this storm."

"Follow him!" he ordered.

I obeyed. But suddenly, Duke stopped. I nudged him with my heels, squinting through the blinding rain in order to see what he was balking from.

"What's the matter?" William asked over the wind and thunder.

"I don't know!" I answered in like manner. "Wait a moment. I think I see something. I'll have to dismount Duke and lead him, he's refusing to move."

"Meg," I heard the concern leaking through William's voice, "be careful. Horses sometimes have more sense than humans when it comes to surviving out in the wild."

"I will," I promised, sliding from Duke's back and wincing at the pain that shot up my cramped legs. I carefully walked in front of Duke, and pulled on his bridle. "Come on," I whispered, "you know you can trust me, Duke."

The horse's soft brown eyes pleaded with me. He remained steadfast, his hooves seemingly anchored into the solid rock beneath them. I sighed, frustrated by this turn of events. All I wanted was a place I could dry out and sleep for a few hours, perhaps even eat a little more bread, and my horse was refusing to let me have even those simple pleasures.

I looked past my horse at William, who sat outlined against the mountainside on his horse as another lightning bolt struck the mountain and teeth-rattling thunder shook the ground beneath our feet. I made a decision. "All right Duke, have it your own way. If you don't trust me to lead you, then I will trust you to lead me." I gave my horse his head and he appeared to understand what was wanted of him. He nickered softly and began walking carefully sideways before walking forward again.

All of a sudden, the wind took the rain directly in front of me away for a moment and I saw, with a shriek of horror, a huge chasm open up at my feet. Had I taken one step more, if Duke had let me lead him a few more feet, we would have both fallen and died. I shouted a warning to William, who followed my advice and now stood on the moderate safety of a ledge that was about three feet in width but stretched beyond what I could see, due to the falling rain.

"Well, that was cutting it close," William said. "Good thing you saw that pit. I'm surprised Steven didn't warn us sooner. Maybe *that* was what he was trying to tell us."

"It's possible," I answered with a frown. "Speaking of which, where is he?"

A look of horror crossed our faces at the same time as the truth hit us like a blacksmith's hammer.

"STEVEN!"

I knelt down on the damp rock by the gash in the mountainside and screamed the boy's name into the pit. Nothing. William joined me as we called out for the younger boy who had led us all safely thus far.

Help us, God, I prayed earnestly. *Please have Steven be all right. Please give him back to us alive. Please don't have him...*

"Milady!" I heard the call, faint but there all the same.

"Where are you, Steven?" I called out again, this time in frantic hope.

"I'm on a ledge about ten feet beneath you," he answered. "I-I think I broke my leg in the fall. My horse is dead," he added in a sorrowful voice.

As William tied a rope to Duke's saddle, I whispered my grateful thanks to the Almighty. Broken leg or not, he was alive and I thanked Him for sparing Steven's life.

William tossed the rope down to where Steven said he could reach it. A few seconds later, a scream of pain split the air along with a crash of thunder. We froze, the rope swinging in the black nothingness.

Steven's voice drifted up to us, but he sounded weaker. "I can't stand up," he said, competing with the wind to be heard.

"The rope can't reach me where I'm laying down. One of you will have to come down and carry me up."

William began tying the rope around himself, but I stopped him. I knew Duke would have trouble carrying the weight of Steven and William together, and I knew he would respond better to my commands.

"I'd better go down," I shouted above the thunder and pouring rain.

"You?" William's eyes were full of disbelief.

I folded my arms stubbornly. "I'm lighter," I told him. "And Duke would have had a hard enough time pulling Steven up without adding another man to the mix. He's used to carrying me."

Rain fell in rivers down my face, neck, and into the soaked fabric of my dress. I was hard put to not shiver in the cold wind while waiting for William's reply.

"I don't think you should," he pressed. Something unreadable lay in the dark storminess of his eyes. "What if I was to lose both of you?"

I sighed and wiped away the water from my face, even though the action was pointless. "You won't," I promised. "Please, William, you've got to let me do this."

My teacher sighed and untied the rope from around himself before securing it around my own waist. "Bring yourself and my brother back up here," he said over the sounds of the storm. "I'd never be able to live with myself if anything happened to either of you."

I gave him a curt nod and lowered myself down over the edge of the precipice. The absence of wind was immediately apparent as I sank slowly deeper into the darkness. I could hear Steven's ragged breathing somewhere beneath me.

"Steven?" I asked the shadows.

"Milady? I'm down here."

"A little more to the left, William!" I called upwards.

"Keep talking," I said, my already raw hands being scraped in other places now as I was lowered towards Steven's place of safety. "If I miss the ledge you're on…" I trailed off with an expressive shudder.

William yelled down at us, "Meg, the rope has no more slack. How close are you to where Steven is?"

I strained my eyes in the dark, as if by sheer willpower they would be able to pierce through the gloom that separated me from Steven. "I can't see," I answered upward.

"You've got about six more feet to go," Steven said morosely. "You'll have to untie the rope and jump."

Terror seized me. Sweat dripped off the end of my nose and onto my folded hands, the salt stinging the raw skin. I would have to jump in the dark, without being able to see, to where I knew not. With only Steven's voice to guide me. Normally, I wasn't afraid of heights. As a child I would climb into the tops of trees where I could be swayed to and fro by the wind. I loved the feeling of being above everyone, seeing things they could not. Right now, I was frozen in fear.

"I don't think I can do it," I whispered, my eyes squeezed shut in fear.

Cloth dragged across stone and Steven spoke again, his voice softer as if he could sense my terror and confusion. "Can you trust me?" he asked.

Above me, William began praying for us. Out loud. The wind stole the words away after a few minutes, before the completed prayer could reach my ears, but somehow, I felt comforted all the same. With astonishment, I realized I almost felt safe hanging over a pit, a few feet from certain death, and the only thing keeping me there was a thin rope. But God was in control. And I found peace.

"Yes, I can trust you," I whispered, answering the quiet voice of God and Steven with the same words.

"Then untie yourself carefully, keeping one hand on the rope at all times," Steven instructed patiently.

The terror that had gripped me now melted as I focused instead on doing as Steven told me. Pain tore through my hands as I fumbled with the knot with one hand while holding onto the rope as though it were the only thing that was between me and death…which, upon reflection, it was.

The meticulous job was finally completed, and I now held onto the rope with both hands. I felt extremely exposed as I lay against the rock face, praying with all that was in me for Steven and my safety.

"Done?" Steven asked.

I nodded, then realizing he couldn't see the affirmative motion, said, "Yes."

"You're directly above the ledge," Steven informed me. "Slide to the bottom of the rope, and then come straight down."

I felt the rope burn my fingers as I let it pass through them. The end came and went. In a moment of breathless intensity, I was alone in the darkness, falling.

15:
Slight Complications

I landed on solid ground a few seconds after my fall, and for the first few moments I lay there thanking God that I was alive, and not wanting to ever touch a rope again. But I had too. Steven needed me.

With a sigh, I heaved myself up off the rock ledge and found Steven's smiling face a foot from my own. "You did well, Milady," he said. "Now let's see if you can tie knots as well as you can fall."

I had to grin at his teasing. "Unfortunately, my ability to fall gracefully and my ability to tie knots well are about the same. I'm horrible at both."

Steven grinned back at me, but then winced. My face paled when I glanced down and saw the unnatural angle his leg was at. It twisted sideways and backwards, obviously causing the poor boy a great deal of pain. I sucked in a breath of air and looked up at Steven's grim face.

"Now you can see why I was unable to climb that rock over there and reach the bottom of the rope," Steven said, bravely trying to mask the anguish in his eyes.

I stood, and helped prop Steven against me with the help of his good leg. One side of the ledge was flat, and the other half slanted upwards, but the floor was rough and impossible for

Steven in his current condition to climb. I tied us together with the rope that hung against the floor of the highest part of the ledge. Apparently, William had been generous with the rope's length when he had tied me up before sending me down to Steven. No wonder I had been six feet above the ledge when the rope ran out of slack.

At my command, Duke began to pull us up with some help from William. I wondered through the mist of pain if I would have any skin on my hands at all by the time we found the princess. I held onto Steven as well as I could with one hand, thankful that his leg had been broken, not his arm, for at least now he could hold himself on once I helped him tie the rope around us both.

Steven's knuckles were white as he held onto me and the rope with vice-like intensity. Sharp intakes of breath and moans caused me to look down into his pain-filled eyes with concern. A trickle of blood wandered down his chin from where his teeth bit down on his lower lip in the effort to not scream aloud in agony. I could only imagine the torture he was going through with movement we made upward.

The climb up was almost more nerve-wracking than the descent had been, since I no longer had Steven beneath me to calm my nerves. My hands hurt so much that I was afraid they would let go of the rope and we would both fall to our imminent deaths.

Minutes later, though to Steven and I hanging over the pit of blackness it seemed like hours, William grabbed my hand and pulled me onto firm ground. I lay there panting, only vaguely aware of my teacher also pulling up Steven and talking to him in a low voice. Water was poured down my throat, and I swallowed it, suddenly aware of an overwhelming thirst.

"Go easy on that, Meg," William cautioned, "save some for Steven."

Ashamed, I stopped and sat up, my head swimming. I was leaned against the mountainside, covered in the same blanket I had found on myself the previous evening. I noticed with

124

surprise that the storm had stopped sometime after Steven and I had made it to the ledge that provided us momentary safety.

William's brother lay next to me, also propped up against the rock face, and his ragged breathing and pale countenance pulled a shocked gasp from me. William's grim countenance that met mine across Steven's prostrate form scared me even more.

"We've got to find shelter and get him warm or we're going to lose him," he said. "His leg's not broken, but the bone is dislocated."

I gasped in dismay. "What does that mean?"

"I'll need somewhere where I can straighten it. This ledge doesn't give me enough room to work, and I want him out of the elements."

"One of us will have to stay with him while the other looks for the shelter," I said.

"You're in almost as bad shape as him," William replied. "I'll go scout out a place. I've been over this pass many a time as a peddler. If I remember correctly, there's a cave not far from here that will serve our purpose. I trust you can keep yourselves safe should the need arise." He patted the sword at my side.

With one last look at first his brother and then me, his face full of concern, he walked along the path and disappeared from our sight. I sent a prayer for his safety upwards even as I tightened the hand on my sword.

"Milady?" Steven looked sideways at me.

"Call me Meg," I told him, and then added, "Do you need anything?"

"No," he answered, with a slight shake of his head which caused him to wince. "I just wanted to say thank you...for going down there and risking your life for me."

I smiled at the fourteen-year-old warmly. "It was worth it in the end. God protected me."

"I thank Him for that," Steven said in relief with a glance heavenwards. He looked down at his leg in disgust. "Now I'm going to slow you and William down in your search for the princess. Perhaps you should just—"

125

I cut him off. "No! We would never dream of leaving you on your own! Especially in this condition!"

"I was going to say," he finished, "that you could put me on a horse and send me back to the castle."

William's voice came from behind me, making me spin around so fast I thought I would fall back down that terrible pit of blackness. "She's right, Steven," he said. "We would never leave you. Or send you back alone. You may think you could make it, but you wouldn't. You lack the strength."

"Did you find shelter?" I asked, recovering from my surprise and willing my heart to cease beating so quickly.

William nodded. "Yes. As I remembered, there's a small cave not far from here. It looked uninhabited still, and though it'll be a bit cramped, I think we'll survive."

I glanced towards Steven. "Do you think he can make it?" I whispered.

"I think so." William's eyes were filled with concern. "But we had better be quick about it."

Together, we tried to make Steven as comfortable as possible on Duke's broad back before leading our horses along the ledge.

William managed to make his cloak into a kind of temporary sling that he hoped would help the short ride to be less painful for Steven. Even so, gasps of pain were sucked through Steven's whitened lips, but I could do nothing to ease him. His eyes closed when we started moving, and perspiration dripped off his pale countenance like so many raindrops. My horse's rocking gait didn't help Steven's twisted leg and I winced every time Duke miss-stepped, causing the young man's body to tense and another moan to work its way out his mouth.

William had been right as usual; Steven would never have been able to travel back to the castle like this.

After a few yards the ledge widened into a safer path before rising into walls on either side of us and above us into the overcast sky.

I led Duke around the various boulders that lay scattered throughout the valley, and over a mountain stream that trickled across our path only to fall through a crack in the other side and create a beautiful waterfall. Steven's breathing sounded labored in my ears, and I sent my worries upward to my heavenly Father as we continued our trek towards the promise of a few hours of peace.

Soon enough, William called back to me that he had re-discovered the cave, and I led my exhausted horse through the narrow opening. William carried Steven off of Duke, and laid him on the blanket he had spread on the damp floor of the cave. I removed the saddles, bridles, and bags of equipment for our travel to a spare corner before tying the horses outside the cave to a sturdy-looking tree.

I entered the cave again, let my eyes adjust for a moment, and was able to see for the first time how small it was. The cave that William had found was about ten feet wide and perhaps seven feet tall, with a sloping floor that was moderately clean, considering it had probably been the home of a wild animal at some point. I noticed William had cut his brother's breeches above his knee and was regarding the malformed leg with sorrowful eyes. I came and stood behind him, hoping to offer my assistance.

William turned when he heard my footfalls, and studied my face for a moment. "I'm going to straighten his leg next," he informed me.

I gave him a short nod. "What can I do?"

Steven's face was almost gray now, and beads of sweat had formed on his brow. He was showing signs of a fever and muttered something incoherent, tossing his head in a restless fashion.

"You've got to keep him still," William said. "Once the leg is set, it will need to be kept straight. Before I do anything, I'll cut a few branches to use as a brace. While I'm gone, there's some wine in the saddlebags. Make him drink some of that. It'll ease the pain a little."

I bit my lip and nodded again.

"You also might want to cover a smaller stick with cloth so he doesn't bite his tongue off while in so much agony."

I shuddered at the thought, nodding once more before he disappeared from the cave to find branches that would be sturdy enough and straight enough to act as a brace for Steven's leg once the bones had been lined up again. I hurried to do as William had instructed me. The wine was easy enough to find, but it was another thing altogether to try to get a feverish Steven to swallow enough to ease his pain. Finally I managed to force half a cup down him by the spoonful. It would have to suffice.

Outside, near the horses, I was able to find a small chunk of wood that was thick enough for the other job. With nothing else handy, I wrapped my own favorite lace handkerchief that I always carried in my pocket around the stick. It would be ruined, but at that moment, I really didn't care about anything other than having Steven back on his feet again. Even the princess and the war that my brother and the king were possibly giving up their lives in fell from my mind.

William came back within a few minutes and stripped the branches of all leaves and smaller twigs, leaving only the main branch. He nodded grimly at the stick I had chosen and covered with my handkerchief.

"How much wine did he take?" he asked while working on getting Steven as immobile as possible with what rope we had.

"Only about a half glass," I informed him. "It was hard enough getting that much down."

"It'll be enough," he said shortly. "He may be sick after it's all over, so it's good he won't have much in his stomach."

My own stomach turned at this possibility, but I only nodded in reply.

William shot me a concerned look. "Can you stomach it?" he asked. "You could wait outside—"

I shook my head. "No. I'll be fine," I answered flatly. I had to be.

William didn't look convinced by my show of bravado, but he turned to Steven's leg and motioned for me to put the stick in his mouth.

I pried the boy's mouth open, and pushed the stick between his teeth. Steven's eyes opened for a moment—they looked so much like William's—but roved around the cave wildly. He fought against the bonds, and then suddenly went limp. I held his shoulders to the floor with as much firmness as I could without hurting him and braced myself.

I averted my gaze as William suddenly put pressure on the bent leg. Steven let loose a scream that I would have been hard put to beat in pitch and volume even as muffled by the handkerchief-clad stick as it was. His body went limp when he passed out, and perspiration dripped off the sides of his face. My tears fell to mix with his sweat. To have seen anybody in this much pain...it was almost too much for me to bear. Steven's eyes flew open a few seconds later and he struggled within the confines of the rope.

William helped me hold him until he faded into unconsciousness. Then he put a hand on my shoulder. "It's over."

I let out a shuddering sigh and turned to look at William's handiwork. The leg was straight now, and the sticks tied around it firmly with the rope that had been keeping Steven's hands to his sides.

I looked at Steven's face. That was a mistake. Pain was etched in every line, in every shadow, and his eyes were closed. His breathing was so shallow, I almost thought he was dead, but his chest rose just enough for me to see that he was indeed still with us, though unconscious.

"All we can do now is pray," William said. "After a few minutes he'll be feeling better, but we'll need to keep him off that leg for a while."

Hearing the pain in his own voice made me lose myself completely. The trickle of tears that had come during the short operation became a torrent. I covered my face in my hands and rocked back and forth in agony. *Why?* I asked. *Why did this have to happen? Why did Steven's horse not warn him as mine did? Why did he have to fall? Why did he have to break his leg? Why can't we just find the princess and everything end happily as they do in minstrel's tales?*

I was vaguely aware when William drew me into a comforting hug, and I continued my waterfall of tears into his understanding shoulder. Then, I felt his shoulder on which I was leaning also shake, and I knew we were both crying. Together, for his brother.

16:
A Time of Healing

After the storm of tears passed, both William and I took turns looking after Steven. He had begun burning with fever only a few hours after William had set his leg, which was now causing us more concern for his life than the previous injury.

I cooked a small meal from our diminishing supplies we had brought with us, and William filled our water skins in one of the many mountain streams he had found nearby.

"If we can keep his fever down throughout the night, I think he'll make it," William said.

It was evening now, and supper had long been eaten. Steven had become conscious briefly and taken some broth I had made him along with some more swallows of wine. Then he had lapsed into a restless sleep. It was a good thing, indeed, that William had made him a brace when he had, for the boy would have dislodged the bone again by this time with all his thrashing if he had not.

I cast a sympathetic glance towards his sleeping form. "Shall I stay up first?" I asked.

William shook his head. "I'll take the first shift."

"Very well," I murmured, attempting to find a comfortable position to sleep on the hard ground and failing. Despite that, I still managed to fall asleep.

However, sleep held no release from the tensions of the day. My dreams were unpleasant and filled with the scream of agony Steven had given when William set his leg. The grinning face of Sir Alfred appeared to mock my efforts in protecting the Princess, and I saw Malcolm and William regarding me in deep disappointment and sorrow.

"I tried to protect her!" I shouted at them. "I thought Sir Alfred was a friend!"

The Princess flashed before me, sobbing in a dark dungeon of a castle somewhere unreachable. "No one can save me," she mourned aloud, "no one cares about my safety or loves me."

"I do!" I cried in frustration, pounding on the wall that separated us. "I tried! I'm still trying! I would do anything to get you back to safety!"

Steven lay dead and cold in an open grave. I stared down on him in shock. His features were frozen in unspoken pain; his eyes met mine, unseeing.

I awoke from the fitful slumber to William's gentle patting.

"If you're not too tired, you can take a turn watching, otherwise I can continue."

"I'm not tired," I answered, stifling a yawn before he could notice. My teacher's face was indistinguishable in the darkness where I slept outside the fire's light, but I could hear the exhaustion in his voice. It would be selfish of me to keep him from his well-deserved sleep at this point. Besides, if sleep held only nightmares for me, I would prefer to spend the remainder of the night awake.

"Very well," William answered, unconvinced. "Wake me when you do become tired."

"I will."

"Good night, Meg."

"Good night, William."

After William had finally gotten as comfortable as possible on the rocky floor, silence fell. I fought off the urge to roll over and let God take the next watch, despite the nightmares, but instead crept to the mouth of the cave after seeing that a cool cloth was laid over Steven's brow. My eyes grew accustomed to the darkness with annoying reluctance. I could see the outlines of our two remaining horses standing in their sleep over by the tree. My gaze was drawn to the heavens where innumerable stars twinkled brilliantly.

"Soli Deo Gloria," I whispered, "To God alone be the glory." From childhood, the congregation of our village church had ended the last prayer of each service with that Latin phrase, so often it seemed almost automatic to me, but now I really meant it as I stared in awe at His handiwork.

Darkness surrounded me, yet I was unafraid. With God above watching out for me, and William within calling distance, I felt safe. I took a moment to go and check on Steven and found him sleeping peacefully. I dipped the cloth in the cool water once more, and then laid it on his head. Once again, I went to the entrance of the cave to look at the beauty of God's creation.

The next thing I knew, a low growl coming from somewhere nearby and the horses' frantic whinnies woke me from a sound sleep. I sat up from where I had slumped against the cave entrance.

Two iridescent eyes shone in the light of the moon. They were fixed on me now, as a possibly easier meal than two frantic horses. *This must be another horrible dream,* I told myself. *I should really wake up. And the best way to wake up is to do something. Or by dying,* I added with a wry smile. Instinctively, I felt for some sort of weapon and found with relief that my sword remained by my side even in my dreams. I slid the blade from the scabbard, relishing the sound it made. Braver by every inch that came, I stood up, a sudden fury flooding my veins.

"Pick on innocent, tied up horses, will you?" I asked the creature through clenched teeth. "Come and fight, coward!"

The shadow slinked closer, and I watched as it lowered itself onto the ground, readying itself for a pounce. I held my breath, clutching Safeguard's hilt with sweaty hands. This dream was becoming too real for my comfort.

It sprang at me without warning. I heard myself scream, an unearthly sound, as though I was somehow detached from my body and watching myself react slower than life. Everything happened too quickly. The creature lunged at my throat, which had let loose a scream rivaling the one Steven had uttered hours before. My sword pierced its hide, and both of us fell to the ground in a heap.

When William rushed from the cave a moment later, rolled the dead body off of me and helped me scramble away, I realized that it wasn't a dream. At the sight of the dead creature's blood all down the front of my dress, bile rose to my throat and out of my mouth. I coughed and shuddered before rising to my feet shakily.

"W-what was it?" I asked when I could trust myself to speak again.

William inspected the creature with his foot after a moment of scanning the darkness around us. "A wolf," he said. "A sick one too by the looks of it. That would explain why he doesn't appear be with a pack and took you on instead of running as any sensible wolf would have done."

"Sick?" My face blanched when I saw the traces of drying foam around the creature's gaping mouth. Quickly, I checked myself for any sign of a bite from the dead wolf, and was rewarded by finding nothing more than a few scratches. One of the sleeves of my dress had been torn off in the struggle, but that was hardly a concern, considering what could have been. I had heard horror stories of people who had been bitten by "mad dogs," and I knew what a diseased animal's bite could transfer into humans.

"You're all right?" William asked. "You should have called for me sooner," he added. "Even with your swordsmanship skills you couldn't have beaten a whole pack of wolves. You were lucky there was only one."

I nodded, my cheeks burning at his reproof. "I'm just little shaken. The horses are safe though." I smiled weakly. "I thought I was dreaming…but I must have fallen asleep somehow and awoken when the horses became restless."

"I'll take over watching now, you go get some rest," he ordered.

I was in no shape to argue. I lay down on the rocky floor, and though it was hardly comfortable, I slept until the gray of dawn had brightened into a brand new day.

My eyes opened to a stream of sunlight pouring through the mouth of the cave. Our fire had dwindled to mere ashes, but that would be easy enough to deal with. William was over by his brother, dipping the cloth again into the cool water and laying it over his head.

I crawled over to their end of the cave. "How is he?" I asked in a whisper.

"Much better than I had dared to hope last night," William answered with relief. "His fever is all but gone, and his leg has set pretty well with hardly any swelling."

"Praise God," I murmured, looking down at the boy's leg.

"Indeed," William said.

Steven's eyes opened slowly, but it took a moment for them to focus on our faces. They were clear, not clouded with fever, or wild with pain. He saw us both sitting over him, and smiled. "Have you been watching over me this whole time?" he asked. "How very touching!"

William grunted in good humor. "If there was any doubt that Steven was still unwell," he said to me, "it's far gone now."

I grinned down on Steven's face, noticing for the first time that his healthy pink complexion was finally returning. "I couldn't be more glad. You had us worried for a moment," I added to the prostrate boy.

"Me?" Steven shot us both a wink. "A little leg injury could never stop *me*!"

William humphed. "Well, it did a good job of it for a while there."

A small frown darkened the younger boy's face. "I suppose this means we won't get the princess from her captors before they reach the Duke of Devonshire's castle."

"I'm afraid not," William answered. "You need at least another day before we can even think about letting you up on a horse."

"You should go on without me," Steven said. "Rescue the princess. Our kingdom needs her!" He bit his lip. "It doesn't need me."

"We're not going to leave you!" I protested. "If Christine were in the same predicament, even if her own father was being kidnapped for ransom, she wouldn't leave a suffering friend by himself."

"She's right," William agreed. "Right now, the princess is safer than you. The Duke won't allow her to be harmed since she's being held for ransom. Though it is true that we won't beat her captors to the castle, I think that even with your broken leg we'll still be able to rescue her before the Duke has time to get a ransom note to our king."

I looked at my teacher in ill-concealed wonder. "How are we going to do that?" I asked.

William gave me a cocky grin that reminded me so much of Malcolm. "Very carefully."

Now it was Steven's turn to humph. He sounded so much like his older brother that I had to smile. "Dream on, oh brother mine. I still think you should put me on a horse and send it toward the King's castle."

Both William and I shook our heads at the same time.

"You're coming with us," I said as firmly as I could. "We *won't* leave you behind."

"Once we reach the King's camp, you can rest while we tell the King what's going on," William said. "Then we'll decide what the next step in the Princess's rescue ought to be."

Despite his protests, we continued to be careful about Steven's injury the following day by keeping the fever down with cool clothes, and making sure he didn't move very much.

In the back of my mind, the same worry over the Princess's condition as captive of Sir Alfred remained. Even when William seemed so confident that we'd be able to rescue her in time, I was still concerned. I could easily imagine how terrified Princess Christine must feel right now, with no idea if we have noticed her disappearance, but I was helpless to do anything except pray that God grant her peace.

By the next day, he was begging us to let him care for himself. William and I took turns helping him hobble around, and his older brother even managed to find him a makeshift crutch from the same tree he had found the branches for his brace.

On the third day in the cave, Steven was proclaimed able to sit on a horse if he was careful, and so we set out towards the Duke's castle. By this time, we realized the princess's captors were too far ahead for us to catch up with, but William had a plan that would save us some time.

"Her captors will have to work their way around King Frederick's camp; that's about a day's journey after we get past the mountains," William said when Steven asked what his grand scheme was. "But we have the ability to go right through, without having to worry about dodging lookouts and watches at night. Like I mentioned before, we'll stop inside the camp and let Steven have some much needed care from a proper healer."

A spark of understanding lit up Steven's eyes. "You may have something," he replied as the idea sank in.

"Of course I do!" William exclaimed indignantly.

Quiet through all of this, I spoke up. "It will help us to meet the king while we go through," I said.

William nodded. "We'll be able to tell him everything that has happened just in case there are more traitors where Sir Alfred and his friend came from."

"Then he'll know to not reply to the Duke's ransom note so quickly," Steven said. "He'll stall until she can be rescued."

"By us?" I shot William a knowing look.

My teacher grinned. "Of course."

"What are we waiting for?" Steven asked sarcastically. "Let's go put our lives in danger. It will be so fun!"

"Well," William said with a snort, "he's definitely better." He helped Steven and me up onto Duke, the bigger of the two horses, before mounting his own.

And then we were on our way yet again.

17:
The Camp

As the days stretched into a week, we did steadily draw nearer to the place we knew the king and his men camped. We stopped frequently to rest and sometimes hunt since Steven still didn't have the strength he was used to having. Any time we did stop, he would protest that he was still fine and that we should keep going. Of course, William paid him no mind. Though it wasn't true, I let Steven declare that the stops were for me and the horses, if only to keep him from wasting more of his waning strength on arguing.

As evening fell, William called another stop under the sparse cover of a few trees and as usual Steven made his loud protests.

"I'm fine! We should keep going!" he told his brother as he was pulled from the saddle, placed firmly against a tree and given one of our water skins to quench his thirst.

William and I exchanged a weary look, and I gave myself the liberty of one longsuffering sigh. He had been riding with me and on *my* horse all this time since his had died in the fall, and I was getting a little tired of his constant pushing of himself, us, and the horses.

"We're going to reach the camp before we rest again," William said. "I'm not going to kill you in order to save the princess. What would our mother say?"

"A little more riding wouldn't kill me," Steven muttered.

I sighed again and sat down next to the suffering boy. "You don't know your own strength," I told him firmly. "We trusted you to lead us up until you injured your leg...can't you return the favor and trust us the rest of the way to the king's camp?"

Steven gave a reluctant nod.

The horses were allowed to graze for a little while, and we ate our supper. Steven's leg was still doing well, and he hobbled with some help from me or with a hand in one of the horses' manes. William told his younger brother to not put any weight on his leg at all. What he threatened he would do to him if Steven did, I don't know...but whatever it was, the threat was effective.

We mounted again, Steven behind me on Duke, William in front with his horse, and we traveled yet again towards the setting sun.

Darkness began to make our traveling harder. The slower we went, the more pain I saw in Steven's face. William mustn't have noticed it with the night falling so quickly, and I was afraid to tell him because it would hurt Steven's feelings.

Thankfully, I was spared that decision.

Out of the trees we were passing under, some men jumped on our horses. Bedlam ensued. Steven's arms tightened around me, and I looked back to see his face white with pain. One of the men was holding onto his wounded leg. Anger bubbled up and out of me.

"Get your hands off of him!" I shouted. "He's got an injured leg! You're hurting him!"

"Leave them alone!" William added from where he was imprisoned by three of the men.

"Who are you and what are you doing here?" One of the men stepped forward, holding a lantern high and squinting at us.

"I'm Lady Megan, lady-in-waiting to Her Majesty, Princess Christine," I informed them haughtily.

William's warning look came too late. It dawned on me that we didn't know if these were the King's men or not. After all, we were deep into the lands of the Duke now, and just as the King was in danger, so were we. I bit my tongue, wishing the words back into my mouth, but knowing it was too late for that.

Behind me, Steven groaned audibly. The men around us burst into laughter. My face flamed in embarrassment and fury.

"Oh, you are, are you?" the same man replied, doubling over with laughter. "Well, begging your pardon, Miss High and Mighty, but let me introduce myself. I'm Solomon the Wise at your service." He turned to his men. "Take their weapons. We'll bring them to the Duke."

I saw with dismay my beloved Safeguard taken from me, though the guards mumbled in surprise that a lady would carry such a weapon. Steven lost his dagger and crossbow, William his sword. We were bound and dragged to the vicious men's camp.

They tied us securely to a stout oak tree, paying little mind to Steven's injury, and I watched in helpless worry as he groaned and bit his lip in pain until blood came. I was sandwiched between Steven and William, and could feel my face still burning in humiliation.

"We've got to escape," I hissed to William when our captors were satisfied that we wouldn't be going anywhere anytime soon and returned to the brace of rabbits they were cooking over their fires.

"I know," William replied grimly. "But how?"

Something cold and sharp was pressed to my hand where they were tied to the tree. I glanced over at Steven in surprise and found his eyes alert and gleaming. "Look away," he ordered. "Otherwise they'll suspect something."

Slowly, as if dejected, I turned my eyes away from him and lowered them to the ground. I looked as if I had no hope, but

141

inwardly, my mind was racing. "How did you get your dagger back?" I asked.

Steven waited until our guard passed before giving me a quick smile. "I didn't," he answered. "It's not mine. The man tying us up had it slip from his sheath while he was working on your feet, Megan, and it landed on the ground by me. I was able to snatch it up and hide it before he moved on to me."

William quietly whistled in admiration. "You'll never cease to astonish me!"

"When should we escape then?" I asked.

"Not until they have mostly fallen asleep," William answered after some thought. "Under the cover of complete darkness we'll cut the ropes and try to slip away."

My brow creased in sudden worry. "What if they happen to all wake up?" I asked.

My teacher gave a slight nod towards a tree about ten feet away that we had seen our captors store our weapons by. "Make toward that tree and grab a sword. I think the two of us could fight our way out. There are only eight men that I counted. Surely my skills and yours combined would at least give Steven a chance to escape before we try our hand at outrunning them."

He paused to let a few of the men drift further away from where they might be able to hear our plans.

"They must be only a scouting group from the Duke of Devonshire. We should warn the king about them though. Where one scout group is, others will follow or they may already be in the area."

We fell silent as the man who appeared to be the leader, the one who called himself "Solomon the Wise," came up to us with a suspicious look on his face. "Here you!" he said warningly. "Enough of your whispering. The Duke's a fair man, and you won't come to any harm as long as you behave yourselves and answer his questions truthfully."

We said nothing in reply to this, and soon he walked away, mumbling something about what terribly thirsty business being a scout was.

142

Three prisoners as we were, food was not a delicacy they thought we deserved. My stomach growled in longing at the sight of the nicely browned rabbits, and I realized the food we had eaten a few hours ago for our supper might have to last until we made it into the king's camp. I wondered if they would even give us water.

At last, the men around us dropped off into drunken slumber. All but the two who were guarding us. I saw our horses on the opposite side of the camp along with the enemy horses, and I realized there was a wrinkle in our plans.

"William," I began in a whisper. "We need a horse to get Steven out of here. They're all tied on the far side of the camp."

My teacher's brow furrowed. "Would you be able to loose the horses while I retrieve our weapons?" he asked.

"Duke could get loose," I said. "I taught him and Prince to untie themselves when they were mere colts so I could play jokes on Malcolm. I haven't asked him to perform since Malcolm began working for the king...so I don't know if he'll still remember the signal." I regarded the oblivious horse with a small frown. "I suppose it's worth a try."

Quietly, I whistled. One long low note, and then two quicker, high notes. Duke's head came up from where he had been grazing by the tree. His ears swiveled towards where I sat. *Please God, have him remember,* I pleaded. Duke nickered, and then his head dipped toward the rope that secured him to the tree.

I held my breath, letting myself hope. One of the ropes to the tree snapped, and Duke was free. As I had taught him, he stood as if he was still tied, but would bolt the minute someone other than me dared to put a hand on his bridle.

Now, I worked on my own bonds. The two guards that remained awake were playing a game of chess, casting glances at us every once in a while, but obviously thought we were a waste of time. Their confidence would be their undoing.

My ropes snapped loose, and I worked on Steven's, freezing my movements whenever the guards happened to look our way. William was next, and soon we were rope free, though our hands were still behind us in pretense.

"Call your horse," William ordered. "But wait until I get my sword. The minute Steven is on Duke, set them towards the king's camp which is due south and come join me fighting. There's no way we'll be getting out of here without a fight."

"At least we'll have surprise on our side," I said.

"They won't be expecting a fight with two sword masters, that's certain," William answered with a wink towards me.

"I'm not a sword master," I whispered.

William waited until the guards glanced in our direction once more, and knowing he wouldn't look again for another minute or so, William bolted as silently as possible toward the tree with our weapons. The minute William made it back to our tree with his sword and mine, I called Duke.

The camp came to life even as Duke trotted towards me. While William kept the guards occupied, I hoisted Steven onto the horse, thanking God again that the boy was as light as he was and still had the use of both hands and at least one leg.

"Ride!" I commanded.

"What about you and William?" he asked.

"We'll come later," I promised.

"I won't leave you!"

I slapped Duke on his rump and the poor horse bolted at the unexpected treatment from his mistress. The boy and horse disappeared into the surrounding trees.

I turned and caught Safeguard from William. A new energy flowed through my veins and I clashed swords with the nearest of the Duke's scouts.

18:
Safety?

William had already taken two men down by the time I joined him, and they were quickly joined by three more when I arrived. I had never killed any person before, but I knew when I began learning how to use Safeguard that there might be times when I would have to kill in self-defense, or for the lives of others, and this was one of those times.

The moon came from behind a cloud and illumined the chaotic scene. Blades flashed in the firelight, and it was soon clear that William and I had the upper hand. We both knew more sword tricks then all eight of the scouts combined. I almost felt as if I was cheating when yet another of the men had his sword fell harmlessly to the ground and was driven to his knees with my blade through his chest.

The remaining guards took to their horses and escaped into the night. William and I didn't bother following them. Two of the six men we had overcome were only wounded, so we tied them up and put them on one of the remaining horses that was still tied to the tree. I regretted leaving the bodies of the men we had killed in the open, but it had to be done. We had a princess to rescue.

We rode together into the night. I sat in front of William while he held the reigns of the horse that carried our prisoners, trying to ignore the painful jab the hilt of his sword gave me at every bounce and the pleasant warmth and security of his solid frame so close to mine.

Thankfully, we didn't have another incident with enemy soldiers. The next time we were stopped in the woods was by one of the king's watchmen, and he only kept us long enough to ask our names and business.

"Who are you?" William demanded this time. He didn't want to risk us being caught by the enemy again.

The man came up and gave him a long look. "William?" he asked as if hardly believing his eyes. "William Price?"

Recognition dawned in my teacher's eyes and he leapt from his horse. "Martin! It's good to see you! Have you seen my brother come by?"

"Your brother?" Martin's face held only confusion. "What would he be doing in our camp? Did he stow away with us to quench a sudden urge for adventure?" he asked with a grin.

"He isn't here?" I asked in concern.

"No," Martin answered, still confused. "Should he be?"

"Yes! We just escaped from a group of the Duke's scouts on our way to trying to reach the king with important information regarding the Princess."

"We'll send out some men to search for your brother," Martin assured him.

"I'll join you as soon as I speak with the king," William said.

I slipped off the horse. "William," I began, "why don't you go search for him now? I can speak with the king and tell him our plans. He'll understand."

My teacher gave me a grateful look. "Thank you, Meg," he answered.

"I'll go warn the king of your arrival before joining the search myself," Martin said, touching his forhead briefly in a gesture of respect toward both of us.

I rode through the darkness into the fire lit camp. Torches were tied securely to stakes located at the front of various tents and to the biggest tent I went, knowing that would be where the King was staying. I took a deep breath and entered.

The sudden light of several different torches and lanterns made me stand in the doorway and blink for a moment. My eyes had become so accustomed to the darkness that they had to have a minute or so to readjust to the light again.

King Frederick was sitting on a wooden stool behind a sturdy table that was also made of a solid oak. Beside him, likewise on a stool, was a bearded stranger. Only when he ran towards me and enveloped me in a great big bear hug and exclaimed, "Meg! What on earth are you doing here? Never mind that. I can't begin to say how happy I am to see you safe and sound!" did I realize that the man was my brother, Malcolm.

Tears of happiness trickled down my cheeks and onto my brother's shirt. "Oh, Malcolm, how I have missed you," I whispered into his comforting figure.

My brother tore out of my hug and pulled me over to a seat in front of the king who had been watching our exchange with a mixed expression that contained amusement, joy, and sadness.

"Sit, sit!" he urged. "Tell us how you came here, why, and what on earth the princess has to do with all of it. Martin was very vague."

I launched into our story. The betrayal of Sir Alfred, the kidnapping of the princess, our journey through the forest, Steven's fall, the scouts we ran into, Steven's flight to the king's camp, the fight, and our arrival to safety only to find that Steven wasn't here.

While I spoke, I watched the king's face. Anger mixed with worry as he listened to our adventures. Once, he even brought his fist down with a crash onto his table, but apologized and urged me to continue when I faltered. Malcolm's expressions were almost identical to the king's, and when I finally finished, his eyebrows were meshed together in a ferocious glower that made me glad I hadn't been the one who dared steal his betrothed.

"So the traitor Sir Alfred is taking her to the Duke of Devonshire?" the king asked in a dangerously quiet voice.

I nodded. "William, Steven and I were planning on rescuing her before they reached the Duke's castle, but his injury put us too far behind to be able to pull off that feat."

King Frederick raised an eyebrow. "And now?" he pressed.

I cleared my throat. "Well, we were hoping to continue as before, only Steven would stay here and recover from his broken leg. But now that he has disappeared..." I trailed off. "Our plans may be all for naught."

The king shook his head. "No, I doubt things are as bleak as that. Surely Steven will be found by our men you said were searching for him. I'll speak with William when he returns and we'll plan our next step to rescue my daughter. Meanwhile, you look absolutely exhausted, Lady Megan. Take some rest and I'll have food brought to you. Tomorrow things will look brighter and more hopeful."

I nodded wearily, all the energy that had mysteriously come to me during our fight had long since been drained from my blood. I now felt the effects of too many nights with little sleep. Malcolm put a supporting arm around my shoulders and led me to a small tent behind the king's. There he laid me on a cot and pulled a blanket over me. Almost immediately, I fell asleep.

* * † * *

I awoke to my brother patting my shoulder. Groggily, I sat up, swinging my legs over the side of the cot and yawning loudly. Malcolm chuckled.

"Did you sleep well?" he asked.

"Better than I have all week," I answered truthfully. "Or all month for that matter…in fact, I slept better than I've slept since you left to war."

He smiled and held out a dress. "This is for you to replace the one you're wearing now."

My mouth dropped open and I took the soft, but durable gown from him in astonishment. "Where did you find it?" I asked, fingering the brown materiel.

"One of our soldier's wives that came to be our cook and help with wounded men is about your size and offered a spare dress to be used by you…since you are in sore need of a new dress."

I glanced down at my ragged apparel. It had a sleeve torn off, the bottom of the skirt was ripped into shreds from all the branches in the forest, and dirt and blood from the wolf decorated the front in gory splotches of brown and rust red. I grimaced at the sight before glancing at my brother.

"Helen, that's the name of the woman I just mentioned, is coming here to help you take a bath," he announced.

"A bath?" When was the last time I had taken a bath? I couldn't remember. That was a bad sign.

As if the woman was waiting for those words to leave my brother's mouth, the tent opened, and she walked in with a pitcher. Following her were two soldiers who carried a large wooden tub. They plunked it down on the ground, and I saw that it was half-full of water.

Quickly, the two soldiers left and were followed by my brother who stopped only to have a few words with the woman. In reply to something he said, she smiled and gave him a gentle shove out the tent doorway. He shot me a quick wink and disappeared. The middle-aged woman fastened the tent flaps securely and turned to me.

"I'm Helen," she informed me. Her warm, brown eyes were twinkling, and crinkled at the corners.

"I'm Megan," I answered, "but everyone calls me Meg."

"So I've heard," she said, her lips pressed together as she took my appearance in with one sweeping glance that seemed to pierce right through me.

I looked towards the dress and smiled. "I can't thank you enough for that dress," I began.

"Posh!" Helen exclaimed in a dismissive manner, motioning expressively to my current apparel. "No decent woman would leave another in something like that when she's in a camp of soldiers. Especially not a young, attractive thing like you," she added with a knowing smile.

I felt my face grow red and I began peeling off my ragged gown in the effort to hide my embarrassment. "Thank you for the bath," I said to change the subject. "I can't remember the last time I had a bath...especially not a warm one!" I exclaimed in delighted surprise as I sank into the water and felt all the grime of the last week loosen from my skin.

"Thank your brother for that," Helen said. "He seems to think that you deserve only the best. He ordered three of the younger men to heat up all that water on the fire and mix it with cold water until he declared it fit for you."

I rolled my eyes, taking the soap from Helen and rubbing the remaining dirt from where it still held onto me stubbornly. "I can't believe he did that. The poor men," I added with pity. "All that work for me!" I shook my head in disbelief. "They'll probably all hate me now."

Helen raised an eyebrow and scrubbed my back vigorously with the bar of soap. No dirt would dare escape her onslaught. I bit back a giggle at her ferociousness and merely smiled at my reflection in the darkening water.

"I highly doubt they'll hate you," she reassured me after my back felt as though she had scrubbed off all skin on it along with the dirt she saw there. "They might be in a bit of awe though. Be prepared to be a bit spoiled by all of them. They'll jump to do whatever you need done."

I stood, and quickly dried myself off with the cloth Helen handed me. The cold air made me shiver, and I hastily pulled the gown over my head to dodge the icy pins that prickled me.

I brushed my wet hair with the comb Helen gave me and pulled it back from my face with a ribbon that she supplied. Ready at last, I opened the tent door. New adventures awaited me.

19:
<u>A New Plan</u>

Malcolm was pacing back and forth in front of my tent and was in a deep discussion with none other than my teacher and travel companion, William Price. He noticed me and walked over with a wide smile.

"You look much more like the sister I left behind in the castle," he said after hugging me.

"I feel much more like the sister you left behind in the castle," I replied. I looked over his shoulder to William, my eyes full of one question: *Did you find Steven?*

William read the question and nodded towards the other tents. "We found Steven last night. Duke was walking slowly and with no guidance whatsoever, due to the fact that my brother was unconscious, about half way between our camp and the enemy's camp."

I gasped in dismay. "Is he still unconscious?"

"No, the healer is with him now. After some wine, food, and a good night of sleep he's improved some."

I sighed in relief. "I am glad. May I go see him?"

"Not right now," Malcolm cut in. "William just came out from talking with the king about his plan for rescuing the princess."

I glanced between the two men. "And?" I pressed.

"The king has agreed to what William put before him."

"Which was?" I asked, hardly daring to hope.

"William will continue to travel towards the castle as was the plan originally, but Steven will stay behind. You will also go with William—"

"I will?" I interrupted him with an excited squeal that I suppressed.

My teacher grinned. "I knew you'd hardly let me leave you behind," he said. "After all, you were the one who insisted on coming with me in the first place."

I nodded. "I feel that it was my fault that the princess was kidnapped," I said. "After all, I was the one who should have realized that Sir Alfred was a traitor. I was the one who shouldn't have let her meet with him alone, and I was the one who should have kept by her side no matter what she said—"

This time Malcolm interrupted me. "Now is not the time for regrets, Meg," he said, "Let me finish what I was trying to say."

My mouth snapped shut, and I gave my brother all my attention.

"You and William will be rescuing the princess, but you won't be the only ones…" he paused for effect. I held my breath without realizing it. "I'm coming with you."

I let out the air in a *whoosh* and grinned up at my brother, giving him a giant hug. He gasped in air at the unexpected action.

"I'm so glad you're coming with us!" I exclaimed, and then shot a mischievous look over his shoulder to William. "I'll feel *so* much safer."

"I beg your pardon!" William said with a wounded air, taking the bait.

Malcolm joined my laughter, and it wasn't long before William gave up his pretense and chuckled.

"When are we leaving the camp?" I asked after the sounds of mirth had died down.

"As soon as we have had lunch," he informed me.

Due to my exhaustion the night before, I had never eaten the food brought to me. My stomach felt as empty as my favorite creek in the heat of summer.

Helen and a couple other women were cooking something that smelled delicious to my famished senses, and the minute the bowl of soup and loaf of bread was handed to me, I sat on the ground cross-legged and began eating as quickly as I could, ignoring the funny looks everyone was giving me.

Malcolm pulled the bowl from my hands and shook his head in mock despair. "Meg, Meg, take your time! We're not going to keep you from eating your fill. There's plenty to go around!"

I realized for the first time what a spectacle I was making of myself and took the bowl back from Malcolm, my face apologetic.

My brother sat down next to me and we caught up on what had happened to him during the month he had been gone. It turned out that Malcolm had had far less eventful days than I had. Most of it had been travel, although they had overtaken and fought a few scouting parties of the Duke's. Currently they were in a sort of stalemate, waiting for the other person to make the next move and begin the war for real.

Once I had eaten, I walked over to where William said Steven was being kept and walked into the tent. Steven lay on the cot, his leg brace back on, and the leg being hung in a sort of sling that was attached to the top of the tent.

I walked over to the side of his bed and sat on a stool beside him, my eyes filling with voluntary tears. I hated to see anyone as helpless as Steven looked.

"How are you?" I asked.

Steven turned his head to me and sighed. "You're rescuing the princess without me," he said, his voice filled with disappointment.

155

I glanced towards his injured leg. "We couldn't very well take you with us," I said in our defense. "Your leg will take over a month to heal properly." I frowned. "Besides, weren't you so set on being sent back to the castle the other day? Why are you set on coming with us now?"

Steven sighed again. "The mind is willing, but the body is weak," he said, then shot me a shaky grin. "I want to come with you, but I knew I couldn't. I so wish that I could."

William ducked into the tent. He noticed me and smiled. "I see you've made it here to visit with the invalid." He pulled another stool over and sat next to me. "Did you fill him in on the new plan?"

I shook my head. "It sounds like he already knew."

"I'm not going," Steven said, proving my point.

William grinned. "Yes, but did you hear that Malcolm is going in your stead?"

Steven frowned thoughtfully. "No, I hadn't heard that." He glanced in my direction. "I'll wager Meg is glad for that."

I nodded. "I am indeed."

"When are you leaving?" the boy asked.

"Now," William answered for me. "I was just coming to collect Meg."

"I came to say farewell," I explained to the prostrate boy.

"Until we meet again then," Steven said as cheerfully as he could muster, putting out a hand to me.

I took it in mine, squeezed it, and then allowed myself to be led from his tent by William.

Glancing back once, I saw him gazing at us wistfully. I hated to have to leave him behind. He had become almost a brother to me, as had William, during the long journey we had taken together, but we had to leave him...it was for his own good. I had a feeling, one that I tried to suppress, that I might never see him again.

Malcolm met us outside, holding onto Prince's bridle with one hand and Duke's and another horse's with the other.

Duke and Prince greeted me with soft whinnies, and even the other horse put his nose closer to me so he could be pet as well.

Malcolm shook his head with a grin. "I always told you that you had a way with horses, Meg."

William nodded in agreement as the horses nudged my pockets in hopes for treats. "Her skill with Duke saved us a great deal of trouble in that scouting camp."

My brother shot his friend a questioning look. "How?"

The story came out and I avoided Malcolm's raised eyebrows when it was finished. "So that's how...no wonder! I was so puzzled back then when my horse seemed to always be getting loose whenever I was late for something."

I cleared my throat. "Well, I was mad that you wouldn't have time to play with me," I said in my defense. "I thought that if I could keep your horse away, perhaps you'd give up on all those meetings and spend more time with me."

Malcolm sighed. "You didn't realize how important they were to my job."

"No," I agreed, pushing the muzzles of the inquisitive horses away when they grew too rough. "I do know now though, and I'd never dream of putting that trick into action...unless, of course, it was absolutely necessary," I added impishly.

"Of course!" Malcolm repeated with a roll of his eyes. He swung up onto Prince. The horse pranced in place, impatient to be off, and I noticed the lack of metallic ringing on the ground.

"Is Prince still barefoot?" I asked.

"Yes, but I hope to get him shod again as soon as we find a worthy blacksmith."

I nodded and mounted Duke. The stiffness had lessoned some due to food and rest, but I still knew I would be glad to have this all over with. In my younger days, I never thought I would tire of riding a horse...but in circumstances like this, riding can be both exhausting and painful.

The men cheered us quietly as we rode away, and soon the surrounding forest hid the king's camp from our eyes. Travel in the woods by day was far easier than navigating it at night; but even so, I wished that Steven had been spared that broken leg. Neither Malcolm nor William matched his uncanny ability to know exactly which way was the fastest, easiest, and least noticeable route.

We almost ran into a few more scouting groups, but Malcolm warned us of them in time. He and the king's soldiers had been keeping an eye on the various groups and which places they patrolled, and when we knew where they went, it was far easier to dodge them.

The Duke's castle wasn't hard to find, though it took us at least an hour of riding before we saw it appear over the tops of trees. It sat high on a hill, surrounded by farmlands and a bustling village. At first glance the fortress was formidable indeed. Towering stone walls rose towards the sky as if they were a giant stone fist, shaking defiance to everyone who dared go against them. The turrets on each corner of the outer wall spiraled upwards to almost touch the sky itself. It was dark, and to fit the mood of our dampened spirits at the sight of such a challenging rescue, rain began to fall.

I was already disguised in my simple brown dress and gray cloak that covered Safeguard from unwanted attention, and somewhere along our trail, Malcolm and William had shed their armor and replaced it with simple peasant clothes. Dirt was rubbed into our horses' coats, and their carefully brushed manes were tangled and filled with burs.

Slowly and wearily, to fit the story we would tell if asked, we rode into the village that sprawled below the ominous shadow of the Duke's castle.

20:
Tricks & Troubles

I was amazed at how well Malcolm and William fit into their roles, and how relaxed they seemed in the enemy's own land. My heart jumped at every soldier that passed by, and fell through my stomach if any of them happened to glance in our direction. I was sure we would be stopped countless times, but no one bothered with the three travel-weary peasants that trudged through their marketplace.

We paid for boarding and food for our horses, and continued through the market unhindered on foot. The busy streets enveloped us and people surged around me, each more busy than the last.

"Have your swords and knives sharp and ready! Two bits to make your old dagger as good as new!"

"Hot potatoes! Baked to perfection! Take one now while they're still here!"

"Lovely trinkets for sale! Come and buy something for that special woman in your life!"

"Fat geese ready for butchering! Have a roasted fowl this Sunday evening to surprise your husband!"

The cries of vendors and haggling men and women as they battled for the best price filled my ears. In our own village, market day was something I had always looked forward to, a day to be spent with friends and talking with familiar faces, but here it seemed utter chaos.

The trinket man grabbed hold of Malcolm and William when he spied me behind them. "Looking for something for the lady, gentlemen?" he asked eagerly. "I've got quite a few things that she might fancy."

Malcolm glanced at William, and then over his shoulder to me. I caught a twinkle in his eyes. He nodded. "If you don't mind, I'm sure she'd love to look at your merchandise to see if there's anything she wants."

The man quickly pulled us over to his stand where all his items lay out on a rickety table. Malcolm motioned to the jewelry and smiled. "Choose whatever your heart desires, Mary," he said.

I accepted the new name without question. Obviously he thought it was necessary. It might take some getting used to, but I could handle it. We didn't know if the Duke knew who we were or not, but Sir Alfred knew, so it was better to be on the safe side.

"Thank you—" I hesitated a moment, my mind racing to come up with a boring, well-used name that would help his disguise. "—Arthur," I finished. I heard that one everywhere.

Malcolm waited until the vendor wasn't watching before giving me a swift nod of approval. I hoped that the man hadn't noticed my second of hesitation. I turned to the table and pretended to take great interest in choosing something from the man's wares.

Then I saw them. Five soldiers headed in our direction. And it looked as if they had a purpose. My hands trembled as I fought to keep my eyes from betraying the fear I felt. Quickly glancing over the rest of the trinkets, I chose a silver necklace that had a delicate cross pendant hanging from its beautiful chain and held it towards the man.

"I think I'd like this," I said, willing my voice not to waver. While Malcolm haggled over the price, as was customary, I nudged William and glanced toward the soldiers. His eyes widened and he tapped Malcolm on the shoulder.

Suddenly, an idea came to me. Before I could have enough time to reconsider, I let out a squeal and tugged on William's cloak. "Oh, Fred!" I exclaimed, ignoring the startled and confused look my teacher gave me. "Look over there!" I pointed to a booth that sold scented pillows, soap, and perfumes which was conveniently far away from the approaching soldiers. "I've always wanted a scented pillow! Do get me one, please? I promise I won't ask for anything else all of today!" I dramatically clasped my hands over my heart, hoping William would know to go along with my ridiculous behavior.

Malcolm shook his head in a helpless manner, but there was a spark in his eyes that told me he understood. "Oh, go get her a pillow, Fred," he said. "If we don't, she'll badger us all the way home."

The trinket man chuckled and so did a few of the people nearby who heard what was taking place.

Without any hesitation, I pulled William towards the booth. "Fred?" he hissed. "That was the best you could come up with? I liked Arthur better."

"I couldn't very well call you *both* Arthur, now could I?" I giggled back. "I can only come up with so many names within a few moments. Anyways, I had to get us away from the soldiers and confuse them somehow. Sir Alfred must have told them to watch for strangers and question them."

William was looking at me in admiration. "Well, you certainly thought of a solution a great deal quicker than Malcolm and I!"

I blushed. "It was a logical solution, and the only one I could come up with at that moment," I answered as if I wasn't quaking inside.

Malcolm joined us at the booth and gave my hand a quick squeeze. The woman selling the pillows was still busy with a different customer, so he took the opportunity to smile at me. "That was quick thinking, Meg," he whispered. "Well done."

I shrugged, hating all the praise. "Thank you," I said. I was eager to have the subject change.

"She thinks Sir Alfred has alerted the Duke's soldiers to search for and question strangers in the town. He suspects that we followed him," William said.

A frown crossed Malcolm's face. "That will make our rescue job harder," he muttered to himself.

"Is there a problem, sir?" The woman who owned the booth was standing in front of us now with a concerned look on her face.

Malcolm stiffened at the unexpected appearance, but kept his cover well. "These pillows seem to be awfully expensive." He glowered. "I wasn't planning on spending a fortune at the market today, but my sister Mary insists upon having one. Do you have smaller ones?"

The woman became all business at once and she smiled. "I do indeed, sir!" she answered, bustling over to another part of the stall. "Here, these ones are small enough to fit into your hand. The fine ladies fancy this kind the most, because they can put them in their wardrobe and their clothes will smell like lavender and pine without the use of expensive perfumes. The scent is very long-lasting, but can be taken out if you wash your clothing in vinegar."

I took the pillow from the woman and inhaled the scent. Lavender calmed my highly-strung nerves, and the pine reminded me of the forests around my home, a smell that always reminded me of my mother. Tears stung my eyes at the memory, but I swallowed them back. I nodded at Malcolm. "This one would be lovely."

My brother haggled the price down to something he "could afford" as a poor peasant, and we melted back into the crowd. The soldiers we were trying to escape had given up on finding us, and were propped against the wall of the nearest tavern. We gave them a wide berth and continued up the road.

Passing into another part of the marketplace, smells assaulted my nose and it wrinkled in disgust. Pigs, horses, cows, sheep, and goats were being herded along the road to be sold to the highest bidder. I kept my eyes turned downward in the effort to keep myself from stepping in animal waste.

Malcolm and William called me to hurry and follow them, so I stepped faster around the disgusting piles. Dodging around stray dogs and loose livestock, I kept my eyes on the ground as a handful of soldiers made their way through the crowds. I allowed myself to be dragged by the crowd and past the soldiers, who paid a lowly peasant girl little mind.

It was because of this that I didn't notice the change in buildings around me, nor the thinning of the crowds. When the road looked safely clean again, I looked up from the cobblestones only to see that I was completely alone. William and Malcolm were nowhere in sight.

Panic gripped my heart, and I sank into the nearest shadow of a tall building. A few people hurried by on their way to the marketplace, but besides that, the street was quiet. Too quiet. Raucous laughter came from somewhere nearby, and I nearly jumped from my skin when three men stumbled by my hiding place from the open door of a tavern I hadn't noticed before.

They passed by so close that I could smell the rank ale on them. I squeezed the little pillow over my nose, letting the smells of lavender and pines drown out the revolting scent. As I breathed in the fragrance, I could almost feel my mother's arms enfold me in a comforting hug like she had so many times during my childhood.

Perhaps they caught a whiff of my pillow, or perhaps they heard my gasp of relief when I buried myself in the better smell, but whatever it was, the men came back, a little too sober for my comfort, and I saw without surprise that each had a sword strapped to their sides.

One of them saw me. He jerked me from the shadows and his face grew a wide smile that showed his crooked, stained teeth. "Well, would you look at that!" he exclaimed to his friends in delight. "Look at what I've found!"

I slapped his hand away from my arm in a sudden burst of courage. "Don't touch me!"

The men surrounding me burst into laughter.

"You caught yourself a lively one, Dick!" one of the other men chortled.

"Aye," the first man agreed, his eyes narrowing at me. "It'll be my pleasure to take her down a bit."

I swallowed. Where were William and Malcolm? *God,* I prayed silently, *help me to escape whatever these men think they're going to do. Give me the strength to stand up to them.*

One of the men ripped my cloak from my shoulders. I pulled away from their grasping hands, suddenly realizing that Safeguard was at my side. As was God. A new courage rose from deep within me.

To the shock of the men who were bent on torturing me, I pulled my sword from its sheath and held it in front of me. "Like I said before," I lowered my voice dangerously, "don't touch me. You'll regret it."

For a moment, the men stood around me in stunned silence. Then, one of them chuckled nervously. "She can't know how to use that sword," he said, trying to convince himself just as much as the other men around him. "And she can't fight all three of us."

My jaw tightened. They didn't know I had fought eight men who were completely sober with William by my side. If I could do that, then with God by my side I could defeat an army. My hands gripped the hilt of my sword, and I faced the men, daring them to come and fight.

As one, they pulled their own swords from their sheaths and came at me. I danced away from their blades, keeping myself out of corners so they couldn't back me into a place where I couldn't fight. One man came a little too close, and I thrust quickly into his side. He sank to the ground beneath a waterfall of curses.

I led the other two men far enough away from their friend so I didn't have to worry about him finding the strength to join back in. I parried and thrust, warding off their countless blows and returning a few of my own. The swords flashed in the torchlight that lit the darkening street. Another man went down when I was able to throw his sword from him and slice his arm.

The last man took one look at his fallen companions and ran away, looking back every once in a while to make sure I wasn't following him. As if I would do anything as foolish as that. I breathed a prayer of thanks heavenward as he left, glad to be alive, even though I was thoroughly exhausted.

I almost walked away, but a groan from the man whose arm I had sliced on the street touched the sympathetic part of my heart, and I knelt a safe distance away, glancing around to make sure neither of his friends came back. I sat gathering my breath and watched the rising and falling chest of my enemy. He was a middle-aged man with shoulder length, graying hair. Only a few wrinkles creased his brow, however, and I put him at about twenty years older than my twenty-four-year-old brother.

"Go ahead and gloat," he said finally, breaking the silence. "I'm sure I deserve it."

I frowned. He had mistaken the reason for which I stayed. "I'm not here to gloat," I answered, coming closer. "I want to help your arm."

He looked at me in disbelief. "No, you don't."

I sighed, cleaning my sword with the cloth on my useless cloak that lay in the dirt, now too ripped and torn for me to wear. Sheathing Safeguard, I turned again to the man who was now sitting up, inspecting the wound.

"You didn't kill us," he said at last.

"I dislike killing when I don't need to," I answered. "You and your friends were cowards enough to pick on a poor defenseless peasant girl, so I knew you'd be cowards enough to give up when you realized I wasn't as defenseless as you thought."

The man snorted his agreement to that statement, cradling his injured arm. "If I said I was sorry, would you believe me?" He looked up at me where I stood safely out of arm's reach.

I studied his face for a moment. He had been the one man who hadn't really said or done anything to me. The man with crooked teeth had a hole the size of my blade in his side and was several yards away, still muttering curses. He had been the first one I wounded on purpose because I saw at once he was the most vicious. The man who had run away was the one who had thought I didn't know how to use my sword; he also was the one who pulled my cloak off my shoulders.

This man, however, stated that Dick had gotten himself into more than he could handle when he grabbed my arm. Of all of them, he was the least likely to harm me. Besides, the beginning of a plan—a plan which would help me find my brother and William again—had begun forming in the back of my mind.

"You knew I was armed," I said after a long silence.

The man dropped his gaze. "I saw your sword under the cloak. Dick didn't. But I thought that the three of us could overwhelm you anyways."

I raised an eyebrow. "Well, you couldn't."

"I realize that now," he said. "What's your name, girl? How did you learn how to use that blade?"

"I'm Me-Mary," I answered, almost slipping up. "I was taught how to fight by my brother and his friend. What's your name?"

"Henry," he answered. "I must say, your brother and his friend did an excellent job teaching you."

I knelt on the ground, my body still ready to jump and run at the slightest provocation. "Will you let me help you? You're losing a lot of blood."

He shrugged, but held out his arm. "Never met anyone who would heal the same person they wounded minutes before."

"Well," I smiled, ripping a few strips of cloth from the already ruined cloak, "I'm not like anyone."

"I can tell," he said.

Even though my hand strayed to my sword every once in a while, as if to remind myself that I could defend myself if Henry tried to hurt me, I wasn't ever in danger. He kept his hands to himself and let me do what I wanted with his wounded arm, his eyes shut tight against the pain he was feeling.

I cleaned the wound as best I could with what I had, and wrapped the laceration with strips I cut with my sword from my old cloak. Once finished, I sat back on my heels and surveyed my handiwork.

Henry opened his eyes and slowly flexed his arm, then winced at the pain. "Thank you."

"You're welcome," I said. "That's all I can do for now…it'll need stitches."

Henry struggled to his feet. "Can you stitch it up for me?"

My brow crinkled as I considered his question. "I can try. I've never done stitches before."

"You've sewn though?"

I thought back upon the years of sewing I did for Malcolm and I in our cottage. A smile twitched the edges of my mouth. "Yes." That was an understatement of the highest level.

Looking around the darkened street, I realized it was no place to conduct a surgery. I at least needed a table.

"I'm going to need you to lay down on something higher up than the street," I finally admitted. "Is there a table somewhere?"

Henry looked at me as if I was daft. "On the street?" he asked.

"Can I have your word that you won't hurt me if we go into that inn?" I asked.

The wounded man eyed me for a moment. "Much harm I could do with your fingers inches from a blade you obviously know how to use," he stated drily. "But if it means that much to you, no I won't harm you. Especially not while you're holding a needle to my skin."

He had a point. I did have the upper hand at the moment. Taking a deep breath, I gave him a nod. "Lead me to this inn of yours then," I said.

21:
A Risky Business

Henry took off at a brisk pace past the tavern, past a few darkened houses, past a butchery, bakery, and blacksmith shop with embers still glowing in the inky shadows. Finally he led me under a creaking sign that read "The Restless Raven: We give hot meals and warm beds!"

The man opened the door for me, and I stepped through into a room filled with smoke and people. Pulling out the pillow again, I pressed it to my mouth, breathing in the sweet scent of lavender mixed with the tangy smell of pine. *Keep me safe,* I pleaded inwardly. That prayer would never grow old, no matter how many times I used it.

The door shut out all fresh breezes so when I tested the air for breathability once it was shut, I only gagged and replaced the scented pillow with all speed. Henry led me to the front desk where a rotund, balding man leaned over and gazed at the two of us through round, owlish eyes.

"What have we here, Master Henry?" he bellowed, eying me up and down like one planning on purchasing a horse or cow.

I winced as all heads turned our way. This was not the entrance I had been hoping for. Thankfully, Henry seemed to know exactly what to do.

"This is a cousin of mine, a healer in training. I got cut in a brawl earlier and she said she would try her hand at stitching it shut. Have you a table nearby that we can use?"

How easily that lie slipped off his tongue...still, it was better to let the people think I was related than for him to say I was his wife or some other outlandish thing like that.

The innkeeper, for so the plump man turned out to be, nodded and led us to the back of his inn. There, he wiped off the top of a filthy table with an equally filthy cloth that he produced from somewhere around his person.

He gave us a wide grin that showed one of his front teeth was half-rotted. "Will that do you?" he asked.

I had always been a firm hand in our home when it came to cleanliness, and the whole atmosphere of this inn was grating on my natural want to be clean, as well as my nerves. But I had no choice. It was this or the street outside.

So I nodded. "May I have some water?"

"That you may, lass," the innkeeper assured me, taking off as fast as his round figure could manage.

Henry found me a thick thread, a bent needle, and a bottle of whisky. I eyed the last item distastefully.

He grinned at my obvious disgust of the intoxicating beverage. "I won't touch a drop without your permission," he promised, handing all the things over to me.

While we awaited the water, Henry situated himself on the table. I pulled out the remains of the cloak to act doubly as a pillow for his arm and a layer between the wound and the dirty table. When the water was brought, I set down the bowl beside me on a handy bench. I washed the cut, wincing as he shuddered. When it was clean enough to satisfy even my high standards, I pulled out the needle and threaded it.

Henry watched me in silence, beads of perspiration already appearing on his face. "I'll need some of that whisky," he said.

I nodded, pouring some of the bottle down the man's throat. He swallowed it with the air of a desperate man. I pulled it away from his open mouth and put it out of reach.

"That's enough," I said.

He looked with yearning at it. "Are you sure? The pain's going to be pretty bad."

"I know," I answered. "But we don't want your stomach too full. This sort of thing can make your stomach do things you might not intend it to do." Almost immediately, I thought back to the advice William had given me offhandedly before he set Steven's leg back into place. My own stomach heaved at the memory.

Henry's eyes widened. "Are you saying I might be sick during or after the operation?"

I nodded grimly. "Yes."

The man closed his eyes, a determined look plastered over his face. I took a breath, steadying my hands.

My stomach squeezed as the needle slid into Henry's skin. I saw black spots sprinkle around the edges of my vision and forced myself to breathe slowly. *In...out...in...out...in...out.* Slowly. Focus. Do not faint. Slowly. *God, give me the strength.* I shut out the smoky atmosphere, the dirty state of the room and table, the flickering light of the candles.

I was back in our cottage on the farm, sewing a new patch in Malcolm's favorite breeches that he wore around the farm. So many places were patched that they were practically a completely different pair, but still Malcolm insisted they had years of wear left in them. He wouldn't let me burn them. So many different shades of brown and blue were mixed together to make one pair of breeches. I wouldn't have been at all surprised if there wasn't a speck of original material on them.

A moan from my patient jerked me back to reality. I was almost done. Only two more stitches. Blood oozed from the wound, but my sewing would hold. Carefully, I pulled the thread tight and the skin closed together. I tied the thread and gave the gray-faced Henry another couple swallows of whisky, wrinkling my nose at the smell.

After a few minutes, his shallow breathing returned to normal as I re-wrapped his arm with the last strip of cloak. He sat up and swung his legs over the side of the table and stood on his shaky feet.

His fingers probed the wrapped cut, and he gave me a lopsided grin. "My thanks."

I smiled. "I hope it holds. I've never sewn—" I shuddered, "—skin back together. Just cloth."

"The textures are different, aren't they?" my patient asked.

My stomach squeezed, and I felt a sudden urge to go outside and lose whatever was inside it. "Please don't," I whispered, swallowing several times to keep my meal.

Henry looked amused at my queasiness, but refrained from saying anything else that would trigger my stomach's current weakness into action. "Can I do anything in return for your kindness and healing skills?"

I blushed. "I didn't do it for pay," was my quick answer.

He looked at me. "Whether you did or not is none of my concern. However, I do feel obligated to do something for you now. I might have lost my arm if you hadn't helped me."

A thought crossed my mind, but I dismissed it almost immediately with a slight shake of my head, shutting my mouth that had opened to frame the question I thought better of. It would be asking too much.

Henry seemed to read something in my eyes and saw the movement. "What were you about to ask?" he pressed.

I sighed, sitting on the bench and propping my head up on my hand. "When you and your friends," I worded the phrase carefully, "found me, I had just realized that I lost track of my brother and his friend. I was wondering how well you knew this village and if you could help me find them again."

Henry sat on a stool facing me and considered my request. "You're a stranger to our village."

It was more of a statement than a question, but I nodded anyways.

"How did you lose sight of your brother and his friend?"

I dropped my gaze. Now I was treading on dangerous ground. But I knew I could never lie with a straight face, so it would be better to tell the truth and face the consequences.

"I was trying to avoid some soldiers."

A light of understanding sparked in Henry's eyes, and he grinned. "I'd ask you why you were trying to avoid them, but I've had to hide from them myself a few times. I understand why you won't want to answer that."

If it was possible, my face turned an even darker shade of red, and I lowered my gaze in guilt.

He chuckled. "Where was the last time you saw them?"

I threw my memory back a few hours. Before I realized I was lost, before the soldiers' appearance, before the fight.

"Where the livestock were being sold at the market."

"Ah." Henry scratched the stubble that sprinkled his chin. "Well, I think the search should start there."

I leapt from the bench with fresh energy. "You'll help me find them?" I exclaimed in disbelief.

He nodded. "Yes. They shouldn't be too hard to find...at least not for someone who knows where to look."

I leapt to where he was now standing, and, forgetting myself, wrapped him in a joyful hug. Coming to myself, I stumbled backwards, my face flaming yet again and my hand over my mouth in shock.

Henry looked almost as shocked as me, and his face matched mine in a fiery red that reached to his ears. His mouth hung open, and he stuttered out, "Y-you're w-welcome?"

"I'm so sorry, I forgot myself," I said.

His face slowly returned to its normal color and he allowed himself a nervous chuckle. "I suppose one can hardly blame you," he answered. "For what it's worth, I forgive you. Shall we go?"

I nodded, following him out the inn's door while ignoring the looks we received from some of the people we passed. I hardly noticed...after all, I was safely on my way to finding Malcolm and William. Or so I thought.

22:

Planning Again

Henry led me from one disreputable neighborhood to another, stopping passersby on the narrow lanes, questioning men who could hardly see straight they were so drunk, and paying some of them for helpful directions. I have to admit, he did know how to glean information, and did a far better job than I would have done. Granted, it helped that he had the courage to talk to a few characters I would have done everything I could to avoid.

Finally, when I had just about worn through my riding boots with all the walking around the village, and my voice was almost completely gone from telling everyone and their cousin what my brother and William looked like, along with their counterfeit names, we found them.

Or perhaps I should say they found us.

Henry was looking worried by the time he came out of the final tavern and walked over to where I stood in the shadows. "I can't get any more people to give me information. It looks as though we've walked ourselves to the end of the road and there's no place to go."

I sighed, rubbing my arms in the cold. "We have to find them," I said, swallowing back the tears of helplessness that threatened to spill out of my eyes and over my cheeks. I had nowhere to go, and night had long since fallen. Trust never came easily to me...and I didn't know how far Henry's gratefulness went. He could be planning on leading me into a corner or to his friends at this very moment.

Instead, hands covered our mouths and pulled Henry and me back into the shadows of an alleyway. I found myself being pushed into a stone wall and my wide, frightened eyes meeting William's. He gasped as if someone hit him in the stomach and stumbled backwards, letting go of me immediately.

"Meg?" his voice was filled with shock and disbelief.

I fell to the ground when I lost his support and sat there, rubbing the circulation back into my arms. Malcolm held Henry still, his eyes wide in surprise. Then, as one, both Malcolm and William turned their glares to Henry.

My brother tightened his grip on Henry, causing the man to wince and groan at the pain he was causing his injury I had so carefully sewn together. "What did you do to my sister?" he demanded fiercely.

"If you hurt her in any way..." William left the threat unfinished, his eyes flashing fire in the darkness.

I leapt to my feet, pulling Malcolm's hands from Henry's injured arm. "Stop! You're hurting him!"

Incredulity at my actions caused them to hesitate, and I quickly glanced over Henry's injury to make sure his cut wasn't bleeding again. The man winced at the probing of my fingers, but his eyes held no malice towards my brother and his harsh treatment.

"He got a cut," I explained, once I was satisfied the wound hadn't reopened. "And he didn't hurt me." My story came out in a rush, and though the air around me was stiff with suspicion, they seemed to accept the fact that Henry wasn't going to harm any of us.

Meanwhile, the man studied me. Once I finished the story and while Malcolm and William decided what to make of it in their own minds, he spoke. "So it's Meg...not Mary?"

I avoided his gaze and stood up.

That alone seemed to be enough of an answer for him. He chuckled. "I *thought* that Mary might not be your real name. You almost slipped yourself."

William glanced between us. "I suppose we should thank you," he said grudgingly.

"For what?" Henry asked.

"For keeping her from searching for us all over the village in the middle of the night by herself," Malcolm answered for William. I don't know what he saw in the look I gave him, but the next thing he said was, "Don't give me that look, you know you would have! Admit it."

Much as I disliked it, I knew he was right. I would have. "Have we found a way..." I trailed off with a glance towards Henry who was watching us with narrowed eyes.

"The Duke is no friend of mine," he said suddenly when he caught my eyes on him.

I shifted my weight from one leg to the other. "Why would you tell us that?" I asked.

"Well, you're obviously trying to do something without his knowledge of it, considering the fact that you were avoiding his soldiers earlier this evening at all costs," Henry answered matter-of-factly.

"We're trying to rescue..." I fought to gather and use the right words. Just in case.

"He kidnapped my betrothed," Malcolm said.

"Ah," Henry replied, his eyes lighting up in understanding. "So you want to rescue her?" At the united nods from us, his brow furrowed, and he scratched his chin, as he seemed to be in the habit of doing when in deep thought.

"A man named Alfred knows we're trying to rescue her," Malcolm put in, in hopes of helping whatever plan the man might have.

Henry sucked in a breath. "If Lord Alfred knows about your rescue plans...that's going to make your job a great deal harder."

My eyebrows lifted in surprise. "A Lord!" I exclaimed, not bothering to hide the shock in my voice.

Malcolm and William's faces sank into smoldering frowns.

"That explains a lot," my brother said.

"The rotten little..." William stopped his verbal abuse of the man and glanced in my direction with an apologetic look.

A smile twitched the corners of my mouth. "No need to hold back too much on my account," I said. "My own vocabulary is sadly lacking in words that I can use to describe his infamous behavior."

Henry interrupted us. "I know you may not want my help at all, but if you are willing, I think I have the beginnings of a plan."

Malcolm's eyes sparked in interest and he leaned towards the injured man. "How could you help us?"

"Well," he hesitated for a moment before continuing, "I have a few friends among the guards in the castle's dungeon, and that is undoubtedly where your betrothed is being held...if she's still alive."

"You think we might be able to slip into the dungeon and free her?" Malcolm could hardly hide the eagerness in his voice.

"Possibly. Or possibly we can work inward from the outside. Tunnels may be a bit common for escaping prisoners to use, but there's a reason for that: it has worked in the past."

The idea of having Henry help was slowly taking root in Malcolm and William's minds. I trusted him more or less, despite the less than pleasant way we met each other. Besides, I was ready to do just about anything to get the princess to safety.

"What is the young lady's name?" Henry continued, looking at my brother.

He froze. We were treading dangerous ground yet again. "Anna," Malcolm said at last.

Henry apparently noted his hesitation. "You'll have to tell me her actual name, otherwise I won't be able to find where she's being kept."

A resigned look came over Malcolm's face and he sighed. "Her name is Christine," he said.

Henry uttered a low whistle. "The princess herself?" he muttered more to himself than us.

"Yes," Malcolm answered. "How did you know that was the princess? Surely there's more than one girl in the kingdom whose name is Christine," he added suspiciously.

Henry raised an eyebrow. "Everyone in this village heard about the Duke capturing the princess to use as a bargaining tool with the king." The man's brow furrowed. "An unfortunate complication…it's going to make our job of rescuing her a great deal harder. Such a valuable prisoner is going to have twice as many guards around her at all times, if not the Duke himself." He paused, scratching his chin again. "In fact, she may not even be kept in the dungeon. The Duke may have her up in his specially guarded tower he keeps for political prisoners."

William chewed on the edge of his lip. "Surely the Duke will have a hard time hiding such a famous prisoner's whereabouts from all the people in the castle. Couldn't we discreetly inquire around until we find out where she is?"

"An excellent plan," Henry agreed, "except that you say Lord Alfred knows about your plans of rescue. If that is so, he'll be sending his own spies to look for people asking about the princess. Once he gets wind of our inquiries, the bloodhounds will follow our trail, and we'll put her life in more danger than it already is…not to mention the fact that we'll be killed."

"What do you suggest then?" Malcolm asked, his face drawn into a worried frown.

"To be able to overcome an enemy, you must find a weakness," Henry said.

For a moment, we looked at him. The man I had almost left to bleed to death on the shadowed street appeared to be as full of surprises as we were of desperation.

"Who are you?" I asked.

Henry sighed. "Who am I? Nobody right now. You should ask who I was."

"Who were you?" William asked without missing a beat.

"I was the Duke's Captain of the Guard."

My hand covered my mouth, muffling my gasp. "What happened?"

"I dared to disagree with his brother."

"On what?"

Henry closed his eyes, as if to shut out the painful memories of his past. "He wanted to send all the soldiers under me into a battle in which we would be outnumbered one hundred to ten. It was nothing short of murder for all my men. I refused, and stated my reasons. His brother was absolutely livid at my refusal and stormed to the Duke who stripped me of my position and turned me out of his army on his brother's behalf from my position without even bothering to hear my side of the story. I have been striving to drown my memories in the taverns since then."

For a moment, there was nothing we could say. Our silent shock hung for a moment, our mouths open in disbelief and horror at what he must have gone through. Henry gave a shuddered sigh and passed a hand over his forehead.

"I would do anything to help avenge these five years I've wasted because of him," Henry continued. "If you wouldn't mind my help that is."

Malcolm grinned and shook Henry's hand. "Consider yourself a part of our rescue plans. We could use another man on our side."

"And one who knows the inside of the castle as well as you do will be invaluable," William added.

The tension melted. Plans were made. Now all we had to do was carry them out.

23:
Unpredictable Circumstances

"Are you sure we can trust him?" William asked, pulling me aside for a moment.

I shrugged. "For now, yes. He holds no love for the Duke, and he had plenty of opportunities to hurt me, but didn't." I leaned against the wall, my stomach full, and the excitement of the previous day beginning to catch up to me. I hadn't slept at all last night and just now I was starting to feel the exhaustion. Briefly, I wondered what had taken it so long.

"Safeguard had nothing to do with it?" William cocked a knowing eyebrow at me.

I laughed softly. "His presence may have helped my cause a little."

My teacher glanced sideways at me, as if studying my face in the flickering light. "I wish somehow that we hadn't separated. So many things could have happened while you were alone…" he trailed off, his sentence fading away like the smoke of the candles that lit the room we were standing in.

We had left Malcolm and Henry discussing further plans in the same inn where I had so recently learned to sew a wound shut. The Restless Raven was chosen as our meeting place because of its less than stellar reputation. Most people who took temporary lodging there were either trying to avoid attention, like us, or only passing through the village on their way and could care less about three travel-weary men and a woman. Not that I could blame them. After all, the inn was hardly a pleasant place. Secretive and a good place to hide, yes, but clean and orderly, no.

Watching Malcolm talk with such animation brought a smile to my lips. I had been gone from his presence for so long I almost forgot how he threw himself so energetically into strategizing. He was brilliant when it came to planning, and this rescue of his betrothed was no different. A certain light shone in his eyes that I hadn't seen there since the last time we had played a game of chess.

"I'll pay you a half-crown for your thoughts," William's voice broke through my reminiscing, and I glanced his direction to find his eyes still studying me. My face must have gone a shade darker pink, because I could see William begin grinning. "Or, perhaps I shouldn't ask," he added.

I rolled my eyes helplessly. Really, the man was incorrigible. "They are hardly worth a whole half-crown," I said with a shrug of my shoulders.

"Now I'm really curious." My teacher's smile reached to his eyes, and I saw them twinkling.

I sighed deeply. "If you must know, I was thinking how glad I was to have my brother with me again. I missed him dreadfully."

"Oh, is that all?" William asked.

With a frown, I looked over at him. He seemed almost crestfallen, but at the same time relieved. I hid a puzzled smile with difficulty. "I told you it wasn't worth a half-crown."

Suddenly, Malcolm appeared in front of me with a half-smile on his face. "Are you done whispering?" he asked.

"We were whispering?" I hadn't realized.

His eyebrows rose slightly. "You were."

"I beg your pardon. It won't happen again, and, yes, of course we're done."

Malcolm shot William a look I couldn't quite decipher, and then motioned toward Henry. "We decided the first step in our rescue is to find out where exactly the Duke is keeping his valuable prisoner."

William mirrored my nod of agreement. It was the most sensible plan of action. *But how?* I wondered.

"As he said before, Henry has some friends who frequent the castle, sometimes even the least used rooms which the Duke inhabits."

Henry walked up behind him, subconsciously holding his injured arm in a protective manner. "They are less likely to attract attention when they inquire about the princess," he explained. "Malcolm pointed out that some of them may even be the very ones who bring food or water to her."

"After we successfully find where the princess is without the Duke or Alfred finding us, what will we do next?" William posed this question to Henry, but Malcolm was the one to answer.

"We will endeavor to find a way to smuggle her from the Duke's grasp," he said. "I agree with Henry. One must find an enemy's weakness if one wishes to triumph over them. That will be our next step: finding a weakness."

"And then," I said finally, "you will swoop in on a white horse in shining armor and carry your future bride off into the sunset."

William and Henry chuckled at this, and I could hardly keep a grin off my own face. Malcolm blushed and ducked his head before quickly gaining control over himself again.

"Of course, it won't be quite that easy." He sighed. "I only wish it was."

I patted him on the shoulder gently. "God will be with us. He will keep us safe, as well as Christine."

A day passed, and then another, before we learned where Princess Christine was kept in the Duke's large castle. Meanwhile, I caught up on much needed sleep and much needed nourishment. The Restless Raven did serve good food, though the dishes' cleanliness was not all it could have been.

At last Henry brought us the news we had been waiting for: the princess was a prisoner in one of the towers within the castle walls. The Duke didn't appear to go near her, except for when he questioned her once or twice to learn all she knew about her father's plans…which, thankfully for us, wasn't anything at all. It appeared that he had no ulterior motives, except to use her as a bargaining tool with the king. We hoped this would continue to be the case until we had a chance to pull her away. Who knew what the Duke would do to her if he grew tired of waiting for the king to demand the release of his daughter.

Our friend Lord Alfred, however, was an entirely different matter. According to Henry's friend, he had gotten a few bruises from the hand of the princess, as well as a few more from her well-aimed kicks, for the trouble he took to whisk her away from her home. Of course, this didn't put Christine in good standing with him.

Worried lines creased Malcolm's brow when Henry finished relaying this information. "We've just got to get her out of there," he said with a hint of desperation, gnawing on his lower lip.

"How?"

My brother's strategizing genius bubbled to the surface yet again. His eyes narrowed in concentration, and he tapped the table we were sitting at with his restless fingers. "We'll have to get inside the castle and gain a better understanding of their defenses."

"Sir...I mean *Lord* Alfred knows what we look like," I pointed out needlessly. I could see everyone was thinking the same thing.

Malcolm held up a hand. "I have an idea."

* * † * *

"This is insane!" I exclaimed when my brother had laid out his "foolproof" plan before us. I stared at the three men watching my reaction with obvious amusement on their faces. "You must be out of your mind!" I added for emphasis.

"I might be," Malcolm chuckled. "But it will work."

I shook my head, sending my long braid of auburn hair flying. "How? Alfred...the Duke *and* Alfred will see right through it!"

"I don't think so." Malcolm looked me in the eye. "Alfred will hardly think that you would allow us to dress you as a boy, cut your hair, and send you alone into an enemy's castle to act as a peasant boy looking for work in the stable as a part of our rescue plan."

"And he'd be right!" I said, holding my hair protectively.

"But you'd do it," my brother continued, "you'd do it for the princess."

"Much as I hate to see all those lovely auburn waves cut off, it's the only way," William added.

Even as a blush deepened the color of my cheeks at the subtle compliment, I gave a heavy sigh. They were both right. I would do anything short of killing myself or denouncing my faith to bring her to safety. It was my duty. With a resigned air, my hand fell away from my braid.

Sitting down on a nearby stool, I surrendered to their plan. "Please do it quickly," I said. "Before I change my mind."

My brother pulled out a wicked looking pair of shears and began sawing my hair away from my head. Strands of waist-length auburn hair fell, only to settle around my feet in a forlorn heap. Already I felt my head lighten, free of the weight of my hair, but that didn't help my mood in the slightest.

As was the case with most girls, my hair had been a source of pride and vanity all my growing up years, and now I was losing all the work I had put into keeping it long and healthy to a whim of my brother's. To say I was distressed would be an understatement of the highest caliber.

"It doesn't look too bad," Malcolm told me when standing back to survey his handiwork. "In fact, it looks quite passable, if I do say so myself."

I took my face out of my hands and blinked away the mist that filled my vision so I could see the final picture in the mirror over the room's fireplace. My sight cleared, and for a moment, I stared in shock at the creature that faced me.

My beautiful hair, the one thing I really had to fuss over with girlish pride, was cut off just below the ears. Malcolm, not being the most accomplished barber by any stretch of the imagination, had cut it jaggedly, the rough ends all different lengths. Some of it hung down over my eyes, effective for hiding my identity, which I realized upon some reflection, but a very unladylike style nonetheless.

Any shred of pride I held had been cut off along with my hair. I pulled my head up and swallowed my pride, still avoiding the image of my new self in the mirror. I gave an expressive moan.

My brother patted me on the back. "You'll get used to it, Meg."

No I won't. I ran a hand through my hair, surprised at how soon my hand came free of the shortened length.

William was regarding me with a lopsided grin.

I met his stare with a glower that came straight from my healthy amount of wounded pride. "Whatever you're thinking, don't say it," I warned. "I'm liable to slap someone, *anyone*, who sees fit to make a joke about how I look at this moment."

My teacher saw fit to ignore my warning. "I was just going to say you look absolutely adorable, Meg," he said with a smirk plastered across his face.

I stomped over and peered up at him, wishing I could be taller and be able to look him eye to eye. "Didn't I warn you not to make fun of me?" I felt hurt by his mocking, and my hand rose on its own accord to slap him.

He caught my wrist and lowered it. "Calm yourself, Meg, I wasn't making fun of your hair." I saw now that William's eyes held only honesty, and I forced myself to listen. "I really do think your hair looks fine." He glanced at my brother and the grin returned. "Granted, Malcolm is not the best hair cutter in the world, but after a few weeks of growing, perhaps trimming it a little after we rescue the princess, it'll look better."

I took a deep breath, felt my shorn head, and gave William a shaky smile. "Thank you."

"I can buy you some boy's clothes, Meg," my brother continued. "And we'll have to fix your face—what we can see of it—and your hair so that Alfred can't recognize you."

I regarded myself sorrowfully in the mirror. "I doubt he'd recognize me as I am now."

Malcolm tilted his head thoughtfully. "Perhaps not, but we'll still have to get you nice and dirty before sending you into the lion's den."

I sighed with a martyr-like air. "I hope Christine appreciates everything I'm going through to get her to safety."

"I'm sure she does," William assured me.

Malcolm grinned and headed toward the door. "William, Henry, meet me outside. We'll split up to gather supplies we'll need for getting into the castle after Meg does her part, and the things for our disguises." He looked at me and a flicker of sympathy clouded his eyes for a moment. "Meg, stay here and rest. Who knows when you'll have another chance."

I waited until the door closed before melting into a puddle of helpless tears once more. It was ridiculous, and I felt ashamed to show my feelings in such a manner, but I knew that if I held the tears inside, my resolve would crumble sooner. Better to let out my emotions now, while no one was near enough to laugh at my misery.

24:
Disguises & Deceit

My tears were spent and dry by the time Malcolm, William, and Henry came back. I was lying on the cot, exhausted and thirsty, but resigned to my fate. Sitting up as they came in, I noticed their arms were loaded with things I couldn't place at the moment.

"Sleep well?" Malcolm asked, taking in my rumpled state.

"Not really, but thank you for your concern."

William plopped a mound of garments on the cot by me, and I shoved it onto the floor instinctively when I saw how filthy they were. Probably the baggy shirt had more than dirt crawling around inside the ragged folds. I shuddered and inched away from the haphazard pile on the ground.

"Tell me I don't need to wear those," I begged.

"I'm afraid you do," Malcolm answered. "Don't worry, most of the dirt is merely for show; they're not as bad as they appear."

I picked up a pair of soiled breeches between my forefingers and thumb in order to regard the offending item with distaste. I could hardly imagine myself in them for a few

189

minutes, let alone the few days it would take for our plans of rescue to be carried out. My pleading eyes met only amusement in the men's faces. Obviously, I would be getting no sympathy from them.

I huffed my disapproval and dropped the garment back on the floor so I could fold my arms stubbornly. "Well, I can't get into these…things with you all in here," I pointed out, giving them all an impatient shooing motion I usually saved for our chickens. "Go on now, I'll let you in once I've changed."

Once the door shut behind them, I gave a heavy sigh and began the unpleasant task of changing into the horribly dirty clothes. I had a much smaller frame than whoever had been the previous owner of the disgusting items. The shirt fell to my knees and hung loosely from my shoulders. The breeches were also baggy, and the boots were too big…I'd have to stuff some rags in them. I tucked in the shirt as best I could, ignoring the funny lumps it created. Now was not the time to worry about my looks.

I avoided glancing at myself in the mirror when I passed it to call the men back into our room, but was sorely tempted to see exactly how bad it was. Things didn't improve when my brother and William arrived either. Upon sighting me in my new apparel, they both simultaneously burst into a chorus of laughter at my expense.

Their sounds of mirth died away gradually once they caught sight of the dangerous glare I was giving them both. "I take it you approve of my new outfit then," I said, my voice dripping with sarcasm.

Malcolm chuckled. "You do look…different," my brother said, apparently at a loss for another word to describe my current appearance.

William was grinning widely. "God knew what He was doing when He made you a girl, Meg," he added. "I'm afraid you don't make a very convincing man."

"Perhaps that's because I'm not one," I shot back. "However, in order for this ridiculous plan of yours to work, you're going to have to help me be more convincing. I've got to fool Alfred, you know, and we all have seen how good he can be at acting. I must be able to out act him."

My brother rubbed his hands together. "William and I will teach you what you need to know."

I rolled my eyes heavenward, asking God silently for the patience I knew I would need. It was going to be a long afternoon.

Several hours later, after William and Malcolm felt they had shoved as many lessons about how a man would act in any given situation down my throat as they could, we stopped to eat our evening meal. I flexed my sore leg muscles that were so unused to taking long, swaggering strides. My arms ached from all the exercising Malcolm put me through; lifting, pushing, and stretching.

Once our meal was eaten, they then put me to work practicing my skills with the blade in the alleyway behind The Restless Raven. For at least one hour, if not two, Malcolm, William, and Henry took turns. Each man had different skills, each better at one thing or another with their own sword, so I got a well-rounded lesson simply from fighting them and finding their different strengths.

Malcolm was better at offense, darting in and out with lightening efficiency, but once I managed to back him into a corner, he was easier to fight in his desperation. I knew he was a superior swordsman, but I also recalled his weakness, namely that he didn't fight as well in a corner and he was better the more space he had to move, it was easier for me to fight him as an equal.

William, as my teacher, was the one I was most comfortable fighting with. I already knew the moves he knew, and could easily work the circumstances around me into my favor. He was still better than me, but not by much, which he told me himself when we stopped to catch our breath and drink some ale that the innkeeper of The Restless Raven brought us on a tray.

"You've gotten better, Meg," he informed me, gulping down a whole mug of the awful tasting stuff. "You're almost as good as I am!"

"Not better?" I teased back, loving the feel of Safeguard's weight in my hand and forgetting for a moment that I had cut my hair and was dressed in too-large boy's clothes.

He shook his head, loose hair falling into his eyes. William pushed it back and shot me a challenging grin. "Shall we find out?" he asked.

My heart warmed in sudden excitement and I nodded. I took a small sip of the ale, but grimaced and pushed the almost full mug back away from me. Malcolm handed me some tea he had made, knowing I wouldn't want to drink the stuff he and the other men were. I smiled at him and drank the hot beverage gratefully before stepping back and getting a firmer grip on Safeguard.

Of course, William ended up winning the duel, but it felt so good to be fighting again that I didn't mind in the slightest.

Henry tried my skills next. Even with a wounded arm, he could duel very well. I was better than he, but he had some skills that tried mine to the extreme. His strength was his ability to fight with both the right and left hand with the same amount of adeptness when not wounded (or so he told me). His weakness was the fact that he didn't know what to do with his legs while he was fighting…that and the fact that he had a wounded arm which made it harder for him to face me.

"I haven't fought much with the sword in a long time," Henry wheezed when we both agreed to stop our fighting for a moment and have some refreshment. "I mostly ordered people to fight back in the old days, but I forgot how thrilling it felt to have a duel." The middle aged man bowed to me and smiled. "I thank you for that, Lady Megan."

I returned his smile. "Please, just call me Meg," I said.

"Mark," my brother corrected. "Remember we're supposed to be peasants, and she's supposed to be a boy."

"Mark then," Henry answered.

"I think Meg—Mark has all he needs to know about the art of being a man," William jumped in with a teasing grin. "When are we planning on setting her—I mean him—loose inside the enemy gates?"

"After I've gotten one last good night's sleep," I informed them before Malcolm had a chance to say anything. "You're not sending me in tonight."

"Of course not," Malcolm soothed. "We'll wait until tomorrow."

Saying the word 'sleep' triggered yawns from all of us, and we departed to our various rooms. Malcolm and I shared one with two cots, and William and Henry shared another like it next to ours. I sank into the dubiously clean sheets with a grateful sigh. Never had I felt so sore. Everything ached from the exercise my brother and friends had made me go through.

However, I knew it would all be worth it—even my shorn head—if only we could succeed in getting the princess back to her home safely.

* * † * *

"Today is the big day!" someone exclaimed, punching through my dreams and scattering them to the wind. *Confounded morning people.* And my brother had to be one of them. I felt his hand shake my shoulder and the mists of sleep cleared for a moment, just long enough to see my brother's face peering down at me. Sitting up, I yawned loudly and rubbed the remaining sleep from my eyes. I blinked a few times in the early morning light that streamed through the one window our temporary residence contained.

"How early is it?" I queried groggily, accepting the mug of tea he pressed into my hand and trying to keep my eyes open by sheer willpower.

193

"Early," my brother answered. "I just came back from awakening William and Henry. I'm heading their way to get ready for the day so that you can have some privacy." He stood and started towards the door. "Don't fall back asleep," he warned with a teasing smile.

I nodded with a reluctant sigh as the door shut behind him. With a glance of longing at the welcoming warmth of my cot, I stood up and dressed myself in the disgusting clothes that formed my disguise. Malcolm had suggested that I not brush my hair, as most peasant boys wouldn't have, so I merely ran a hand through it a few times to make it all lay more or less flat after a night of sleeping on my side.

Because I didn't bother washing my face either, I was ready for my adventure within a few minutes. Breakfast consisted of some broth, leftover from our supper the night before, and a few slices of bread to dip in it as well as more tea and a small pitcher of cream from the innkeeper's private milk cow.

Just as I finished my meal, the men came in, all dressed in equally shabby clothes and looked as if they hadn't had a bath in months. At the smell they were emanating, a smell that caused my nose to wrinkle in revulsion, that guess wasn't far off when it came to whoever the previous owners were.

"You look just as bad," Malcolm said, catching sight of my grimace.

I gave him a look of obvious disbelief. "I don't think that's possible."

My brother grinned good-naturedly and gave a suggestive nod in the direction of the mirror. I glanced at my reflection briefly, but looked away quickly with a shudder, a blush mounting my cheeks. I did look terrible. With a knowing smile, my brother ate his breakfast with William and Henry. I huffed my impatience and fiddled with Safeguard's handle while I waited for them to finish.

Before long we were walking through the village. I was doing my best to copy my brother's easy stride that consumed

194

distance like fire consumed fuel, but my already sore muscles began shouting their complaints at the unnatural effort I was making them give.

When we finally reached the castle gates, I was just about ready to drop. I braced myself, receiving my brother's hug in silence, as well as William's promises to pray for me while I was inside. Henry shook my hand and wished me luck. I gave them all a tight-lipped smile.

"You'll do fine," Malcolm assured me.

I swallowed my fears and nodded.

"God will give you the strength you need," William added.

I nodded again, not trusting my voice to be steady if I tried to reply.

With one last reassuring squeeze of my arm, the men disappeared into nearby shadows and I faced the castle gate by myself. From now on, I was more or less on my own, and if the princess was to be rescued, I would have to be ready for anything.

25:
A Job for a Boy

It wasn't until I had practically worn the skin off my knuckles rapping on the huge wooden door of the castle that I got an answer to my noise. A short and stout man with a grimy face and scraggly beard opened the smaller part of the door. He regarded me for a moment, suspicious and wary.

"What are you doing here?" he demanded in a rough voice. "No stragglers allowed on his Lordship's doorstep. Get along with you or I'll summon the soldiers!"

I swallowed once, willing my voice to keep steady and lowering it for effect. "I'd like a job, sir," I answered with as much boldness as I could manage at the moment.

He seemed taken aback. "A job? Why do you want a job here?"

"I'd like to be a stable boy, sir, I do well with horses."

"You've got nerve, I'll give you that!" he exclaimed after considering my request for a few moments. "I'm not the one you want to ask about a job. Wait here while I get Lord Alfred. He'll be the one who'll tell you if you're needed or not."

I hid my fear of meeting Alfred so soon with an abrupt nod. "Thank you."

The door shut in my face and I remained standing in trepidation, praying with everything that was in me for Alfred not to recognize me. When the man appeared at last, it was with as much suddenness as he had disappeared. He opened the door wider and motioned with his head for me to come in.

"He'll see you," he said. "Follow me."

I obeyed the man in silence and walked a respectful distance behind him as he led me through a tall archway into what would have been a sunny courtyard, except for the fact that the high walls kept it in shadow for most of the day. We continued on to another stone building that rose in the middle of the courtyard and was surrounded by several guards. I could smell horses, and heard a few whinnies, but couldn't see them. Somehow, my courage was lifted after hearing the familiar sound. My head lifted higher, and I gave a bold nod of greeting to the soldiers who watched my passage with wary, untrusting eyes.

I kept my eyes open for which tower might be *the tower* where the princess was being kept prisoner, but there were too many places for my eyes to look, and I didn't want to appear suspicious. Turrets, topped by fearsome battlements, towered in the four corners of the daunting outer walls that contained the courtyard and inner castle.

A guard opened the solid looking door which led into the main part of the castle and the man led me through. We walked down a dusty hallway and took a few turns. I tried to keep some sort of map in my head of which places I went, but it was a fairly hopeless task with all the different directions I was taken.

At long last, the man halted in front of a door and knocked on it after muttering more to himself than me, "Here we are at last."

Alfred—my mind refused to give him any honorary title—opened the door. I tried to mask the anger in my eyes from the cowardly traitor before me, realizing I had to act as if I didn't know him.

The gatekeeper ducked his head respectfully, and, seething inside, I did the same. "Lord Alfred, here's the boy I was telling you about."

Alfred studied me for a moment. I kept my head down, my hands folded to keep them from trembling, and stayed silent. His fingers tapped against one of his legs in a thoughtful manner.

"Thank you, Burns, you may go now."

The gatekeeper bowed once more before walking back down the long hallway. I was now at the mercy of Alfred. I closed my eyes and prayed he wouldn't know me.

"You don't have to look so terrified, I'm not going to eat you." Alfred's light tone sounded so out of place in the dark rooms that I forgot myself for a moment and looked up.

The traitor had an amused smile tucked about his vain features. He flicked an imaginary speck of dust from his spotless jerkin. "I assume you know who I am," he stated finally with a self-satisfied air.

I swallowed back the bile that rose to my throat at his pride. "Yes sir," I muttered through clenched teeth. *More than you know,* I added to myself. I took a deep breath and forced myself to relax. The last thing I wanted to do was make a bad impression. "I do, sir," I repeated in a firmer tone, daring to look him in the eyes.

"I, however, do not know who you are. What's your name, boy?"

He didn't recognize me. *Thank you, God.* "I'm Mark, Your Lordship."

"And a fine lad you look to be too," he said easily, patting my shoulder. His hand paused there, and squeezed critically. I winced at the power of his grip, shuddering to think what the full power of his strength would be like. "Not much muscle to speak of," he muttered more to himself than me. "How old are you?"

199

"F-fifteen," I said, kicking myself inwardly for sounding so frightened. *He can't be suspicious. He can't have any reason to watch me closely.* "I turn sixteen this summer," I added.

"Excellent. You say you wish to be a stable boy here in the Duke's castle?"

"Yes sir," I answered, letting eagerness leak through my voice and brighten my features. "I'm very good with horses, sir!"

"Why do you need this job?"

I kept my face downcast and sniffed, wiping imaginary tears from my eyes as if angry to show emotion. "My papa died almost a year ago, sir, and my mum...she used to be a seamstress, but her eyes aren't what they used to be. I need to work so she can rest and keep what little strength she has."

"Have you been looking for a job ever since your father died?" His astonishment was evident, and I hoped that would work in my favor.

"Not quite that long, sir, just since mum could no longer do her sewing work because it hurt her eyes. I decided I was plenty old enough to find a job and help provide." I straightened, putting my shoulders back and lifting my head as I envisioned a fifteen year old boy might. "I am the man of the house now, sir."

Alfred smiled thinly. "So you are." He glanced over me a few times, up and down, somewhat doubtfully. I bit the inside of my cheek. He just *had* to give me that job. Otherwise Malcolm would be starting his planning all over again and my hair would have been cut for no reason.

"I'm a quick learner," I added hopefully. "I can do more than just watch horses. I can run errands, I can wash clothes, and I can even do a little mending... I've helped mum before with her sewing you see, before I began searching for a job of my own. I can cook, too...a little."

Alfred considered me in a new light. "We may need someone with your variety of skills around the castle. You'll be expected to work hard and not show any amount of laziness or slothfulness." His gaze swept over my outfit, and his nose wrinkled in revulsion. "I'll have Burns get you new clothes and help clean you up in a warm bath."

My eyes widened in horror at the thought. "I can wash myself, sir," I said hurriedly. "I'd hate to be an inconvenience to you or your men, sir."

Alfred sighed, and to my relief, shrugged with a careless air. "Very well," he said. "I'll still have him bring you new clothes, though. The rags you have on will hardly do as a stable boy for our beloved Duke."

I nodded mutely, and hoped inwardly that I would never have to refer to the princess's abductor as "beloved."

The despicable man beckoned me to follow him down the hallway, back the way Burns had taken me. After a few minutes of walking in silence I finally ventured to speak again.

"Sir?" I began.

"Yes? What?" Alfred's impatience showed in his voice, as if I had been pestering him nonstop with questions when I really had stayed mostly silent.

"What will I be paid for my services?"

"Two shillings a week," he answered promptly.

"That's not very much," I whispered under my breath.

Alfred spun around and grabbed my shoulders until I had to bite my lip to keep from crying out in pain. His grip was every bit as strong as I had imagined it to be. "We don't have to pay you anything...I could have Burns put you out onto the street where you came from."

He no longer hid his cruelty; it flashed in his eyes openly. I lowered my eyes in the pretense of being meek and also to hide the anger simmering in them that might give me away.

"I'm sorry, sir," I muttered.

Releasing me from his viselike grip on my shoulders, the mask slid back into place and he smiled thinly. "Just remember that you should be grateful for your position here and not forget who your new masters are."

We walked a few more minutes in silence. Suddenly, he turned to me. "However, now that you mention it, how is your mother going to cope with being alone while you work here?"

I shrugged, hoping the story my brother had given me wouldn't flee my mind when I needed it the most. "She knew what I was planning and I promised to go see her once-in-awhile. Her sister, my aunt, has been living with us since papa died, so she isn't all alone."

"You'll have your meals in the kitchen with the other servants," Alfred went on as if he hadn't heard my answer to his question. "And I hope you don't mind sleeping with the horses."

"I've slept in worse places, sir," I said, inwardly exulting. Sleeping in with the horses would help me escape possibly awkward situations as a girl acting as a boy. God was with me and heard my frantic prayers. I glanced upwards with a thankful smile as soon as Alfred turned back around.

He seemed pleased at this show of quick submission. "Well said, Mark."

For a few more minutes we were silent again, and I tried to get my bearings. The surroundings were unfamiliar, and the torches flickering along the stone walls did little to brighten the shadowed passages. I could count the number of windows I saw on one hand, and those I did see were high up and very small. The doors we passed were closed and made of wood. Not entirely soundproof; I could hear muffled voices and movement behind a few and this fact I stored away for use later.

At long last Alfred led me through a door and into the courtyard. It was a different entrance than the one the gatekeeper, Burns, had taken me through, and I at once saw that I was now at the back of the building. Somehow, during the twists and turns, I had managed to make it through the entire bottom floor of the castle.

The stables were immediately to my right, and I could see the horses' inquisitive muzzles turned in my direction. Probably the smell of my clothing was the main source of interest. I could hardly blame them. At least by this time my own nose was used to the stink.

I was led to an enclosed stall and Alfred opened the door. "This will be where you'll sleep," he said. "You'll be close enough to the horses so that you'll be able to help them during the night if they need it. A few of the mares will be dropping foals sometime during the next month, so you'll have to keep a watchful eye on them especially."

With a quick nod, I soaked in the surroundings. This would be my home for the next week or so. Saddles, bridles, and such things were hung about on various pegs. There was a cot in one corner, a few blankets, and a washstand with a pitcher and bowl on top. A chair was wedged between the open doorway and a saddle that lay on the floor. It looked as though the saddle was waiting to be polished for some special occasion, because a small cup of oil sat on the chair next to a rag.

My suspicions were confirmed when Alfred motioned to the saddle and asked, "Can you polish that?"

I had seen Malcolm polish his once or twice before riding to the castle, so I nodded. "Yes, sir."

"Excellent. Start on that while you await new clothes. I'll give Burns the rest of your instructions for the next few days. See that you obey him."

"Yes, sir," I repeated, ducking my head as he left.

The door slammed shut behind him, and I immediately sat down to work on polishing the saddle.

I was still at it when Burns opened the door an hour later. I noticed his glance of approval and smiled as I stood.

"I see his Lordship gave you something to keep you busy," he said. When I merely nodded, he continued. "Here, he sent these clothes to you. You'll need to change right soon or this whole blessed stable's going to smell like a pigsty."

I nodded again. "Thank you kindly, sir." Taking the clothes, I set them on the bed.

The gatekeeper grunted. "Don't need to thank me," he said gruffly. I could tell he was pleased, though. "I'll be sending my boy in with a tub and water for your bath. His Lordship's orders," he added a little apologetically.

"That's all right," I assured him. "He warned me about it earlier. I told him I could wash myself so as not to inconvenience any of his men."

The gatekeeper sighed in something akin to relief. "John'll be glad of that, poor boy."

So am I, more than you could ever imagine. "I look forward to meeting your lad, sir," I said.

The man shrugged, trying his best not to look pleased again. "You can stop calling me 'sir'," he said, "Burns'll do...that's what everyone else calls me." He abruptly went out the door. "I'll be back once you're freshened up and ready for your first few jobs as the new stable boy."

I went back to polishing the saddle and finished it just as a boy about Steven's age, perhaps a little younger, burst through the door with a huge wooden tub. "Here*th* your tub," he said with a small lisp. "I'll go fetch *th*ome water for you."

"I can help," I offered quickly.

A look of gratefulness mixed with reluctance split the boy's face. "Lord Alfred ordered me to *th*ee to your need*th*," he said slowly.

I rolled my eyes, reveling in the fact that it was an act I could now safely commit since I was not a lady at the moment. "For goodness' sake! I'm supposed to be working here, not a fancy gentleman to be helped through every little thing. Let me help," I pleaded.

A grin took the place of his indecision, and I saw with a start that his two front teeth were missing. No wonder the poor boy lisped. "*Thinth* you in*thitht*," he answered with a nonchalant shrug.

We walked back and forth to the castle's well, located inside the courtyard, loaded down with buckets of cold water. My bath wasn't going to be warm, but I could hardly complain. At least I would be cleaner. Once the tub was full, John took his leave, and I washed quickly, lest one of the other servants happen upon me. I needed my disguise as a boy to last until the princess was safely in Malcolm's arms.

Even at the lightning speed with which I took my bath, I only barely managed to slip into the new clothes before John knocked on the door. I was shivering violently from the ice-cold water, and my fingers were hopelessly numb as they frantically tried to fasten buttons they couldn't feel.

"One moment," I said, finishing the last few buttons and trying to calm my shivering and racing heart. "C-come in," I added once I felt safely covered.

John poked his head in. "Are you fini*th*ed?" I nodded. A look of remorse crossed the boy's face when he saw me shivering. "I'm afraid we don't have the privilege to wa*th* in warm water."

"It's all right," I hastened to assure him, touched by his obvious sympathy. "Once I start working I'll warm up."

He gave me a once over, and I shrank. Did he see I was a girl? The clothes were less baggy than the ones I had gotten out of. "What's wrong?" I asked, trying to hide the anxious note in my voice.

"Nothing," he said finally, then paused. I felt perspiration collecting on my forehead. "Tho*the* clothe*th* look too big on you...I could try finding you a *th*maller..."

I interrupted him quickly. "These will do just fine."

He shrugged. "Very well," he motioned towards the stables. "Are you ready to learn what hi*th* Lord*th*ip want*th* you to do?"

I followed him outside. And so the true deception began.

26:
A Plan & a Prisoner

A few days went by as I learned what I needed to know as a stable boy in the Duke's castle. Meanwhile, during the meals in the castle's kitchen, and as I wandered about the castle grounds on various errands, I kept my ears open to learn all I could about the princess's whereabouts.

John and I became good friends, and we worked together on most of the jobs we had. I relaxed in the knowledge that if he didn't know I was a girl, then I was probably safe from both the Duke and the traitor, Alfred. It was a good thing John became my friend, for he turned out to be the best source of information about the princess.

One day as we were both working on brushing down some of the horses after a company of soldiers came back from a scouting trip, we fell to talking about what it was like working under the Duke and Lord Alfred.

A dark look passed over John's face for a moment and he sighed heavily. "I don't like working here," he stated.

I raised a surprised eyebrow. "Why not?"

"He'*th* a bad man," John said in a whisper after glancing around for possible eavesdroppers

Both eyebrows reached for the sky. "Who? The Duke? Your pa?"

He shook his head. "No, Hi*th* Lord*th*ip."

"Why do you say that?" I queried.

John sighed again. "I didn't alway*th* talk like thi*th* you know," he said at last.

I frowned. "Lord Alfred did that to you?"

"He knocked my teeth out when I refu*th*ed to lick hi*th* foot. I wa*th* lucky to e*th*cape with only two mi*th*ing teeth."

A disgusted look crossed my face, and my careful brushes halted halfway down the horse's back. "Why did he want you to lick his foot?" I asked as a frown at the boy's treatment clouded my face. Very unladylike thoughts were forming in my mind against Alfred.

John looked at me as though I had suddenly grown a third arm. "Have you ever looked in hi*th* eye*th*?" he asked instead of answering my question.

I nodded slowly. "Yes, I have."

"What do you *th*ee in them? I mean when he'*th* not pretending to be a gentleman around the Duke, but when he'*th* being him*th*elf."

"Cruelty," I said after a little reflection.

"And the de*th*ire to be great," John added. "He think*th* he de*th*erve*th* our ab*th*olute honor and wor*th*ip." He paused for a moment, checking for eavesdroppers again before lowering his voice. "*Th*ome *th*ay that he will get the Duke'*th* po*th*ith*on if he die*th*. If I were the Duke, I'd wat*th* my back."

My strokes on the horse's back continued as I reflected upon this bit of information. So the traitor was power thirsty, was he? "Are the rumors that the Duke keeps a princess as prisoner true?" I asked as nonchalantly as I could, careful to continue my work as if I was only curious about what he might answer.

John nodded, and my heart leapt in hope. "Ye*th*," he answered, "the rumor*th* are true."

I frowned in a puzzled manner. "Where on earth could he keep her?" I wondered aloud, keeping an eye on John's reaction.

My new friend lowered his voice again. "I've never *th*een her my*th*elf, but I've heard that he keep*th* her in a *th*pe*th*ial room in the very top floor of his ca*th*le."

So she wasn't being kept in a tower as I had supposed. "Why?"

A strange look crossed John's face and I tried to hide any interest that might have possibly showed in my own expression. "They *th*ay that the Duke i*th* u*th*ing her to get our king to allow him hi*th* own private kingdom…but that'*th* only par*th*illy true."

"What do you mean?" I reached for a comb and proceeded to work the burrs out of the horse's mane.

John appeared to be in want of someone to confide in, and frankly, I was overjoyed to hear all the secrets he had to offer. "Apparently, the Duke attended a fea*th*t the king held in honor of the prin*th*e*th*'*th* eighteenth birthday, and for him it wa*th* love at fir*th*t *th*ight."

I couldn't help the disbelief that filled my next question. "He claims to love her?"

"Ye*th*," John shrugged as if someone falling in love with the woman my brother loved was an everyday occurrence. "I've heard *th*ee'*th* very beautiful and ha*th* a kind heart toward*th* everyone but the Duke and hi*th* Lord*th*ip."

I hid a smile at this. If I had any doubts that Christine was here, they were gone at that statement. "Who looks after her?"

"*Th*ervan*th* that the Duke hold*th* in confiden*th*."

"I don't suppose I could ever get a look at her?"

John gave me a knowing look. "Perhap*th*. Mo*th*t of the men around here wi*th*e*th* they could *th*ee her. We've heard a great deal of her beauty, *th*o we all want to *th*ee if it'*th* true."

"Do you suppose…" I paused for a moment, unsure of how to continue. "Do you suppose I could offer to be a companion for the princess? Someone for her to talk to?"

John snorted. "You could try, but I wouldn't hope for *thucctheth* unle*th* you can find a way to make the Duke think you'll get her to like him."

I finished combing the horse's tail, and a sudden idea came to me. I must have shown my elation, because John asked me what I was thinking. I could hardly contain the excitement from him. "I just had an idea, thanks to you…but I'm not sure yet what will come of it. If everything goes according to plan, you'll be the first to know," I assured him.

We moved on to the next set of horses, cleaned out the stalls, and had our evening meal without speaking much to each other. I was thinking, and too busy working out my plan to waste any effort talking. Though John was obviously curious, he refrained from asking any questions, a trait of his for which I was very grateful.

"You think you could convince the princess to consider my suit?" the Duke leaned forward and watched me in an odd mixture of hope and worry.

I had come to the Duke's presence in fear and trembling. After a night of sleep, and after more planning the next day, I finally got up the nerve to speak with the Duke. My idea, thanks to John's statement the prior day, was to convince him that I might bring the princess around to the thought of becoming the Duke's wife in order to stop the deaths that would come from the battle which would take place otherwise. I thought blackmail would be something a villain like himself would understand.

However, the Duke wasn't at all what I had expected. In my mind I had thought of the Duke as a middle aged man, with cruel, glittering eyes, perhaps a golden earring or two. A man with bad breath and rotting teeth; a man who would be shifty, smooth as oil, and wicked. What he turned out to be took me somewhat by surprise. His neatly combed black hair reached his shoulders, and he sported a carefully trimmed beard. He was older than Malcolm by at least five years, if not more, but he didn't have any gray hairs sprinkled through his beard, or wrinkles tucked around his face. He was handsome, a fact I immediately took note of as a girl, and had an air of constant melancholy about him that made me almost pity him.

"I will try," I said. "I know the circumstances surrounding her stay here, and, take no offense Milord, but I think she may listen better to me than you."

The Duke gave a sigh and pinched the bridge of his nose. "I will take no offense against your bold statement because I know only too well how true it is." The man sighed heavily as if carrying a great weight on his shoulders. "I only wish she would believe me when I say that I love her and would give my right arm for her to be happy as my wife."

"Well," I ventured, "I can hardly blame her for being doubtful of your true intents...you did take her away from her home in a rather..." I thought for a moment, searching for a prudent word to describe the princess's abduction. I finally settled upon, "unusual manner."

A frown darkened the Duke's face, and for the first time I saw a look full of both jealousy and hate enter his eyes. "That," he answered in a clipped tone, "is because of his Lordship Sir Malcolm."

I almost jumped at the sound of my brother's name coming from the mouth of the Duke. "Sir who?" I asked as if I hadn't heard him.

"Sir Malcolm," the Duke spit out again. "He was going to take her from me. Lord Alfred was there at the engagement feast when..." he trailed off and glanced in my direction, lowering his voice to a sinister whisper. "I will kill him if he tries to take Christine from me." He ran a hand through his hair and sighed, the melancholy air falling over him again, the hate leaving his eyes and only sadness remaining. "I don't know why I'm telling you this," he said.

I took advantage of his uncertainty, still a little shocked at his promise to kill Malcolm if he tried to rescue the princess...which of course was exactly why I was here. "Perhaps there's something about me that makes people want to confide in me," I said. "Which is why I think that the princess might enjoy my company. It might profit you too," I added, as if almost an afterthought.

The Duke considered my offer. "Very well. I'll let you up there..." his eyes narrowed and he stood up, the chair letting loose a groan when relieved of his weight. "Would you try to win her for yourself?"

The idea was ridiculous from my perspective, I knew I was a girl, and that she was deeply in love with my brother, but of course the Duke was unaware of both those facts. I drew myself up. "Of course not, sir. Not only am I far too young for such thoughts, but I have no desire to court a princess...I wish to find someone of my own station when the day comes for me to marry."

His face relaxed. "Then follow me."

We walked from his private quarters, located on the third floor, up another flight of stairs, and down a long hallway. He stopped at the end of the hallway, spoke with one of the four guards lining the passageway, and continued to the farthest door. From what I could tell, the princess would be impossible to free from this direction. I had better keep my eyes open while I kept Christine company.

The solid door opened, and I saw it was at least three, if not four, inches thick and made of stout oak planks. He knocked on the now-open door.

"Christine?" he called softly into the darkness.

"I already told you my answer. Go away." The princess's voice sounded tired and strained.

The Duke turned pain-filled eyes towards me. "She's been like this ever since she realized she wouldn't be able to escape. I almost preferred her when she was fighting me."

I swallowed. He really did love her, however strange his way of showing his love was, and I saw it in his eyes. Still, he had promised to kill my brother for rescuing his betrothed, and

Christine most certainly did not return his twisted love. "Let me see what I can do, sir. Do you mind leaving us alone?"

He shrugged. "It's not as if you can help her escape. The only way out is through this door, and I've warned my guards to be careful. I'd hate for my bride to escape when our wedding plans are coming along so nicely."

I stifled a gasp of horror. "You are to be congratulated then?" I asked in a strangled voice. "I thought you said she didn't wish to marry you."

"She will learn to love me as I love her," he said. "Even if it takes a few weeks, months, or even years."

"When is the marriage to be?" I tried to hide the desperation in my tone.

"In three days," he said with a smile. "And then not even Sir Malcolm can take her from me."

I stared at the man with a blank expression on my face. A slight worry crept into the back of my mind that the Duke was losing his hold on reality. The man was going as mad as the wolf that had tried to bite me in my journey. He was picking the worst possible way to show his love. And I knew just how worthless his efforts were. I had to get the princess out. I had to get her out before the wedding.

27:
Three Days Left

The Duke gave me a gentle shove into the room. "See if you can pull her out of this mood she's sunk into," he pleaded. "I'm only asking for a chance to show her how much I love her, how much I want to make her mine."

"I'll talk to her," I promised vaguely.

The door shut behind me, and I was enveloped in utter darkness except for a thin line of light that illumined a few inches of stone floor just inside the otherwise unlit room. I leaned against the door. I could hear absolutely nothing. If I pressed my head to the stone floor, I could hear the vibrations of the Duke's feet getting farther away and one of the guards taking his place in front of the door. The thin crack of light was lost for a moment, and then I could distinctly see the bottoms of two boots silhouetted against the light of the passageway.

"Who are you?" the princess spoke out of the shadows.

"A friend," I said in my normal voice softly, just in case the door was less soundproof than it had proved so far.

"Meg?" Disbelief and hope threaded her question. "How did you get here? Why did the Duke let you in here with me? Where's Malcolm? How is my father?"

I hushed her quickly. "For heavens sake, Christine, light a torch. How many days have you stayed in the darkness?"

Some scraping and a hiss sounded through the silent room and a flame burned bright suddenly. I squinted in the light, catching sight of the princess's sheepish face behind it.

"I keep it dark in here so that the Duke can't see me. I thought that perhaps if he couldn't see me, he'd stop..." she trailed off with a sigh. "Well, anyways, I'm glad you're here, Meg." She studied me for a moment. Suddenly, she let out a shriek which was quickly muffled by my hand over her mouth.

I glanced fearfully toward the door. My hand remained clamped firmly over the princess's mouth and I could hear her soft whimpers. When nothing happened, I slowly relaxed. Once the danger seemed to have passed, I brought my hand away from the princess and spun to her with a glower.

"What was that for?" I hissed. "You could have gotten all our hard work wasted."

"I'm sorry," Christine said, her eyes brimming with tears. "Your hair..."

So she had seen my hair. I sighed, running a hand through the shortened length. "It is a bit of a shock the first time," I said ruefully. "You should have seen me when I first caught sight of myself in a mirror."

"Who did this to you?" she asked sorrowfully.

"Malcolm," I answered. When her eyes widened in shock and disbelief, I added, "It was with my permission. I had to, you know, so that I could get a job as a stable boy here and learn more about the inside of the Duke's castle. My job is to find a weakness and tell Malcolm and William along with another friend who are still outside."

"I see," she said, although she didn't really look as if she saw. "And so the Duke and Alfred think you're a boy?"

"I would certainly hope so!" I answered. "They act as if they think I'm a boy at any rate."

"And you have some way of communicating with Malcolm and William?"

It came back to me…I had to warn Malcolm that the wedding was supposed to be in three days. Would I, a mere stable boy, be allowed out of the castle any time I wished? Supposedly, I had a failing mother that would want to see me at some point. I gave the princess our plan as it was so far, adding that I would need to find some way to warn Malcolm of the impending wedding ceremony soon, seeing as he didn't know about it yet.

Christine's face blanched as all blood drained from it. "What wedding?" she demanded.

I frowned. "The Duke didn't tell you that you're supposed to be marrying him in three days?"

She shook her head and sank into a nearby chair. "I won't!" she exclaimed. "I'd rather *die*," she added dramatically.

I patted her on the shoulder. "Malcolm won't let it happen," I said. "However, I do need to warn him."

"You don't know how you're going to communicate with them yet?"

"Honestly, I was so certain Alfred was going to recognize me that I didn't bother planning more than obtaining the job as a stable boy," I admitted.

"Well, you'd better hurry about finding a way," the princess said.

I nodded my head. "Yes, although I have the beginnings of a way already…I just need to find out if it will work."

"Well, good luck." Christine sounded doubtful. "I'll be praying for you…and your brother and friends." She stood up again and hugged me. "I can't tell you how relieved I am to know that you're here to rescue me. I had almost given up all hope."

217

"Don't ever give up hope," I admonished her gravely. "Even in more dire circumstances than yours, God is always there. He will never leave you nor forsake you."

Tears gathered in the princess's eyes and she smiled. "Thank you, Meg, I don't know what I would do without you."

"I don't know what you would do, either," I replied with a wide grin.

We laughed together. Suddenly, the door burst open and the Duke came in. The princess's eyes went wide and she looked like a mouse about to be caught by a falcon.

The Duke stepped forward, taking in our positions and the lighted torch with one sweeping glance. "You lit a torch!" he exclaimed in surprise.

"I asked her to," I said.

He smiled. "Well done, Mark. You've accomplished more than I already. I am pleased, but you must attend to your other duties now." He turned to the princess. "Lord Alfred is going to be bringing you some food. Darling, please eat this time." The Duke looked truly concerned about her wellbeing.

Christine cringed, whether from the Duke's term of endearment, or the mention of Alfred, I wasn't sure. I would find out more the next time I visited.

I followed the Duke in silence out of the princess's temporary residence. As soon as the door shut behind us, and before I could possibly react, he slammed me up against the wall, his hands were at my throat and my feet were at least three inches up off the floor.

"Does she love you?" he demanded, his face twisted in outraged jealousy.

My look of shock must have convinced him that I was telling the truth when I gasped out, "No!" for he set me back on the floor and straightened his clothing.

"She is mine," he said with deadly calm. "No one can take her from me."

I rubbed my sore shoulders where they had been slammed against the wall. "I won't try, sir," I said in a show of humility. *But I know my brother will do his best,* I added silently.

His face eased into a smile. "Then we understand each other?"

"Perfectly, sir." *Better than you might think.*

As I followed him and then after we parted ways, him to his private chambers, and me to my stable duties, I thought of how I might get word to Malcolm. Speed was of the utmost importance now.

$$* * \dagger * *$$

"What'*th th*ee like?" John demanded as soon as I joined him.

Still deep in thought, I absentmindedly picked up a brush and began grooming the nearest horse. It wasn't until after John had repeated his question twice more that I looked up and said, "Hmm?"

"What'*th th*ee like?" he asked yet again, with a hint of impatience.

"Oh, she's very beautiful," I said.

"How beautiful?" he demanded. "What doe*th th*ee look like?"

"*Very* beautiful, she has long black hair, and sparkling blue eyes." I gave the answer I hoped a boy would want when curious about a girl. I really was terrible at being something I was not.

John sighed. "I don't *th*upo*th*e the Duke would let me come with you on the nek*th*t vi*th*it?"

I shook my head. "It was hard enough to get him to let me visit with her," I said.

"You're lucky," he growled, attacking his horse's mane with a vengeance. The horse sidestepped his onslaught with a nervous whinny at his unexpected behavior. John softened his yanks immediately, remorse sweeping across his face. He patted the horse gently and crooned to it softly until it calmed down.

I studied him a moment, wondering if he was someone I could confide in. It was time for the next step to take place in our rescue, and I needed John as an alibi. From the time we spent together, I was certain he was trustworthy. I prayed he was trustworthy. "She's not happy," I said finally.

He looked up at me with a frown. "Why not?"

"Well, if you think about what it would be like if you were in her circumstance, you'd see," I said. "She was stolen away from her home, kept as a prisoner against her will, and then told she was going to marry the Duke."

"And *th*ee doe*th*n't want too," he said.

I nodded. "She's in love with someone else."

His brow crinkled. "Who?" An eyebrow arched upwards and he grinned. "You?"

My eyes widened in shock. "Heavens no!"

The puzzled look came back and his teasing tone disappeared. "Then who?"

I glanced around for enemies before lowering my voice. "She's in love with my brother."

"Your brother i*th Th*ir Malcolm?"

I nodded. Apparently, more than the Duke and those at the princess's castle were aware of my brother's love for Christine. Not that it surprised me that much. My brother would have been eager to spread the news that he was engaged to the princess. No wonder the Duke had kidnapped her when he did.

A hurt expression crossed the boy's face. "You're lying to me," he said flatly.

I shook my head. "I'd never lie to a friend like you, John."

He frowned. "Everyone know*th Th*ir Malcolm ha*th* only one *th*ibling, and *th*e'*th* a girl with legendary beauty which i*th* rivaled only by the beauty of the prin*theth* her*th*elf."

I blushed at this description of myself, and wondered if my brother had started the rumor for the express purpose of making things awkward for me. "I'm not lying to you," I declared.

For the first time in the few days I had worked with him, John really studied me until a look of realization replaced the one of disbelief and was followed by one of shock. "You're a girl!"

I hushed him. "No one else can know that," I said. "I'm only telling you because I need your help."

"How can I help you?" John asked, resigning himself to the fact that I was a girl so quickly I was suitably impressed.

"I need to warn my brother that the Duke is planning on marrying the princess in three days."

"And how can I help you with that?"

I glanced around again. "If I try to contact Malcolm, the Duke might suspect something is up and I'll lose the ability to help the princess if he finds anything suspicious about me."

"He i*th* rather *thuthpithiouth*, ain't he?"

"Indeed," I answered dryly. "He's *very* suspicious."

"How can I contact your brother? He doe*thn*'t know me."

I nodded. "I realize that. I'll give you a letter explaining everything in my hand including my signature. He'll recognize that. If he asks any questions after reading the letter, tell him that Meg sent you."

"When?" John asked. He seemed doubtful, yet willing enough to do the dangerous task I asked of him. I shuddered to think what might happen to the lad if he was found with my letter on him.

"As soon as I can write the letter."

"Where is he?"

"Outside the castle gates somewhere. He won't be far." I studied my friend, a sudden idea coming to me. "We're about the same build," I said at last. "If I gave you the clothes I arrived in, you could very well pass off as me. Once he gets close enough, he'll know it's not me, but by then you can give him my letter."

John shrugged his reluctant agreement to my farfetched plan, and I went to my temporary living quarters in the stable. Upon my return, I found him still grooming a horse in the pretense of being busy and handed him my old clothes that I had worn when Malcolm and William had sent me into the fortress. While he changed in my room, I pulled out the paper I had carried with me all this time for the express purpose of this and hastily wrote a letter explaining everything to Malcolm. I warned him of the wedding plans, and included a rough sketch of what I had seen and remembered of the inside of the inner castle.

John came out later, clothed in my old things, and I had to swallow my laughter. The clothes were every bit as baggy and ill-fitting on John's slim, gangly figure as they had been on mine. Worse in some places. No wonder my brother and William had laughed at the sight of me in them.

He glowered at the laughter that must have shown in my eyes. "It'*th* not funny."

I tried to wrestle down my mirth. "I know," I said with as straight a face as I could muster. "I was just thinking how awful I must have looked in them."

A glimmer of amusement lit the boy's eyes and he snickered at the picture of me in the same garments. "Girl*th* don't belong in men'*th* clothing," he said at last. "No offen*th*," he added quickly.

"No offense taken, I assure you," I replied quickly. "I completely agree. If the princess hadn't been stolen away, I would never have dreamed of wearing the awful stuff." I shuddered for good measure, then passed my letter to him. "Don't let this fall in the wrong hands," I warned him.

He tucked it into his oversized boot and shot me a grin. "I'd die fir*tht*, Lady Megan," he said valiantly.

I shook my head. "We will hope it doesn't come to that."

He nodded his agreement before dashing off to the gate and somehow managing to get his father to open it for him. With a sigh and a prayer for the mission to be accomplished, I turned back to the stables and began cleaning them. It was in God's hands now...and John's.

28:
Two Days Left

A soft knock on my door in the middle of the night woke me instantly. I reached for Safeguard as I called out quietly, "Who's there?"

"It'*th* me, John," a voice replied with equal quietness.

I sheathed my sword and slipped out of bed, realizing with a start that I was still dressed in my work clothes and smelled like a stable. Wrinkling my nose, I shrugged. It showed how exhausted I was and how much I really didn't care how I looked at this moment. I tiptoed to the door and opened it. John glanced around outside before slipping into my room.

Lighting a candle and setting it on the washstand, I motioned to the chair by the door. "Please, make yourself comfortable," I whispered with sarcasm.

John's appreciative grin flashed white in the darkened room. "Thank you, I will."

"Well?" I prodded once he had sat down. "What happened?"

As John launched into his story, I could almost picture what had taken place. The boy had walked out of the castle and almost immediately perceived three men, whom I knew to be Malcolm, William and Henry, coming toward him. Soon enough they realized that John wasn't me and must have frightened him with their terrible scowls upon thinking that something bad must have happened to me. Malcolm probably assumed a trick from the Duke or Alfred.

"Where did you get those clothes?" one of them (*William,* I thought to myself) had asked in suspicion.

"Meg *th*ent me," John had answered immediately, giving the letter to the man who spoke. (*An intelligent answer, John, probably the only one that saved you from getting a black eye or an equally bad injury in some other part of your body. Well done.*) He had glanced at it and handed it to the man beside him, a dark-haired fellow, whom John realized must have been my brother. From the description, I knew his assumption was correct.

"It's for you, Mal-Arthur," the first man had said, correcting himself from saying my brother's real name out loud in the street where who knows who might hear it and report to the Duke. Without a doubt, my suspicions that the first man who spoke was William were confirmed with this new information.

My brother had read the letter very quickly, glancing up at John ever so often. When he finished it, he turned to the third man, whom I knew by process of elimination to be Henry. "Take this. We'll need her sketch of the castle, but destroy the letter."

Henry had taken the letter and disappeared into a building where they must have been staying in order to keep their promise of being close at hand. My brother looked John over for a few silent, intense minutes before nodding shortly. "You're John?" he had asked.

"Ye*th th*ir," John had told him.

"My sister seems to think that you can be trusted," he continued. "So I'll give a reply to this letter. Wait here a moment."

The other two men had left, and John had stood alone on the mostly empty street. After a few moments, Henry had come back after carrying out his orders to burn my letter. In his hand was a new letter and John at first assumed it to be the one he would be told to take back to me.

"Take this to the Duke," he had said instead, confusing John for a moment. "Leave now and don't ask any questions." He took out a bag that looked to be full of gold coins and dangled it temptingly in front of my friend. "It'll be worth your time."

At this point John began questioning Henry's loyalty and so replied, "I can't, *th*ir, I'm to wait here until Meg'*th* brother return*th*."

"Very well," Henry had replied in an angry manner. "I'll report you to the Duke, too. I had thought better of you, John." He had then paused as if to see if John would say something, but when he didn't, Henry stormed off into a tavern.

Malcolm had come out of the same building as they had first come out of with a letter in his hand and gave it to John with a smile. "Take this to her and let her know that we're praying for her every moment of every day. Tell her God is with her even when her brother can't be."

"I will, *th*ir," John had replied, then after a pause had continued, "I*th* that man loyal to you, *th*ir?"

"What man?" my brother had asked, raising his eyebrows in surprise.

"The one that tried to have me take a letter to the Duke, *th*ir."

"That was a test to try your loyalty, John," Malcolm said with another smile. "But you passed it well. It seems my sister has not placed her trust senselessly. Your loyalty will be rewarded once the princess is safely home again."

"I didn't do thi*th* for pay, *th*ir," John had answered indignantly. "I'm doing it for Lady Megan."

A knowing light would have appeared in my brother's eyes at this point as he said, "As is fitting for a man of honor. I am convinced more than ever that we can trust you."

I could almost see John's face darken into a crimson hue at this compliment. "Thank you, *th*ir."

My mind drifted back to the present as John finished his tale with, "I took the letter, hid it in my boot, walked back through the gate*th*, caught up on chore*th*, had *th*upper, went to bed, and then came out to tell you everything after my parent*th* were *th*afely a*th*leep." He fished around in his pocket for a moment before pulling out a somewhat rumpled piece of parchment. "Here'*th* your brother'*th* letter, *th*afe and *th*ound. I'll leave you to read it in pea*the* now."

I gave the boy a grateful look. "I can't thank you enough for doing that for me," I said, receiving the letter and smoothing it over my lap as I sat on my bed.

"Anytime, Milady," he said, ducking his head quickly. My sharp eyes saw the effects of my compliment before he was able to hide it entirely though, and I held back an amused smile.

Once the door had shut behind him, I opened the crinkled letter eagerly, hungry for news from my beloved brother and friends. As I half expected, the letter began with Malcolm's even script and carefully drawn letters, but ended with William's easy scrawl and dashing signature.

Dearest Meg, it was wonderful to hear from you again. I am so glad you have found a friend and ally inside the enemy's fortress. How is Christine doing? Tell her I have been praying for her safety. If the Duke or Alfred so much as touches her roughly I swear that they will regret it by the time I get my hands on them. Pray for me. I am so angry right now that I am terribly afraid I will do something now that I will regret later.

You are doing a wonderful job as our inside spy. I shall have to tell the king about your skills when this is all over. Perhaps you will receive a full time job under him.

We plan to sneak our way into the castle tomorrow in time to stop the wedding. Henry says he knows a few men who will help us fight. Be prepared to join us if we cannot succeed without fighting. Keep your sword with you always, just in case.

All that said, know that I am keeping you in my prayers. God is with you. Stay strong.

Much love, and a giant hug,

Malcolm

My dear friend Meg, can't stay out of trouble, can you? Well, it's a good thing Malcolm and I have been watching out for you. Poor Malcolm is gnawing his fingernails to the bone over this new complication, what with the Duke planning on marrying the princess in three days and all. Not that I can blame him. If someone was to kidnap or harm the woman I love, they would be sorry for it a hundredfold by the time I was finished with them. God help me.

Speaking of that, I hope you're all right in there by yourself. I think John is a trustworthy fellow, if a little moonstruck over your obvious charm and beauty. Never knew that would come in handy, did you?

After this is all over, I hope we can sit down and have a good talk. I miss those times more than I ever thought I might. You've become a very good friend of *mine...perhaps someday you'll become something more than that.*

Know that God is watching over you as I wish I could. Don't give up. You're doing a fine job.

Wishing I could be with you,

William Price

I treasured each word my brother and William had written, reading their loving and teasing sentences over and over until I knew them by heart. Then, I held the paper over the flame of my candle and watched as the fire licked up their words, burning them away into nothing. Once the paper dropped from my hands onto the dirt floor and disintegrated into small specks of gray ash, I felt a small part of my heart go with it.

When at last I laid down, I fell asleep wondering what on earth William had meant when he said *"you've become a very good friend of mine...perhaps someday you'll become something more than that."*

* * ✝ * *

The next thing I knew, someone was pounding relentlessly on my door, shouting things at me that my tired mind could not comprehend.

"Just a moment," I grunted finally, realizing there was no way I would get back to sleep. I was still in my day clothes, so all I had to do was roll off my cot and half walk, half stumble to my door. I opened it and blinked slowly in the bright sunlight.

Burns stood outside with a frantic look on his face. "Do you realize what time it is?" he demanded glancing down at my clothes. "I'm glad you're dressed already."

A puzzled frown appeared and rested between my eyebrows. "Why are you so upset?" I asked. "What's the matter?"

"What's the...? What's the...!" he trailed off into a string of swear words. I cringed inwardly, but knew he wouldn't apologize since I wasn't a lady to him. He seized my arm in a painful grip and began dragging me towards the castle.

His bad language had toned down to the occasional mutter as he marched me through the courtyard. Other servants stared openly at us in great astonishment, and I couldn't help still being confused.

"Are you going to tell me what's going on?" I asked, suddenly frightened. Had Burns caught John out of his bed last night? Had he guessed the secret we held between us?

"I'll tell you, all right," Burns growled. "The princess is in hysterics over her impending nuptials, which the Duke finally told her about, and refuses to let the Duke's seamstress measure her for the wedding gown. She's resorted to throwing things at anyone who comes near her and won't eat or sleep. The Duke's been taking it out on the rest of us, and demanded that we find you, since you appear to be the only human in the world who can calm his feisty bride-to-be."

I gulped. Of all the days to sleep in, of course I would choose the worst. Without ceremony, I was taken to the Duke who met me outside the princess's room with a mixture of relief and suspicion etched across his features.

"Ah! Splendid! Mark, I need you to go in there and calm her down. I *will* have her marry me properly in a white gown, as is fitting for a bride." The Duke's eyes dared me to contradict him.

I lowered my head in a respectful bow. "I'll do my best, sir."

He opened the door and shoved me in before shutting it quickly behind me; as if afraid I might try to escape my duty. I frowned. The Duke was acting like a jealous madman. I sighed heavily.

At the sound, a plate flew towards me, missed my head by an inch and crashed to the floor, shattering into a thousand miniscule fragments. "Heavens, Christine! Are you trying to kill me?"

When she heard my voice, the princess lit a torch to make sure it really was me before running to me and falling into my waiting arms with a gasping sob. "They're trying to get me a wedding gown!" she wailed. "I won't do it! They can't make me! I'd rather *die* than marry that horrible Duke! I hate him! Oh, I know it's terribly wicked to hate someone, but I really hate him! I do!"

I hushed her, wiping away the strands of hair that fell over her wild, desperate eyes. In my arms she settled down, her sobs dying away into sniffles and an occasional hiccup. "I won't marry him," she repeated in a calmer manner. "They can't make me."

I patted her back in the effort to reassure her. "I'm afraid they can make you marry him. However," I added when she stiffened and pulled away from my embrace, "they won't. Malcolm will see to that."

She sighed and melted back into my hug. "Thank God you made it here, Meg. I don't think I could possibly have survived all this without leaving my senses."

"What has he done to you?" I asked in sudden apprehension.

The princess shuddered. "Nothing yet. Except to keep doggedly saying how much he loves me and how happy we'll be together once we're married." Christine rolled her eyes. "There's only one man in the world I want to marry, and that's your brother Malcolm." She paused. "No, the Duke has mostly been annoying more than anything. It's Alfred that makes me feel strange."

"Has he done anything to you?" I asked.

"No," the princess answered, slower this time, and with less certainty.

My eyes narrowed as I regarded her irresolute expression. "Explain," I said.

"Well," she began, "he comes sometimes when the Duke isn't around and asks me questions. If I refuse to answer, he comes closer until his face is next to mine," the princess shut her eyes and shuddered expressively, "before whispering threats and telling me I should be thankful I wasn't about to marry him because he'd be looking forward to teaching me a few lessons in submission."

I gasped at the audacity of the man and wondered if the Duke knew this was going on. Probably not, or Alfred would never be allowed near the princess again. "Have you told the Duke about his threats?"

She shook her head with disdain. "And speak to him? No. I've been doing all I can to ignore the Duke and his offers of a happy married life with him. Alfred is cunning and vain, as well as power-thirsty and used to getting his way, but he can do nothing to me or the Duke would kill him. And he knows it."

"Unless the Duke is disposed of…" I thought aloud suddenly. "Then nothing would be between you and Alfred."

A look of utter shock and horror passed over my friend's face as the realization dawned on us at the same time. "Do you suppose that Alfred would try to…" the princess covered her mouth with a shaking hand.

I nodded grimly. "It's entirely possible that Alfred might try to kill the Duke. I do believe the man would do anything to gain something for himself in the end."

"Should we warn the Duke?" Christine asked.

I chewed on my lip in an absent minded fashion for a moment. "I'll think about it. Even the Duke is better than having a man like Alfred for a husband."

The princess nodded her wholehearted agreement.

"I'll try to speak with him next," I continued, turning to the door. "Let the poor seamstress make you a dress. You might as well, you have nothing else to do with your time here in this room."

"And it doesn't mean I'll wear it ever," Christine added with a lift of her chin.

I smiled. "Exactly. God be with you, Christine."

She smiled back. "God be with you, Meg."

I opened the door into the astonished faces of the four guards standing outside. "The princess is hungry," I said, "and don't worry about her throwing things at you when you bring her food to her. She's in a much better mood now."

Without another word, I marched down to where I knew the Duke spent most of his time during the day, my promise to the princess still fresh in my mind.

As I neared the door which separated the Duke's private residence from the public hallway, I heard a murmur of voices. Not all the doors were soundproof, and apparently this room was one of those. Against all better judgment, I knelt down and pressed my ear against the door.

29:
More Than I Bargained For

The muted tones of two men reached my sharp hearing. The voices I recognized as belonging to the Duke, which I had expected, and the traitor, Alfred. My curiosity bubbled to the surface, wanting to know exactly what they were saying. Had my brother been there, he would have given me his best impression of a mother and said: "You know the saying, Megan, 'curiosity killed the cat'." I rolled my eyes heavenward at this thought, smothering a grin. *It's a good thing I'm not a cat then.*

"...Only slowing down your chances, Richard," Alfred was saying. "Why put it off any longer?"

The Duke replied in anger, muttering a curse. "I love her, Al. I don't want to force her into this marriage, I only wish she would learn to love me before the ceremony instead of after."

Alfred grunted. "Why marry her for love? The vixen pretends to be in love with someone else out of spite, she deserves your displeasure. If I were the one marrying her instead of you—"

"If you as much as lay a hand on her, I swear I'll kill you, be you my brother or not. That woman is mine, and mine alone!" the Duke's voice rose, and I was glad it did, because I had given an involuntary gasp at the sound of the Duke calling Alfred his brother.

Upon reflection, I realized they did look similar enough to be brothers, even their personalities matched in some ways. Although, if I had to be stuck in a room with them, I'd choose the Duke every time. At least he still had some scraps of gentleman's honor, however thin and sparse the strands were.

A slap of skin against skin rang out, clear even through the door, and I winced at the sound. "You'll regret that someday," Alfred said, his voice low and dangerously calm. "I won't put up with this much longer."

"You won't put up with what?" The Duke's words had a wild, taunting sound to them. "You wouldn't dare lift a finger against me. I'm the keeper of Father's will, and I can change it to suit me if you do anything I don't like."

"You can't if you're dead," Alfred replied in the same, even voice that hinted at far darker intents.

I could almost see the blood drain from the Duke's face. "Y-you wouldn't dare," he protested, no doubt enraged by this turn of events.

At this point I wondered if perhaps I should make myself known to the room's occupants…and then realized I would probably get myself killed as a witness. I didn't doubt Alfred's sincerity. He meant every word he said.

"I would dare," the traitor continued. "To be honest, I'm sick and tired of following your every order, obeying your every whim, carrying out your every wish. As the second son, I've never had a lot. You've been given everything. Everything," he repeated emphatically, spitting out the word bitterly. "The land, the castle, the servants, a place in the king's court. Even the right to rule over your younger brother. But not now."

I heard a swish of cloth and the distinct, familiar sound of a sword being drawn. In horror I sat motionless where I knelt, frozen in shock.

"When you declared you no longer would serve the king, I felt proud of you. Proud to call you my brother, a man who could stand on his own two feet. But then I learned that you really only wanted to get the king and most of the men away from the castle so you could steal away the princess for yourself, and I began to doubt you, Richard. I obeyed your command to capture the princess for you, even if it meant losing my good standing with the king as one of his most trusted knights because I hoped you would use her to gain the throne, and therefore I would gain your title as the next Duke of Devonshire."

The Duke interrupted him. "You wanted me to gain the throne so you could have my title?" he repeated in a disgusted voice. "I forgot how obsessed you always were over power. You always were a bully, Al, even when we were children."

"I hardly think that you are in a position to speak to me as you are," Alfred continued. "I know I wouldn't if I had a sword pointed at my neck."

I heard a gulp, and a sudden intake of breath before the Duke answered in a weaker voice, "I always suspected you would try to overthrow my authority to gain this position, but I never thought you'd have enough gumption to kill me for it. I rule with a fair hand, Al. My subjects won't be happy with you when they hear about my death at your hand. They love me."

"Who says they'll know it was me? You of all people should know how well I can hide my tracks if I wish to leave none."

"You'll regret this," the Duke pressed. I could hear panic building in his voice.

I closed my eyes, willing my legs to push myself up and my hand to open the door and stop the murder I felt was sure to happen, but nothing happened. It was as if someone had tied my feet to the floor. Desperately, I tried to do something, anything to help the Duke. He was less of an enemy to me than Alfred was, and I shuddered to think what might happen if Alfred was able to carry out his sinister plan and marry the princess in his brother's stead.

My numb body finally gave some signs of life and the same mysterious energy that had come to my aid when we had been captured by the Duke's scouts flowed through my veins. I jumped through the door, thankful it wasn't locked. A shriek tore from the Duke's throat even as the wooden door swung open.

Alfred looked up, bloody sword in hand, a look of utter shock across his features. Then, a cold mask fell over his face and he walked toward me. My eyes were fastened on the fallen Duke; on the blood that poured out of his chest across the stone floor.

"You killed him!" I gasped out, forgetting that I was supposed to be a boy.

The traitor shrugged while peering at me suspiciously. "He was in my way. It had to be done."

Anger flooded all good sense out of my mind and with a cry I pulled Safeguard from his place at my side and faced the man I hated with every fiber of my being. An icy feeling of determination chilled my heart.

Alfred held back for a moment, studying me. "You're not a boy," he said at last as if he had finished solving a great puzzle. "I wondered."

"What of it?" I shrugged. "You were not a loyal subject of the king, nor to your brother as I now know. Appearances can be deceiving."

"Who are you?" he asked, circling my wary blade, careful to stay out of reach.

"Does it matter?" I bit out through clenched teeth.

"It does to me," he answered, his eyes watching, always watching. Waiting for me to drop my defenses so he could come in for an easy kill. "You look vaguely familiar, despite being in disguise."

"If you must know, I'm Megan, lady-in-waiting to the princess and sister of the princess's betrothed," I said irritably.

Recognition dawned at last. "Ah! I see the resemblance now. So you did follow me all the way to my brother's castle. I'm sure the princess is touched with your devotion to her." Sarcasm dripped from his voice like honey off a slice of bread.

"More so than your brother is of your devotion," I said scornfully. "I can't imagine how he managed to not see through your falsity before this." I burned with an angry fire, unquenchable and too deep in my soul to be put out by any water of compassion. "You are not only a bully and a cheat, but a coward and braggart," I stated coldly. "God will make you suffer eternal damnation for this."

"And you will be glad to speed His wrath no doubt," Alfred answered drily.

A sudden feeling of guilt pierced through my anger. Was I really ready to kill this man? What had happened to my senses? Wouldn't God's eternal punishment be enough? Couldn't I trust Him to deal with the man? With disgust I realized that in my anger I had become like the man across from me, a man whom I despised for acting in the same way I was now.

I lowered my sword and felt a sudden urge to pray for the man's soul. Shocked at my own thoughts, I did exactly that. At the sound of my first whispers of a prayer, a look of deeper hatred leapt into Alfred's eyes and with what sounded like, "You fool!" he jumped towards me.

My reflexes acted immediately, and Safeguard blocked his thrust with the ease of much practice. Almost unconsciously, I parried his blows with ones of my own, and soon our blades were flashing faster. I could tell at once that Alfred was a master swordsman and knew many of the same tricks William had taught me to avoid and counterattack. With a slight start, I realized that William had probably taught Alfred much of what he knew. After all, my own teacher *had* taught a great number of the nobles and knights in the castle at one point or another.

Suddenly, I saw out of the corner of my eyes, one of the Duke's hands move. It was slow, and painful. His eyes were open and he was watching his brother. When I noticed what he was reaching for, my body felt as if someone had poured a bucket of cold water over me.

He was reaching for his dagger. He was alive.

For a moment, I felt almost glad. But apprehension overcame that feeling. Who was he trying to use his dagger on? Me? Or his treacherous brother? Was he even conscious enough to see what he was stabbing at? Could he even find the strength to stab someone? How would he even stand up?

My questions were all answered when he gurgled out, "You have underestimated me, Al. You may be a better swordsman, but I have always been a better shot with a dagger." With a sudden heave, he threw the weapon.

Alfred's confident sneer turned into one of shock and disbelief when he heard his brother speak. He spun around and the expression froze as the dagger sunk into his chest and he slipped to the floor, landing with a metallic thud as his chain mail scraped on the stone and his sword clattered to his side.

I saw a glazed look pass over the Duke's face and his arm fall to the side. A hesitant hand on Alfred's pulse told me that he was, as I had predicted, suffering eternal damnation for all the pain he had given others. However, the Duke's life still clung to him by the thinnest of mortal threads. I watched his labored breathing for any signs of pause before laying him as gently as I could on the stone floor. I took Alfred's cloak off his shoulders to make a pillow for the prostrate nobleman.

Once I felt he was as comfortable as I could get him, I rushed to the open door.

"Help!" I cried, while mentally shouting a similar message heavenward. "Lord Alfred has nearly murdered the Duke! I need help! Quickly!"

A guard appeared out of nowhere and rushed past me into the room. He took in the scene at a single glance before rushing out again. He returned a few minutes later with a healer, but as I paced the floor worriedly, it seemed hours had passed.

"You did well not to move him, my boy," the healer told me as I leaned worriedly over the dying man. "He would have lost more blood, and he has barely enough as it is."

I hardly heard the praise. "He'll live, won't he?" I asked.

"I can't know for sure," the healer replied grimly. "But if the man is anything like his father, we might have some hope." He turned to the dead man on the floor and shook his head. "I'm afraid young Master Alfred was nothing like his father."

The guard grunted his agreement and covered the traitor's face. I was glad of this, but somehow I knew the horror of the unseeing eyes and frozen features would return to haunt me in nightmares.

"Ch-Christine," the Duke gasped out suddenly. He immediately had all our attention. "I-I want to-to speak with the-the princess."

The healer looked at me in confusion, and I bolted towards the door. "I'll be right back," I assured the wounded man.

Up the hallway I dashed, taking the stairs two at a time when I came to them and nearly running over the four guards watching over the princess's cell.

"The Duke asked for her," I wheezed, fighting for air. At their dubious looks, I shot them a pleading look. "You've got to believe me," I said. "He's dying and he wants to say something to her."

I could see their wall of resolve crack. "We'll take her to him," the one in front of the door said. "Our lives are nothing if she escapes."

Without hesitancy, I nodded. "Please hurry, I don't know how much longer he has to live."

At this, the remainder of their resolve crumbled away into ashes and they opened the door. Christine looked at us in confusion, but I motioned her to be quiet and told her to come without questions. Amazingly, she obeyed me.

The four guards stood around us, making it impossible for us to escape, but right now, the rescue plan was the farthest thing on my mind. Somewhere, deep down inside me, I held onto the frail hope that perhaps, just perhaps, the Duke would die a forgiven man.

30:
Death & Deliverance

As we rushed back through the hallways and down the staircase, I explained all I could to the princess. Once the tale was finished, I saw the compassion I felt for the dying man reflected in her own eyes.

"Why would he want to see me?" she asked finally.

I shrugged. "I suppose we'll find out."

We entered the room again. I noted with relief that Alfred's dead body was gone, and most of the blood had been mopped up off the stones. Servants carried water and bandages to and from the healer, and a priest knelt by the Duke's side. He looked a little stronger...pale, but sitting up and wrapped in bandages.

At the princess's entrance, all went suddenly still. The guards took their positions faithfully outside the door, even though I could see they were longing to see what took place on the other side. Christine's eyes were filled with tears as she regarded her helpless captor.

"Christine." The weakened man lifted an arm off the ground only to let it fall back to its original resting place on the floor. "Come closer. You have no need to fear me anymore."

A strangled sound escaped the princess's mouth, even with both hands placed firmly over it. She fell to her knees beside the prostrate enemy and let out a sob. "I was never afraid of you. Only what you tried to make me become."

The Duke's eyes grew full of pain. "I never wished you to be unhappy."

"Then why did you take me from my home? Away from the only man I could ever love?"

The whole room was shocked when the Duke slapped Christine across the face. Hatred mixed with the pain that crossed over his features from the sudden action. "Never speak of that man to me again, darling," he said forcibly, "You are mine."

Christine's hand covered the flaming red mark that spread over her otherwise pale face and she stared at the man in horror. "I will never be yours," she whispered vehemently. "I love Malcolm, and I could never love you. Not if we were married for a thousand years."

"Say no more," the Duke hissed. "I would kill that man if I ever met him, kill him for stealing your heart that should belong to me."

A sudden commotion from outside in the courtyard snagged my attention momentarily from the drama in front of me. A frown creased the healer's face as he worked on the Duke's wound, and he shot occasional looks of apology toward the princess. The Duke also lost his concentration for a moment and waved away all the guards but one.

"For heavens sake go and stop that ruckus. Do whatever it takes to make it stop," he ordered, wincing in pain as the healer probed his injury which was still bleeding but didn't appear deep.

Obediently, the guards dispersed towards the sound. Those who remained focused again on the Duke and the princess as they fought their verbal battle.

Christine had her head held high and her eyes were blazing with a hidden flame of confidence that I had never seen before. If this was what love did, I wouldn't mind it so much.

"I will obey you and say no more," she said haughtily, all compassion gone from her icy gaze. "I will say no more," she repeated coldly, "because no more needs to be said. You know my answer. I have told you often enough. Now it is time for you to believe me when I say that I mean it."

From behind me, I heard a metallic clank and the thud of a heavy body hitting the floor. In surprise I spun around only to see William and Malcolm standing in the doorway. My brother's eyes shone with a proud light as he looked at his future bride kneeling majestically beside her fallen enemy. Love emanated from his being and engulfed everyone in the room.

The princess felt it and glowed as if a candle had been lit inside her. William grinned like an absolute idiot. The Duke had a murdering glare fixated on my brother and too late I noticed his hand inching towards a dagger in his belt. It was then that I realized my mistake of not taking advantage of the wounded Duke and checking the wounded man for more weapons while he was so helpless.

"Malcolm, he has a knife!" I yelled in desperation, launching myself at the wounded man in order to throw off his trajectory.

My brother jumped sideways at the warning, and William followed his example. As I had hoped, I crashed into the Duke's arm and the dagger flew away from my brother.

The next few moments seemed to go twice as slow when I noticed with horror that the dagger, though safely away from Malcolm, flew directly at William. My mouth opened in a scream, but no sound came out. The Duke's breath came in ragged gasps and his wound was pouring blood onto the floor even as I felt Christine drag me away from his dying thrashes of frustration.

William slipped to the floor, his eyes fixed on me, his hand holding on to the handle of a dagger that stuck out of his chest. Numbing shock spread through my body as I hung limp in Malcolm's arms. The healer moved from his dead master to William.

I relived those moments three more times before a scream finally erupted from my mouth. I flung myself towards William. "No! No, no, no!" I shrieked. *God, I can't take any more! Stop having people die around me! I need to breathe. You are in control. I know that. Breathe. I need to trust. But I can't. Breathe. I can't...I can't...*

Then blackness descended and I knew no more.

I was drowning. Water filled my nose and I coughed so hard that I sat up. The ocean dripped off of me, and I realized that I wasn't swimming. I was on something soft. Sand? No, sand was grittier.

My eyes opened, and I glanced blankly around the room.

I heard a voice whisper: "I told you dumping water would do the trick." And another voice whispered back: "Really, Malcolm, you shouldn't be such a tease. She's been through so much in the last few months."

Then everything came back and a sudden panic gripped me.

"William? Where's William?" I tried to stand up and walk out the of the room, but firm hands pushed me back onto the bed.

"He's resting and not to be disturbed," my brother's voice replied from somewhere behind me.

I turned and saw him looking over me with his arm around Princess Christine. "Is he alive?" I demanded.

"Yes," my brother answered with slight hesitation. "The Duke is dead, as is Alfred, and we have been told all about what happened. No one holds any malice toward us for what took place, only sorrow that we had to be dragged into it. We are free to go home. As soon as you are ready, that is."

"What about William?"

My brother sighed and looked at his betrothed, seeking help with his eyes.

"He isn't strong enough to travel so soon," she answered.

"I'm not going until he goes," I said, crossing my arms stubbornly.

Malcolm cocked an eyebrow at me. "Why are you so concerned about William's health?" he asked.

I felt my face heat in a blush, and I dropped my head without a word.

"I see," my brother said drily. "Well, I think he'll be glad to hear that. He's been in love with you long enough; I'm relieved you finally realized that you love him back."

"I didn't say that!" I exclaimed, my face heating further.

A knowing grin stretched across my brother's face. "No, but you are. You just don't want to admit it."

I huffed, crossing my arms. The healer came in and walked over to me with a relieved look.

"I've never lost so many patients in one day," he muttered to himself as he checked my heartbeat and felt my head for signs of a fever. "Especially not such highly ranking ones." He glanced up at me. "You have a very eager visitor waiting outside. Can I show him in?"

A puzzled frown brought my eyebrows together. "A visitor? Who on earth…"

"You could let him come in, and then we would all have our curiosity satisfied," Malcolm interrupted.

I glared at him and gave a stiff nod of approval. Though hardly in a state to meet visitors, I didn't care…not with William so close to death.

The healer went to the door and opened it to reveal a nervous, red-faced John standing outside. Relief flooded his features for a moment when he saw me sitting up in bed awake, and then one of embarrassment replaced it as he stood shuffling his feet and twisting his hat in restless hands.

"Please come in, John!" I said with a forced smile. "How are you?"

"Better, knowing that you're *th*afe and *th*ound." He took my invitation to enter and stood just inside the doorway, glancing at my brother and the princess uncertainly.

I smiled at him. "This is my brother, Sir Malcolm, and his betrothed, Princess Christine."

Something akin to awe flickered in the boy's face and he bowed to both my brother and the princess. "It'*th* a plea*th*ure to meet you both," he said.

Malcolm stepped forward and shook his hand in a friendly fashion. "And to meet you again, John! I can't tell you how glad I am of your help in rescuing my bride. We couldn't have done it without you."

The boy ducked his head in embarrassment. "Lady Megan needed my help, *th*ir. How could I refu*th*e?"

"Well put, John, well put," my brother replied, sending a wink in my direction. I shot him a look of disapproval. His teasing knew no bounds. I wondered if most of his cheerfulness was put on to help my own worries, or if William was out of danger. I hoped for the latter, but feared the former was true.

I was beginning to feel impatient. Seeing John was all well and good, but I needed to see for myself how William was doing. Malcolm must have noticed my fidgeting because he drew John towards the door while whispering something about me needing to rest.

Within moments, Christine and I were alone in the room. "Where is he?" I asked.

"Follow me," she answered without question.

31:
A Friend & Something More

The door creaked open painfully slow, but Christine assured me that it was because William had such a pounding headache from hitting his head on the stone wall in his fall that even the slightest sound might hurt him. This scared me into doing whatever she told me to.

Every scrape of my leather shoes on stone caused me to wince in fear that it might hurt him somehow. I came over to the bed and looked down on William's pale face. His hair was lying damp against his clammy forehead and his eyes were closed.

I sat gently on the edge of the bed and instinctively reached out to push his hair off his face. My teacher's eyes flickered open and he let out a shuddering breath. For a few moments they searched the room, but upon sighting me, he stopped and a weak smile brightened his features.

"Meg? You-you're all right?" he asked hesitantly.

I nodded, relieved beyond measure. "I should be the one asking you that question," I said. "Are *you* all right?"

William sighed, then winced. "As well as someone who got a dagger thrown at them can be."

A soft whisper of noise distracted me for a moment, and I saw Christine glide out of the room, leaving me alone with the wounded man. His eyes met mine for a moment, and I saw something in them I had never noticed before. Something that looked almost identical to what I had seen in Malcolm's eyes every time his gaze rested on Christine.

William's hand reached out for mine. When his fingers enclosed over them, a warm wave of contentment washed through me. I felt safe. Loved. And I wished that the moment would never go away.

"I love you, Meg," my teacher whispered gently.

I lowered my eyes for a moment, contemplating a reply to his confession. "I know," I said, looking up at last and meeting his eyes.

A question filled them, and he spoke it aloud. "How?"

"You just told me," I answered, not bothering to hide my smile of amusement.

"You didn't know before?" my teacher asked, his eyes sparkling with silent laughter at my answer.

"Well, Malcolm told me when I woke up an hour ago," I informed him. "And I suppose I should have realized it sooner."

William searched my face for a moment. "I suppose I ought to thank him," he said.

"For opening my eyes?" I asked. "For showing me something I should have noticed a long time ago?" I nodded. "Yes, you ought to, as should I."

"You're very welcome."

I spun around to see my brother leaning against the doorframe, his arms crossed and a lopsided grin making him look like a little boy who had just managed to get something he wanted. He sauntered toward us and glanced over William.

"How are you, my friend?" he asked.

"I've been better," William answered drily. "But Meg is the best of nurses."

My brother's amused eyes met mine across the bed. "I would imagine so if she can make you forget about that wound of yours. You nearly bid farewell to this world yesterday evening. Thank God the dagger missed puncturing your lungs."

My tendency to worry rose to the surface at this revelation. "You almost died last night?" I asked. "Why didn't any of you come and get me?"

"I told you she was worrying about you," Malcolm said, ignoring my questions and grinning at William.

"How sweet," William answered, his eyes still on me.

"I'll leave you two to talk about me in peace," I said stiffly, standing up in order to go.

"Don't, Meg, please stay," William pleaded, his hand held out towards me in a mute appeal.

I could hardly refuse him. Taking his hand in mine, I sat back down on the edge of the bed, worriedly noting how even the small effort he made when urging me to stay made perspiration drip off his face to dampen the cushions beneath.

Malcolm was watching us with a self-satisfied air about him that put me on my guard. "Have you asked her yet?" he asked in a loud whisper towards William.

William sighed, then winced. "Not yet. I was about to when you came in."

A look of remorse crossed my brother's face and he exited the room, turning back only to give me a quick, "I'll speak with you later, Meg."

My teacher and I were alone again. Well, as alone as two people could be in a busy castle.

"Meg?" William's weakened voice had my immediate attention.

"Yes, William? Can I get you anything? Water? Food?" I glanced around the room in order to see if there were any of these items on hand.

"No. I want to ask you something." His quiet voice brought my attention back to him again. He had a hopeful, almost worried expression on his face.

"Well, ask away," I said.

"I'm being serious, Meg," my teacher reproved.

My eyes dropped to my lap, suddenly interested in the fine weaving of the brown material.

"I wanted to know if..." William trailed off, and I dared glance up only to see my teacher's face was a strange shade of red. Was it possible that William was *blushing*? "Would you be willing..." he halted again.

"Go on," I said, hoping to encourage him to just get out the obvious proposal attempt. The poor man looked about to choke on the unspoken question lodged firmly in his throat.

My teacher rubbed his eyes and sighed, taking in a shaky breath. "I've never been at a loss for words before, Meg," he said.

"That sounded more like a statement than a question," I said, pointing out the obvious.

William groaned. "For goodness' sake, Meg! I want to know if you'll be my wife!"

I stared at him. A few silent minutes passed, and a crestfallen look began to show on my teacher's face.

"I understand if you want to say no," he continued, the words appearing to cause more pain to him than the wound in his chest. "But I do love you, and I want you to share the rest of my life with me as my wife."

A slow smile spread over my own face and I squeezed William's hand. "Nothing would give me more happiness and pride than the ability to call you my husband," I said at last. "I would love to become your wife."

Joy and disbelief mixed in William's features, and the result was so comical that I burst out laughing. Without completely being sure why, he tried to join me, though he could only chuckle without causing himself unnecessary pain.

Gently, with a tenderness that made me swallow back more tears, William kissed my hand. "I love you, Meg," he said with complete earnestness.

"I-I love you too, William," I answered back.

"It's about time!" a new voice joined in from the doorway.

I spun around, nearly losing my place on the side of the bed, and saw Malcolm and Christine watching us. Malcolm was grinning like an idiot again, and Christine had tears in her eyes.

"I believe congratulations are in order," my brother continued.

"Oh, I'm so happy for you, Meg!" Christine said, flying across the room and throwing her arms around me.

"Thank you," William and I said at the same time. My eyes met his over Christine's shoulder and we shared a contented smile.

I noted how William's face was shockingly white again now that the blush had faded away. With concern, I felt his forehead. "You're burning hot," I said in horror.

"Malcolm, go get the healer," Christine ordered, taking charge immediately. I stared at her in astonishment. Where was the girl so frightened of leading her father's kingdom while he was away at war? I smiled. This new Christine was a vast improvement of the old one.

My brother bolted from the room.

"What can I do?" I asked, beginning to panic when I saw the worried expression on Christine's face.

"Go to your room and pray," she said.

"I want to stay and help."

Christine gave me a knowing look, but shook her head. "You won't do any good staying here. Please understand."

I nodded. "William..." Tears threatened to spill out again.

His eyes met mine. "I love you."

My sight blurred and I whispered back, "I love you too." Somehow I managed to get into the room I had woken up in hours earlier and the door shut behind me. I stared vacantly into space before sitting down on the bed.

Go to your room and pray, she had said. Well, that was something I could do. Falling to my knees, I pleaded for William's life. The life of the man I loved.

32:
A Journey Home

With a start I awoke, slumped over the bed. Sometime during my prayers, I had fallen into an exhausted sleep. I looked toward the one window in the room only to discover that I had slept into the evening. No light shone in from the inky sky outside.

For a moment, I lay there, listening. Far off I could hear quiet footfalls, the scuffling of leather shoes over stone, hushed voices. A slight frown rested between my eyebrows, and a sense of foreboding fell over me. Something was wrong.

The door creaked open, and a head peeked through. It was Christine. She was crying. Panic clawed at my insides, tearing me up as I rushed to her.

"Tell me how he is," I ordered.

"I-I came to get you," she whispered. "He wants to say…" she paused. "He wants to see you. Now."

The princess ducked from the room, and I followed her, my worry rising steadily as the people we passed bowed their heads when we went by. No one made eye contact.

We reached the room at last. Christine opened the door and shoved me gently inside. It was dark, except for one lit torch by the bed. The healer was kneeling by William's side, and a priest was on the other side. My worst fears surfaced, but I shoved them forcefully away. William couldn't die.

Could he?

Labored breathing rasped across the room, and I could see the barely visible motion of his chest rising and falling...rising and falling...so slowly that I had first thought that I had imagined it. The healer glanced up and saw me. He stood and walked toward me.

"He wishes to speak with you," the healer whispered. "Don't overtax him. He's got little enough strength as it is."

I nodded. The healer left the room, and the priest followed him. I walked toward William and stood at the foot of his bed. The bed curtains cast shadows over the blankets and the flickering light of the torch added to the eerie effect.

"Meg?" William's eyes were open a slit. He had seen me. The whisper was even weaker than when he had spoken to me before.

My dress rustled as I sat on the edge of the bed. His searching hand found mine and he gripped it with some of his former strength. His half-opened eyes met mine, and I smiled with whatever hope I still had hidden in the wrinkles of my torn faith.

"They tell me I don't have long to live," he said bluntly.

I felt as if the dagger that had wounded William sunk instead into my own chest. The flicker of faith I still had died away into wisps of grief. Tears smarted in my eyes.

"Don't say that," I urged. "You can fight this! I know you can!"

William shook his head and sighed. The effort made his body convulse into a coughing fit. Once it was over, he brought his hand away from his mouth and I saw with horror that it was covered in blood. He tried to hide it, but I took it and wiped it off as best as I could with my handkerchief.

"Stop, you'll ruin it," William pleaded.

I shook my head. "It doesn't matter." I finished and looked up at him. "Why is the healer so certain you're going to die so soon?"

"I've lost too much blood, and as you can see, these coughing fits don't help matters." William lay back on the cushions, pale and spent. He turned to me with a smile. "I had to have you near me again. I had to be able to say goodbye."

The tears that had been blurring my vision up to this point finally made their way down my face and off the end of my jaw. "It's not fair," I sobbed.

One of William's hands gently wiped away my tears. A shadow of his old grin flashed across his face. "You know, Meg, you really shouldn't cry; your face goes all red and splotchy."

Tears burst out anew. "H-How can you t-tease me at such a time?" I wailed. "I don't c-care what I look like! I d-don't want you t-to die!"

"I think the overall effect is rather adorable," he continued in a whisper without paying any heed to my previous statements.

"William!" Anguish over the situation made it impossible for my sense of humor to take the sting from the truth I had been told so abruptly.

He sobered in an instant. "I'm sorry, Meg. I don't want you to be so sad. You're making..." He took a moment to breathe. "You're making it sound like the world will end!"

"It will...for me," I answered.

"I'm going to be glad to be rid of this pain." His gaze softened and he touched my face again. "I will miss our life together. I'm sorry I proposed. It has caused you too much pain."

"No," I whispered. "No, I'm so glad you proposed. Otherwise, I never would have believed it possible that such a man as you could love me."

His hand dropped to his side and he coughed again. Blood dripped from the corner of his mouth onto the pillow. I wiped it away, crushing the sudden urge I had to shudder at the horrible sight.

God, must it really end like this? Why would You put this man into my life only to take him away again? What am I to do? I shall miss him so terribly. Do You really know what You're doing?

"Meg," William whispered, gaining my immediate attention. His eyes were fixed on mine and filled with concern. "Please, don't feel sorrowful about my departure." He smiled and continued, "I'm going to be with my heavenly Father!"

"Aren't you afraid to die?" I asked.

A haunted look appeared in his eyes for a moment, but it passed and he shook his head. "I was at first, and I'm sad, devastated in truth, to not be able to share the rest of my life with you, but I do look forward to meeting our Lord."

My emotions took another turn again and unbidden tears filled my eyes once more. "I'm going to miss you so much," I said at last.

William took an unsteady breath and coughed again. I wiped the blood away tenderly. "I'll miss you too, Meg, and if it's possible, I'll watch over you in heaven. I'll make sure to thank whoever your guardian angel is for keeping you alive all these years."

"God's going to be putting up with a lot when you finally get there," I stated, my dry humor coming back to me at last.

"That's the spirit, Meg," William approved, patting my cheek.

His hand dropped to mine and he held it for a moment. "I couldn't have picked a better death scene," he added. "Lying mortally wounded in a bed with a beautiful maid sitting next to me, declaring her undying love. It's hopelessly romantic."

"Really, William!" I exclaimed in shock. "I was hardly declaring my—"

"You said you loved me, didn't you?"

256

"Well, yes, and I do, but—"

"Just so," William interrupted me with a smug look.

"You're hopeless," I responded with a grin that belied my words.

William leaned back and closed his eyes. "Sing me a song, Meg."

I frowned at the unusual request. "A song? What song?"

"Anything," he answered. "Pick one of the ones you like. One you know well."

I searched my mind for a song that I liked and knew well.

"Greensleeves is my delight, Greensleeves is all my joy, Greensleeves, my heart of gold, And who but my lady Greensleeves?" I began the song from my childhood haltingly, stumbling over a few of the words.

William was smiling, his hand gripped mine. I took encouragement from this and continued. *"I have been ready at your hand, To grant whatever you would crave, I have both wagered life and land, Your love and good will for to have.*

"Well, I will pray to God on high, That thou my constant sea may see, And that yet once before I die, Thou wilt doth say to love me."

By the time I finished the song, my voice had broken. Tears streamed down my face and I did nothing to stop them. William's hand still held mine, and his eyes were closed. I thought him to be asleep and leaned over to gently kiss his damp forehead.

I waited for him to open his eyes and look at me, but the moment never came. He didn't move at all. I gently pried my hand from his and leaned over, placing my head to his chest. Nothing. He was gone. Torn from my life, leaving a gaping hole in my heart too large for anything else to fill.

I cried out my grief into the sheets that surrounded his body until I had none left to cry. Anger at God for taking him from my life, frustration that I could do nothing to save him, overwhelming sorrow that I would never be able to be his wife, all poured from my soul as I lay there. I shook with sobs in the cold room.

I awoke to raindrops dripping through a window above the bed. Everything from the night before came back to me. William's stiff body still lay on the bed, his face frozen in a contented smile. Somehow, seeing him die happy brought some comfort to me. I couldn't prevent his death, but at least I had made the start of his journey heavenward easier. Or so I hoped.

In silent respect and reverence, I pulled the blanket up to cover his face.

"He's gone." Malcolm's voice came from behind me, flat and emotionless.

I nodded, finding no words to say.

"When did it happen?"

"About an hour or so after Christine brought me to see him."

My brother sighed, brushing his fingers over the stiffened figure. "I'll miss you, William my friend." Malcolm turned to me. "You were with him when—?"

I nodded again. "He," I faltered, "He asked me to sing to him."

"He looks like it was a peaceful passing," my brother added, noting William's facial expression. He let the blanket fall back over William's face.

A strangled gasp sounded out across the room and Christine entered. Upon seeing the tell-tale cloth over William's face, she began crying.

"Oh, Meg!" she sobbed, allowing Malcolm to comfort her.

My tears had already been used up the night before, and so my eyes stayed dry, even while a few guards took the body away, even as they buried the body, even as the priest recited a prayer, even as they covered him with dirt.

I knew he was where he belonged. But I would miss him so, so very much.

* * * *

As the crowds who had come to watch him be buried wandered back to their jobs, I stood over the newly turned soil with an aching soul.

"Come, Meg, we must be getting back," my brother said, pulling me away.

I forced my feet to move. "Getting back where?" I asked listlessly.

Malcolm and Christine exchanged a glance before he answered in surprise, "Home of course!"

"Oh." My answer held no emotion. "Home."

We saddled our horses and left. As Duke's muscles bunched and stretched beneath me, I stared straight ahead, my mind somewhere far, far away. A place where William was still alive.

33:
In the Company of Friends

When we reached the king's camp, it was well into the afternoon. Malcolm had stopped our small band only once before then, ordering us to eat our afternoon meal.

Henry, by now a good friend—he who had once been my enemy—was now a part of our little group. He and Malcolm had become fast friends, both of them sharing a love for strategy. They could talk for hours on one method of battle.

The gatekeeper's family had also joined us, in order to seek a new job in the same village I had spent all my life in. Malcolm assured them they would be able to find employment with ease. I would have enjoyed their company more, but I was sadly missing William's presence.

"Meg, you've got to eat," Malcolm said, setting a plate of food down in front of me.

261

"I'm not hungry," I answered with a sigh, eying the meal with disinterest.

"William wouldn't want you to starve simply because you miss him," my brother continued. I read pain in his eyes at the mention of our friend. "He'd want you to be happy here."

I gave him a thin smile. "I know…and I'll do my best to eat something…but not yet. Please let me wait until we reach the king's camp."

Malcolm sighed, running a hand through his hair. "Very well."

Our journey to the king's camp was relatively trouble-free. We had some difficulties crossing a river, but other than that, God spared us. No bandits attacked, which was my greatest fear when travelling, and none of my friends received any injuries other than the occasional scratch from a branch or bite from an insect.

Upon arriving in King Frederick's camp, we were given a hero's welcome. Flower petals fluttered around us, and cheers echoed across the forests and valleys before fading away in the mountain passes. News of the Duke's death and princess's release had spread faster than we had travelled.

Princess Christine had jumped from her horse only to throw her arms around her father and weep with joy. Tears stung my own eyes as I watched their reunion. Malcolm was grinning so wide I thought his head had been cut in half, and the new friends were quickly greeted and made comfortable by the soldiers and their wives.

I saw Helen and waved. She came over and looked me up and down with a practiced eye. "You've lost some weight, my poor girl. What have they done to you?"

"William's dead," I said in a whisper.

A shocked expression flew over Helen's features, followed by one of motherly sympathy. "You poor child," she said, opening her arms.

That was all the permission I needed to sob my aching heart into her comforting embrace. The tears that had been

262

building up inside me since I had spent them all the night William died now poured out afresh. The soldier's wife held me until the storm passed and I wiped my eyes.

"Better?" she asked.

I nodded. "Yes, thank you."

She gave me a sad, knowing smile. She, too, had seen death, and so I felt she understood what I had gone through. "Let's get you some food."

I opened my mouth to protest, but she waved my objections aside as one might wave aside a terrible smell. "No, no, don't even try to refuse. You need a good, wholesome meal in your belly, my dear."

Too tired to say anything against her wishes, I plopped down on the nearest seat and waited for her to hand me a bowl of soup and a few slices of bread.

"That's what I like to see!" Malcolm said. "William would be proud of you."

I swallowed the food, giving it the silent command to remain in my stomach. "I only hope I don't become sick," I muttered. Malcolm gave me a hug, his eyes full of understanding, before walking towards the king's tent. I returned to my meal, forcing it down with a determination I couldn't feel.

From behind me, without warning, I heard a thump. My nerves, already a wreck from everything I had put them through during the last few months, twisted themselves into knots of tension. I spun around to see Steven behind me, propped up on a long, thick stick, a grin stretched across his face.

"Scared you, did I?" he asked, plopping down on the log next to me. "What on earth happened to your hair, Meg? You scared me almost as much as I scared you!"

"I was only startled," I corrected with a stiff nod of greeting. "As to your question about my hair, Malcolm cut it."

"You let your brother cut your hair?" Steven asked in obvious disbelief.

"I had to. It was so we could rescue the princess."

"Oh. I see." Steven still sounded unconvinced.

263

I eyed the stick he brandished with some suspicion. "What's that?"

Steven looked at it nonchalantly. "This? It's a crutch, Meg. Haven't you ever seen one?"

I shook my head. "Not one that looked like that. Does it help at all?"

"Of course!" Steven sounded a little wounded. "I made it myself," he added with pride.

I was impressed. "It looks sturdy enough to withstand everything you would put it through," I admitted. "And now that you mention it, how is your leg?"

"Better than it was a week ago," Steven said with a sigh. "Helen's been doing an excellent job making me rest."

"I'm glad someone took you under their wing," I said with a smile, glancing towards Helen who was bent over the soup pot, stirring some kind of spice into it.

She raised an expressive eyebrow. "Well, someone had to," she said. "Otherwise the good Lord only knows what trouble he would have gotten himself into, not to mention his poor leg."

I giggled even as a dark scowl fell over Steven's eyes. "I know how to take care of myself," he muttered.

"Just like you did five minutes before falling over that precipice and almost breaking your leg?" I questioned with a raised eyebrow.

A blush mounted the boy's cheeks and he dropped his head. "I stand corrected," he answered.

At Helen's pointed stare, I finished off the rest of my meal and handed her the empty bowl. She looked at its lack of contents in satisfaction before handing me a mug of fresh tea. I took a sip of the refreshing beverage.

"Where's William?" Steven asked. "I was told not to leave my tent when you arrived," he added, glancing towards Helen. "So I missed welcoming you all. I haven't seen my brother. Is he with the king?"

I choked on the tea half-way down my throat. For a few blessed seconds I was physically unable to answer his question.

After that, a few minutes passed when I was mentally unable to answer his question. I stared into the distance, swamped by memories.

"Are you all right?" Steven's voice broke into my thoughts and I turned to see his concerned eyes searching mine.

"I'm fine." I sighed heavily, wishing I had a way with words like Malcolm. But I didn't.

"So where is my brother?" he persisted. "Is he with the king?"

"No," I said. "I mean, yes, I suppose he is."

"Meg, you're not making any sense," Steven complained. "What do you mean?"

"I know, I'm sorry," I answered in misery. "I meant... Steven, William is with the King of Kings, with God his Father. In heaven."

Steven stared at me for a moment before the news really hit him. "William's dead?"

I nodded, tears springing afresh to my eyes. "I'm so sorry, Steven."

"How did it happen?" Steven demanded. I could see the same shocked disbelief I had first felt when William died, pass over his features and I impulsively grabbed his hand as if my physical touch could ease the pain.

I started at the day when we had left to go to the castle, then continued through the many ups and downs of our rescue, including the disguises, the deceit, the tricks, and the troubles. The tale grew as I added the conversation I had overheard, and the ensuing battle. His eyes widened as he heard about the Duke's stubbornness and his jealousy and hatred towards my brother, then hardened when I went on to describe how his brother had been killed by the stray dagger.

"He died the next evening," I finished, my voice catching as I relived the moments before William's death. "However, he died happy and unafraid, Steven. He knew where he was going and went to meet his Lord with a contented smile."

I fell silent, and Steven did nothing to break it. Finally, he looked over at me and I noticed unshed tears glimmering in his eyes.

"Thank you for telling me, Meg," he said in a controlled voice.

I stood up, understanding what he would want next. "I'll leave you by yourself now. Don't wander too far."

He gave me a shadowed smile. "Thank you again, Meg."

"It's a lot to process," I said. "There's a William sized hole in both our hearts now where no one else will ever fit. I miss him, just like you."

Steven nodded, and I left him alone in his grief.

It was evening when Steven showed his face again. He looked pale and gaunt as he hopped into the circle around the fire and ate the food Helen gave him listlessly. I sat on the far edge, and watched as he went through the same grief I had gone through hours earlier.

"I*th* he William'*th* brother?" John asked from beside me on the log.

I nodded. "Yes. His brother was the only sibling he had in the world. And now he's lost him."

John studied Steven from his vantage point beside me. "He look*th* like hi*th* brother," he said suddenly. "But he ha*th* darker hair...and darker eye*th*."

"Yes," I said again. Steven *did* look like William. I hadn't noticed until John had pointed it out. Perhaps a tad thinner, more like a hitching post than the oak tree William had been...but the way they smiled...and the way they spoke...

My brother came and sat on the other side of me, interrupting my scrutiny of Steven. "We're going to be riding back to the castle tomorrow. Will you be ready?"

I shrugged. "I'm not the one you should ask," I answered, nodding slightly in Steven's direction. "*He's* the one you should ask."

"And I will," Malcolm said. "Were you the one who told him?"

I nodded. "He took it better than I did."

"I'm glad. I would have told him…but I think it was best that you broke the news. I think he would have reacted in more anger towards anyone but you."

"Perhaps so, but I am glad that he knows now."

"You should get some sleep, Meg, it's been a couple of very hard days for you."

"Try months," I suggested. "Ever since you and the king left for what we thought would be a war but that instead ended in months of stalemate."

Malcolm smiled and gently kissed my forehead. "Go to bed, Meg."

"Yes, sir," I answered with a teasing smile. Getting up to obey, my eyes swept over the people around the fire. "Where's Christine?"

"She's with her father. She's hardly left his side at all since we got back."

"Tell her goodnight for me, Malcolm."

"I will."

My body suddenly decided that it was exhausted and the minute I climbed into the sheets, hardly finding the time to change into a clean nightgown, my eyes closed and my mind slipped from the realm of reality to one of dreams.

34:
Home at Last

The next morning, after packing up the entire camp—which took a great deal longer than I had thought it would—we started our journey home. I was so happy to finally be returning to a place I could call my own, but a part of me stayed behind, buried beside William's body in the shadow of the Duke's castle.

As we passed places I remembered from our previous journey to the king's camp, memories came back to haunt me. The decaying remains of the men William and I had been forced to kill during our escape from the scouting camp that we now took time to bury. The mountain pass where Steven had so nearly lost his life and the cave where we had spent those three long days waiting for him to become strong enough to travel again. The forest where Steven's horsemanship skills had been put to such a test.

Steven was riding a few horses in front of me, and I could see his mind churning with the same thoughts mine was. My heart bled, wishing I could somehow comfort him, but knowing I couldn't. As quiet as Steven had been in comparison to his older brother, he was even more so now.

Days passed as we travelled almost continually, stopping only to eat our meals and sleep through the night.

By the time we stopped for one of the afternoon meals, not only was my stomach growling, but all my bones ached from sitting astride Duke for so long. I ate Helen's meal with a relish I hadn't felt for quite a while, something she noted with obvious approval. Steven still wasn't eating much, but I shot him an understanding look because I knew only too well the things he was dealing with.

"How are you doing, Meg?" Malcolm asked, coming up next to me.

I sighed. "Better."

He gently squeezed my shoulder. "Excellent."

"I never knew I had the ability to miss someone as much as I miss William," I said.

My brother held me in his arms for a moment, allowing my tears to soak into his cloak. "Love is a wonderful thing," he replied softly, "but it can be cruel to those who choose to embrace it."

"I loved him."

"I know that. In fact, everyone knew that. It was also fairly obvious how infatuated William was with you." Malcolm looked down and I met his eyes. "Always know that he loved you. No matter what happens in your life, never doubt his love. He would have gone through flood and fire for you."

My smile at this assurance was seasoned with sorrow as we stood there a moment, watching the men saddle horses and the women pack up the tents and food. Time spent alone with my brother were getting more rare, so I treasured the few stolen minutes while the rest of the camp got ready to travel again.

"When are we hoping to get back to the castle?" I broke the silence first. "We've been travelling for a week already."

"It takes a long time with all the people and horses to feed. I predict at least a few more days of travel...possibly another week."

I groaned. "I don't know how much longer my backside is going to take all this riding," I complained.

My brother cocked an eyebrow at me. "I thought you liked riding horses!"

"I do!" I agreed. "But not every morning, every afternoon, and every evening, only stopping to eat meals and to sleep each night. Especially not for weeks at a time."

"I think you'll live," Malcolm answered with a parting squeeze of my shoulders as he caught sight of Christine and the King coming out of their tent.

"Perhaps," I answered doubtfully toward his retreating form.

* * † * *

Two weeks later we arrived at the castle. Like we had at the king's camp the day after William died, we were given a hero's welcome. Trumpets blared across the streets, children danced and laughed, women smiled through tears of joy as they welcomed their men into their arms. Young women threw flowers and garlands at the returning soldiers, and I saw as a few of them watched with envy as Christine and my brother rode in next to each other.

An older woman dashed through the crowd and flung herself at Steven's horse. The beast stopped obediently, and I was suddenly glad that Malcolm had been so stubborn about having Steven on one of the more tame horses.

"Steven, my boy! Welcome home!" the woman cried. I realized that she must be his mother.

This thought was confirmed when Steven slipped off his horse and onto his crutch in one smooth, practiced movement and hugged the little woman with a cry of "Mother!"

Through the loud noises surrounding me, I could barely make out her next question as her eyes scanned the soldiers parading past their small reunion. "Where is William?"

Steven's eyes clouded and he ducked his head. "William's with both Papa and his heavenly Father now, Mum. He was killed during a battle."

A hand flew to cover the woman's mouth, and her eyes searched Steven's for any hope that what he said was wrong. Apparently, she saw none, for the next moment she was sobbing out her sorrow into her younger son's shoulder.

They were lost from my sight for a moment and I was pulled with the crowd toward the castle. In vain I searched for Steven and his mother, but could see them no longer. With a sigh, I turned Duke back to follow the flood of people.

I finally made it to the castle and from there to Malcolm's side as he stood holding Christine's hand. Bitterness reared its ugly head when I saw this simple show of affection. If William had lived... Immediately, I forced that line of thought from my mind. Of course, I was happy that Malcolm and Christine were together and safe back home. How could I begrudge them their joy just because I couldn't share it?

King Frederick was standing on the wall of the castle while all his subjects spread out about him.

"He's going to make a speech," Christine informed me in a loud whisper.

My eyes centered back on the king as he waited for the crowd noise to quiet down more.

"My beloved subjects," he began in a loud voice that echoed over the sea of faces beneath, "I have returned."

Here, cheers erupted and it was another couple minutes before he was able to continue again. However, the king showed enormous patience and waited with a smile across his face.

The King went on to talk for another few minutes, but my mind wandered rebelliously back to the short, sweet moments I had shared with William before his death. When I pulled my focus back to the present, King Frederick was just finishing his speech.

"My friends," he was saying, "I would like to end this return speech happier, so I shall now announce the engagement of my daughter, Her Royal Highness Princess Christine, to my military leader and strategist, Sir Malcolm Hall."

Cheers erupted again from the thousands of throats around me, and I joined in, though my effort was halfhearted at best. I was happy for my brother and Christine, but I missed William.

Later that evening, once the princess was in bed and all was quiet, I stood by my window overlooking the peaceful night. Stars lit up the sky, sparkling in the midnight blue darkness. A single, soft snore reached my ears from where the door opened between my chambers and the princess's, followed by a contented sigh. She was safe.

I closed my eyes and breathed in the silence. I relished the smell of fresh flowers which climbed up past my window from the courtyard's garden beneath and the hint of rain on the breeze that lifted the tendrils of hair off my forehead. I was safe.

William was gone. Steven had a lot of healing yet to happen, both inside and outside. Burns was given a new position as gatekeeper of the castle, and John was a stable boy. He and Steven had become best friends, which helped with Steven's sorrow over the loss of his brother. In a few weeks, Malcolm and Christine would be getting married. My life was never going to be the same.

Yet, somehow, I didn't really mind all that much. Whatever happened in the future...God knew what He was doing, and my life was safe in His hands. I knew I could trust Him. No matter what.

Epilogue: Six Years Later...

"Auntie! Auntie! Take me outside! Please?" The voice of my three-year-old nephew, William Price Hall, woke me from my daydreaming. The black-haired imp was tugging on the skirt of my dress and he was regarding me with his large brown eyes that were so hard to resist.

Yet, resist I must. "I'm afraid I can't, Little Will. Your auntie has some very important things to do."

"Looking out the window doesn't seem very important to me," William huffed in disappointment, his arms folded over his tiny chest.

"Let Auntie alone," the serious voice of my older nephew came to my rescue as its owner appeared in the doorway. Five-year-old Frederick Malcolm, or Freddie as he preferred to be called, came and took his younger brother's hand. "I'll take you out to the garden," he offered sweetly. I thanked the boy with my eyes.

"Will you help me catch frogs in the moat?" I heard William demand as they left my room.

Christine came around the corner just as the boys disappeared from sight, her arms full of beautiful baby Megan Christine who toothlessly beamed at me from across the room. "Have they been bothering you, Meg?" she asked, eying my half-finished letter.

"Oh, heavens, no!" I answered with a laugh. "I could never get tired of having your little ones around me. I love them all so dearly!"

"Who are you writing?" she asked curiously before a teasing light appeared in her never-fading eyes. "Or perhaps I shouldn't ask."

I rolled my eyes, and then was dismayed to see my namesake copy me. "I'm afraid your children are going to have terrible habits from me," I said with a laugh, touching Megan's nose briefly and earning a giggle from the tiny bundle of joy. "But to answer your question, I'm writing a cousin of mine. I was thinking about visiting her this next summer. I haven't since…since my parents went to be with our Lord."

"Ah," Christine answered, understanding lighting up her sympathetic eyes. "Just don't be late for the swordsmanship class you're supposed to be teaching in an hour."

I laughed. "I wouldn't want to miss it!"

The princess left the room, probably in search of her elusive husband, and I turned back to the letter I was supposed to be writing. Thankfully, after some practice, writing letters was coming easier to me. Still, sometimes I found it hard to concentrate.

My Dear Cousin Susan,

How can I begin to tell you how I am doing? So much has happened to me since the last time you wrote me. Malcolm has married Princess Christine, and they now have three beautiful children. Two boys, Freddie and William, and a baby girl who was named after me! I have been enjoying the joys of being an Auntie every day. Malcolm sold our cottage by the farm to our new gatekeeper and his family, just so we can be near King Frederick in the later years of his life. I moved in the castle a while back, as you probably remember, and have stayed ever since.

This was where I had stopped and my mind wandered into the past. I reread what I had written and dipped my quill in the ink before continuing to write where I left off:

There are times when I miss the quiet life of the country, but overall, I am vastly content with my new life with Malcolm and his family. Of course, Christine has been trying to match me up with practically every bachelor in the kingdom, but so far I have successfully evaded her efforts.

A smile tugged at the corner of my mouth as I recalled the times my sister-in-law had tried to introduce me to potential husbands. All of them had been failures on her part, but I often gained new friends from the trials. The trouble was, I couldn't help but compare the men she introduced to me with William... and none of them were him. It wasn't their fault, the poor men, and I watched as Princess Christine's efforts doubled and tripled in urgency as I became older.

Just a month ago I celebrated my twenty-fourth birthday, and I think Christine has finally reconciled herself to the fact that I can never marry anyone with William gone. I now help her with her children and watch them when she has to go to important banquets with Malcolm or the king.

Malcolm has also started training some new soldiers and guards which I have been helping with, along with a few nobles who want private swordsmanship lessons like William used to give. Sometimes, when Malcolm is busy, I can take over for him, and it's always interesting to see their reactions to a female teacher. Most of them react first in disbelief that someone like I would have the ability and knowledge needed to teach swordsmanship, but then gradually come to the realization that I can and do.

So, as you can see, I have been keeping myself very busy. How are you? How are Aunt Diana and Uncle Richard? Is your life very busy right now? Have you found your true love yet? If you have, what is he like? Remember when we were younger and made up stories about meeting the man of our dreams? That one time when I came over to your house for the summer and we laid under the bedclothes and pretended we were fine ladies on our way to a fancy banquet is one I will never forget. How we used to tell the most outlandish tales to each other!

I miss the innocence of childhood. We spent so much time wishing we were grown up that we forgot to enjoy all the little moments of simple pleasure we had. I was thinking about coming and visiting your family this summer. Would that be possible? Please let me know!

Much love,

Megan

I folded the letter carefully and sealed it with warm wax. Pressing the family seal into the moldable red blob that held the edges of the letter together, I pushed it from me with a sigh. I would make sure it was put in the hands of the very next messenger Malcolm sent towards Susan's home.

This done, I sat by my window and let my mind wander into the past again. The memories of William came to me easily, but with less pain now than they had in the past. A fresh breeze cooled my skin, and I shut my eyes. My hair had grown back, and was now almost to my waist. I ran my fingers to the ends, relishing the feel of it being back to its normal length.

A polite cough startled me into spinning around with a gasp. Steven Price stood with his arms folded and his head bowed in respect. Now a young man of twenty, he had changed from the horse-loving boy I once knew into a responsible adult. Granted, he still loved horses, and he was often the one I chose to accompany me when I rode Duke around the countryside.

"Yes, Steven?" I asked after recovering myself.

"I was told to come and tell you that the men are almost ready for your lesson in swordsmanship."

I sighed. "I'll come in a few minutes, Steven."

"I'm supposed to escort you, Meg," he added with an ill-concealed smirk. "Malcolm's orders."

I stifled the urge to huff my disapproval. "I think I'm perfectly capable to find my own way down the staircase and into the courtyard," I said.

"No doubt," Steven agreed, "but I believe Malcolm doesn't wish you to be lacking in friendly conversation. Apparently you've been spending a great deal of time up here by yourself. You haven't been spending enough time with other people...at least, not enough to please the princess."

"Even if I went to every gathering the princess invited me too, I don't think I'd spend enough time with people until I marry somebody. Christine's set on me being happily paired with a nobleman." I gave an exaggerated groan.

"But you can't find anyone like William," Steven said, sitting on a chair by the fire.

I nodded. "I don't think Christine understands."

"Of course not, she never lost her true love," Steven said, arching his eyebrow at me. "I miss him, too," he added with a sigh when I sent him a scathing look. "He was my only brother. I've only got mother now."

Steven appeared so lonely. I walked over and set a comforting arm on his shoulder. He covered it with his own and pulled it lower so he could hold it more comfortably. "Sit down," he offered, half pushing me into the other chair by the fireplace.

I sat down and gave him a puzzled frown. "What was that for?"

Steven sighed, running his free hand through the dark hair that waved carelessly in the breeze which came through the open window. "I've wanted to talk to you about something," he said.

I smiled. "Well, go on," I encouraged.

Steven licked his lips in obvious nervousness. "I'm not sure how to say this," he began, "but I have admired you for a very long time. You have been a constant ray of light in my life, ever since I met you that first day I worked as a stable boy in the castle. You have always been there to encourage me when I'm feeling low, and can bring a smile to my face no matter what I'm going through.

"I want to know if—when you're ready to love again—you might consider me as a possible future husband?"

For a few moments, I sat in stunned silence, regarding the young man across from me with astonishment. "Are you proposing to me, Steven Price?" I asked.

Steven nodded, his face heating into a darker red. "I understand if you don't feel comfortable marrying someone so much younger than you. I'm sure William was a lot more mature than I'll ever be. I want you to know that I'll be here, whenever you need me."

I considered his question. Steven had been an almost constant companion during the days after William's death, and I knew him to be both compassionate and interesting to be around. Of course, he wasn't William…Steven was quieter than his brother, but just as passionate when it came to things he cared about. A home with him would never be as lively as a home shared with William, but I felt sure we would find things to keep us busy. Steven had a sense of humor, an appreciation for beautiful things, and a love for all animals, horses in particular. All three of those traits he shared with me. We would not lack things to enjoy together.

"I'll think about it, Steven," I promised. "I do like you as a friend, and I believe it could become something more, but you'll have to give me time. I need to pray about it."

"I'll give you time if you promise to give me a chance," he said with a grin.

I stuck out a hand with a grin that mirrored his own. "That's a deal," I said, and we shook on it.

"Now, shall I escort you down to the courtyard, Milady?" he asked with a deep bow and twinkling eyes.

I laughed before offering him a beautiful curtsy. "Why, thank you, good sir."

We walked down the shadowed hallway and staircase before we turned to an open doorway and into the sunshine. There, along the side of one of the walls, about seven men mingled.

I felt my side where Safeguard still hung, as he had every hour of every day. His cold, metallic handle fit snugly in my hand. A new confidence came to me and I strode with purpose toward the waiting students.

Steven spoke first. "Greetings, Milords, this is Lady Megan, and she will be teaching you all she knows about swordsmanship."

One of the younger men eyed me in obvious disbelief. "*She's* our teacher? I thought this was an advanced class."

I raised my eyebrows at the man and a hint of a smile appeared on my face. I had dealt with men like him before. "It is," I answered.

"And she will be expecting all of you to treat her with the respect due her as not only a teacher but also a lady," Steven added, looking pointedly at the man who had first objected.

"What is your name, sir?" I asked the young man.

"Sir Harold Ridgefield the third, Milady," he answered with pride.

"Would you mind being the first to duel me? I usually fight with each student before you begin working with each other so I know what your different strengths and weaknesses are."

The young man shrugged. "Of course I can." He sent me a cocky grin. "I'll try not to be too hard on you in front of your other students."

"I predict his pride will be his weakness," Steven whispered to me with a frown.

I bit back a giggle. "I somehow remember that you weren't all that different when I first taught you," I pointed out.

"Was I really that bad?" he asked in astonishment.

I patted his shoulder. "Sometimes worse." With a parting grin, I walked to the middle of the dueling circle, and drew Safeguard from his sheath by my side.

At my apparent lack of fear, Sir Harold had lost some of his insolence and followed my lead by pulling out his own sword. "Shall we begin?" he asked.

"Whenever you're ready," I answered graciously.

"I'm ready NOW!" he cried, coming towards me with an unearthly yell.

I cringed at the horrible sound before easily blocking his thrust. A startled look passed through his eyes before he recovered himself and lifted his arm for a swipe through my midsection. My eyes narrowed. Sir Harold was too open with his moves. I could predict them a mile away.

I dodged his next three thrusts without difficulty, and slipped away from his slice long enough to come in with a few moves of my own. The feel of Safeguard in my palm was so natural that dueling like this was the most effortless thing I'd ever done...except perhaps using my bow. I still enjoyed that, and Christine had vastly improved; we had tied in the last archery tournament we had held between each other.

My mind pulled itself back to the fight and with a smooth arc, I caught his blade with mine and pulled it out of his hands. It clattered to the floor. The dust settled as Sir Harold and I sucked air into our lungs.

I sent the young man a smile. "Well done," I said. "You should work on being a little more subtle with your moves. I could predict what you were going to do a few seconds before you did it. That's bad. Also, don't try to aggravate an enemy before fighting them. Angry men are likely to fight in a far deadlier fashion."

"Thank you," Sir Harold answered; sweat dripping down his forehead and over his cheeks. "It..." he paused, holding out his hand with reluctance, "it was a good fight. You're better than I thought you would be."

"Is that an apology?" I asked, my eyebrows reaching upwards again.

The young man reddened. "Yes, I...I suppose so."

I grinned. "Don't worry; I have surprised a lot of people with my ability to fight with a sword. You're not the first, and you certainly won't be the last." I turned to the other men and smiled. "Who wants to be next?"

* * † * *

Once the class was over, I felt as if I would never be able to lift Safeguard above the ground again. My throat was sore from all the shouted commands and advice, and I felt as if I had swallowed a cup full of small rocks and a great deal of them had refused to be swallowed all the way.

Christine brought me a mug of tea and a sympathetic smile. "I take it your class must have gone well?" she asked.

Dinner was over and the children had just been put to bed after badgering me with requests for a story before they had to be sent away. I had regretfully told them that I couldn't, but kissed them each on the head to make up for it, promising I would try to read to them the next night, hoping my throat would be in full working order by that time.

"Will you read *Beowulf?*" William had asked. "I love that story!"

"Perhaps," I had answered.

I took the cup of tea from Christine and sighed happily as the soothing beverage cleared the rocks from my throat. "Yes, class went well. As usual, there were a few doubters, but I managed to get them taken care of."

"Oh, to see their faces," Steven chortled from his place beside the fire where he was watching Malcolm and Henry play each other a game of chess. "Especially when she could so easily unarm them of their swords," he continued, grinning.

Ever since he had returned with us after the exciting and sorrowful events that led to the princess's escape, not only had he been knighted for his efforts in rescuing the princess, but he had earned himself a place in the King's Court. He now often joined us for family meals, and afterward, too. Malcolm had taken an immediate liking to him, and the two had become as good of friends as my brother and William had been.

"That's my sister," Malcolm said, coming over and tugging on my hair in his teasing manner. His hand lingered on the ends, and his eyes met mine, alight with an amused twinkle. "See? I told you it would grow back."

I let out a *humph* and folded my arms. "It took long enough," I muttered.

Henry moved his horseman forward and shot a triumphant look toward Malcolm. "Check," he declared.

Steven peered at the board. "I do believe you have met your match in chess strategy, Malcolm," he said.

My brother ran a hand through his hair after sitting back down across from the older man and pursed his lips as he contemplated his next move. "Well, Megan wasn't enough of a challenge," he said, throwing me a grin.

"Enough teasing," Christine admonished her husband. "Meg is probably exhausted, and deserves some rest."

Malcolm let it go, turning back to his game with a determined look. He would do his best not to let Henry win.

I sighed and stood up. "Christine is right, I am exhausted. I think this will be a good night to you all."

Christine, Malcolm, Henry and Steven all wished me a good night as I left the room. The hallway was lit by a line of torches, and I found my way to my room with the same ease as I had won all the duels fought that afternoon.

With a contented sigh, I sank into the warm bed after changing into my nightgown. I let my sore muscles relax and my body melt into the comforting softness of the mattress beneath me. My old life had been a wonderful thing, but my new one was also wonderful…if in different ways.

As I drifted off to sleep, I heard Princess Christine singing *Greensleeves* to little baby Megan, and I smiled serenely. Here was where God had put me. Here was where I belonged.

Just like Christine.

Even though she had hated the idea of ruling the kingdom while her father was gone, she was able to realize that here was where she was needed. We both belonged where God intended us to be.

The princess and I.

In Appreciation:

There are so, *so* many people who deserve a place of honor in my book as a thank you for all the work they put into this story. Writing a book is a huge job. A fun one, I'll grant you, but a *big* one as well. There are so many little steps in a project like this one that require a large amount of people. Every little typo, every weirdly structured sentence, every detail I missed had to be caught and dealt with. And I had a wonderful group of fabulous people who gave their time and effort into making this book a possibility.

First, I'd like to thank my family: my parents for letting me take the time to bring my crazy imagined characters and world into a book, my siblings and cousins for being my own private fan club asking me if I was finished with it yet and begging me to "read another chapter to us!", and my grandparents for encouraging me to live my dream.

Second, I'd like to thank Mrs. Miller, Grace, and Kathryn for reading the final copy of my book and encouraging me to release it to the world.

Next, I can't begin to say how thankful I am for my team of editors. Jesseca, Faith, Megan, Kaitlyn, Abigayle, Deborah, Soliel, and Jonathan, you all were so much fun to work with and each of you were able to catch different flaws and bring them to my notice. Your encouragement meant so much to me.

I want to give a special thank you to Alea Harper for the time she spent designing the beautiful cover. I am so pleased with how it turned out. Her amazing work deserves recognition.

My amazing circle of friends from the blogosphere have played a huge part in encouraging me to finish my book and get it published. Without their constant pushing, I would have taken twice as long to complete the editing process on my book. Many of them willingly volunteered to take part in a cover reveal and a blog tour which played a huge part in getting my story out to a larger audience.

Last, but not least, I'd like to thank my heavenly Father who created me with a love of both reading and writing. May all the glory go to Him.

~Rebekah Eddy

About the Author:

Rebekah grew up surrounded by family members who appreciated and read good literature. First, she fell in love with the stories her parents read aloud to her from the Bible and books like The Chronicles of Narnia, Great Expectations, The Hobbit, and Anne of Green Gables. After learning to read on her own, she discovered other fantastic books which helped to build her ever growing imagination.

She completed her first written work at the tender age of eight and now uses it to humble herself whenever the need arises. The story did serve to show her that God had given her a desire to write, however, and from that moment on Rebekah has never looked back or regretted picking up her pencil and becoming an author.

This eighteen-year-old homeschool graduate lives in rainy Western Washington and is currently working on receiving her BA in English in order to further her passion for creating worlds on paper.